BLUE BALLS

RC BOLDT

Enjoy the final
release !
RC Boldt

Enjoy the trail !

BLUE

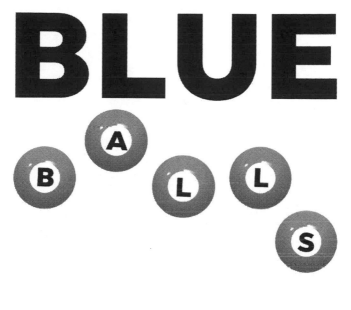

RC BOLDT

Editor: Editing4Indies
    http://www.editing4indies.com
    Proofreader: Judy's Proofreading
    Proofreader: Julie Deaton
    http://jdproofs.wixsite.com/jdeaton
    Cover design: RBA Designs
    http://rbadesigns.com

and are used only for reference. There is no implied endorsement if one of these terms are used in this work of fiction.

If you upload this work to any site without the author's permission, it indicates piracy which is stealing. Both are ridiculously uncool and if you do so, then you understand that you'll forever be labeled a pirate (and not the super hot Johnny Depp kind) and the Book Loving Gods will be watching you. And when I say that, I mean they'll be watching EVERYTHING you do. Especially when you do *those* kinds of things. Just a heads up.

Visit my website at www.rcboldtbooks.com.
Sign up for my mailing list: http://eepurl.com/cgftw5

DEDICATION

Matty,
*Thanks for **not** being the inspiration for this story. And for*
giggling with me like we were two school girls every time I said the
title of this book.
P.S. I still love you more.

A,
You are—and will always be—my favorite girl in the whole,
wide world. Never change—except for that whole temper tantrum
thing. For real, though.
And, don't forget, I love you "more than the world and the
universe".

This book is dedicated to anyone who has ever dealt with blue balls.
May you find your relief soon.

NOTE FROM THE AUTHOR

Since this is a fictional story, some liberties have been taken and names have been changed to protect the innocent.

Just kidding about that last part. Kind of…

Okay, the truth is that some of the incidents in this book *might* have occurred in real life to my friends. Or myself. But mostly my friends.

Enjoy the crazy shenanigans ahead.

INTRODUCTION

BLUE

Truth: A painful condition caused by a prolonged state of sexual arousal without release.

Myth: Only affects males.

SARAH

I'm beyond frustrated with the man who's left me high and very far from dry. Multiple times. But, somehow, even though I'm not interested in a relationship, Mr. Tall-Dark-and-Handsome keeps me coming back for more—one crazy, sexual debacle after the next.

Come hell or high water, the stars will align, and the release will be out of this world.

JACK

I'm captivated with the woman who's left me sixty-nine shades of blue, and she's only in this for one thing. The first time, I blew it—and not in the good way—but I'm going to ensure we finally see it through. I need to put an end to this "plague" of sexual calamities and prove to Sarah that we can have more.

It's time to grab the universe by the balls and show it who's boss.

PROLOGUE

SARAH

I know you're wondering what the hell you're getting yourself into. I mean, I can practically hear you thinking to yourself. *Blue Balls? What in the holy hell is this?*

I get it. I really do. If anyone had told me I'd be faced with this dilemma, I would've laughed in their face.

Hold up! Where are my manners? Sheesh. If we're going to discuss blue balls, I should at least introduce myself properly.

My name is Sarah Matthews. I'm a nurse, my favorite movie is *The Princess Bride*, I love chocolates (the ones that come wrapped in foil with special messages printed on the inside), I love men, and I love sex.

Wait just a minute before you go all Judgy McJudgerson on me. I simply happen to like sex—*safe* sex, mind you—and I'm particular about who I sleep with. I consider my vagina to be more of the free-range variety. You know, like those chickens who lay better eggs without all the hormones and crap. Or at least that's what the packaging claims when I pay nearly five bucks for a dozen eggs. (And seriously, how do those people sleep at night, charging that much for twelve damn eggs?)

Basically, my vagina's picky and doesn't like restrictions on where it can, *uh*, "graze."

This is getting weird, isn't it? What I'm trying to say is, I have requirements. I don't consider myself a slut—my vagina isn't open to the public nor does it experience high volumes of, *ahem*, "traffic" like Times Square in New York City. My vagina is *selective*.

Besides, I don't do relationships; not only because of my childhood, but also because I've been far too busy. I'd decided being a physician assistant wasn't for me and switched gears to become a nurse anesthetist. Studying for my certification while working my full-time job didn't leave time for much else. Sure, my best friend found the guy of her dreams, but me? Meh. It's not in the cards. I just want a guy who's fun to be around and happens to have the gift of burning up the sheets with me.

When Maggie and Ry first became roommates, I met Ry's best friend, Jack. The two were pretending to be gay lovers —*long* story there—but Jack always intrigued me.

Jack's different. I've been interested in him from the start, and I'm almost certain he reciprocates that interest. Sure, circumstances threw up a few roadblocks, but once the stars aligned and we could act on our fierce attraction, I figured it would be smooth sailing. We'd get a little hot and sweaty, a *whole* lot of naughty, and I'd get to experience whether he would live up to my expectations.

Except that's not the way it turned out. Instead, we fell prey to a terrible illness, so to speak. And this "illness" wasn't minor. Nope. It veered more into the realm of a plague.

What you're about to read is our journey—and attempted battle—of the blue balls plague.

CHAPTER ONE

SARAH

Tall, dark, and deliciously handsome. That's Jack Westbrook.

I've known him for over a year now, and ever since the mutual acquaintance of our best friends thrust us together, I've wanted to include other types of thrusting in our equation. However, we'd been tiptoeing around the attraction with neither of us making any moves—*until now*—for multiple reasons:

1. I can finally say I am a nurse anesthetist <does happy dance> and at the point where work and school won't nix any existence of a social life.
2. Jack had been seeing someone in Boston, and it'd been casually mentioned in passing that they'd amicably ended things. (And I can neither confirm nor deny this news made me do a hearty fist pump. <avoids eye contact> Okay, fine. I confirm it.)
3. Do I really want to date the best friend of my best friend's fiancé? And does that question sound as incestuously confusing to you as it does to me?

Let's just say I'm certain I wouldn't scoff if his penis were to get "busy" with the inner workings of my vagina. In fact, my anticipation of this is at an all-time high. It's been far too long since I've been with a guy. My poor hoo-ha basically has cobwebs—that's how long it's been. Frankly, it wouldn't surprise me if the next guy who parts my legs to go "downtown" hears a crypt opening, complete with dust and bats suddenly flying out.

That was pretty graphic, actually. Especially with the bats. I think that's what pushed it overboard. Sorry about that.

Since it's Maggie and Ry's engagement dinner party, I went above and beyond to ensure that I look presentable for my best friend's special night.

It has absolutely nothing to do with a tall, dark, and handsome six-foot-plus of sexual manliness. Nope. Not at all.

Lieslieslieslieslieslies. That's what you chanted, right? Don't worry; you're not alone. I called bullshit on myself, too.

Can I just have a quick moment, please? Because Jack Westbrook is one hell of a freaking hot male specimen. He's one of those guys who looks phenomenal wearing a sexy as hell business suit and just as delish wearing some jeans and a Henley. Jeans that cup him in all the right places. Allllll of them. Especially his ass and that *other* place.

Don't shake your head at me. I can't help that I'm a perv. I was born this way, just like Lady Gaga's song. Yeah, I know. Now you're pissed because you'll have that song stuck in your head all day.

Anyway, back to the topic of Jack. Just saying his name makes me do that swoony sigh—the one all us ladies make fun of. But trust me when I say this swoony sigh is one hundred percent warranted.

I feel the doubt pouring off you in waves, so let me explain. Picture this: Dark hair that's artfully tousled with enough length that you can imagine gripping it while he's "downtown" and going all out in an "I'm eating you like it's my last meal on earth" kind of thing.

Hey, now. I warned you that I'm a perv.

Then there's his body. While I admittedly haven't seen it uncovered—*yet*—I can tell he's rocking some seriously hard muscles from playing racquetball with Ry at the gym. Racquetball is something I just don't get, though. Who wants balls flying at their face at Mach speeds? Not this girl. In fact, I'm not a big fan of balls in general. They're not nearly as interesting as penises.

Whoops. There I went—off on a tangent again.

Now, don't get me wrong. I'm not entirely superficial. More than just Jack's good looks enamor me. He happens to have a wicked sense of humor and can be a perv like me, too. I appreciate that in a guy. He's also smart as hell and is an independent business consultant. From what I can tell, he's in high demand and nearing the point where he may have to turn some jobs down because of his jam-packed schedule.

Maggie and Ry's engagement dinner party gave me the perfect excuse to get beautified...and show Jack what he's been missing. I pulled out all the stops with my hair, makeup, and attire to ensure I'd hold his rapt attention.

Surrounded by the family and friends of Ry and Maggie, we're sitting in the large banquet room of the historical restaurant, Longfellows, situated in downtown Saratoga Springs.

Jack's deep voice carries over the audience. "Maggie and Ry met in an unconventional way. Their story is unique, filled with endless shenanigans, laughter, and most importantly"— he breaks off to smile down at the couple seated to his right—"love."

Shifting his gaze, it dances across the rest of the audience before resting on me an extra beat, and he continues.

"These two are perfect for one another because they're the best of friends who know each other inside and out and love each other, not in spite of their imperfections but in addition to them. They love one another for the good qualities as well as the not so favorable ones.

"They savor every quality the other has because that's what makes each of them unique. That all those qualities combined have *made* the person they've fallen in love with. That those qualities have come together to make that person real. Imperfect, flawed yet..." Jack smiles down at Maggie and Ry before his voice lowers a decibel, becoming softer, more intimate. "Two imperfectly, flawed individuals found their other half. Together, their imperfections, their flaws, disappear. Instead, all you can see when you look at them is simply love."

Raising his champagne glass to toast, he appears to have a slight sheen in his eyes. "To love, laughter, and happily ever after. To Maggie and Ry!"

"To Maggie and Ry!" we all chant in return before taking a sip of our champagne.

To love, laughter, and happily ever after.

Huh. Apparently cute guy rhymes, too. Not to mention, he totally showed me up. Damn it. My speech pales compared to his.

Not that I'm bitter or anything, but geez. Can't a girl have a moment to shine?

At least I've got this fancy strapless dress. It's blue and satiny, fitted, and I'm pretty sure my boobs look great with this new push-up bra I'm wearing. Who knew these things could be so amazing? I'm not gonna lie; I've totally been sneaking peeks at my own chest tonight because I think I'm falling in love with these girls and the way they look.

The blue of this dress matches my eyes, so I'm working that angle because I figure it's worth a shot. If my chest doesn't mesmerize Jack, then maybe my eyes will do the trick. Aside from my phenomenal personality, of course.

Yeah, I think I rolled my eyes at myself on that last one.

After the toast, the wait staff places a dessert at each seat, and I make my way to the restroom. As I head off to the quieter section of the restaurant—Ry's dad rented it out for this particular occasion—my eyes take in the authentic, rustic feel of this place given by the ceiling's large crisscrossed wooden beams and the stonework.

After washing, I reach inside my small clutch to retrieve my little guilty pleasure and quickly take a tiny bite of chocolate. I swear these suckers are the best after some champagne. As much as I love Maggie, her choice of dessert—red velvet cake—is not my favorite.

I check the foil wrapper for the little message written on the inside—**Chocolate cures everything** (Isn't that the truth?) —before replacing the remainder back in my purse.

Exiting the restroom, I only make it two steps before someone snags my wrist, and I'm tugged over to a small alcove. My back against the smooth, wooden accent wall, I'm instantly caged in by one hundred percent, USDA choice male. And when his gaze drops to my chest before returning to my eyes, I mentally high five myself while uttering a gracious thank you to my bra.

"I haven't had a chance to talk to you." His deep blue eyes flicker to my lips for a moment. "To properly say hello and... congratulations on everything."

God. Not only is his voice pure sex, but the fact that he's congratulating me on becoming a nurse anesthetist, the fact that he's *clearly* paid enough attention to know this, sends warmth running through me. Also, in case you're wondering if it's possible that he made me orgasm simply by speaking to me, the answer is yes.

Okay, *fine.* Maybe it wasn't a full-fledged orgasm, but it was definitely a mini one. Like a tiny little jolt, not a full-blown one that would leave me an embarrassed and sweaty mess.

"Thank you." Heat suffuses my cheeks, and I try to play it off like my panties aren't damp as hell. "So is it true?"

He cocks an eyebrow and… *For the love!* How is practically everything he does so damn sexy? It's just not fair.

"Is what true?" His tone is playful. "That Maggie's realized she's planning to marry the wrong guy?" He scoffs playfully. "Of course."

With a smirk, I swat at his chest. "As amusing as your response is, no, not that." I pause, tipping my head to the side inquisitively. "Is it true that you're back on the market?"

Jack offers a slight shrug. "Guess so. At least that's what they tell me." Then he grins. "Why do you ask?"

I mimic his shrug. "Oh, because I might know someone who's curious."

"Really?" He leans in closer, and that grin turns even hotter. "Might this someone have silky blond hair and a wicked way of speaking her mind?"

"Mmm...quite possibly." Reaching out, I tuck a finger beneath the waist of his suit pants. "That someone might be dying to see"—I give a slight tug—"exactly what you've got going on beneath these."

His head descends slowly, bringing his lips to the shell of my ear. They brush lightly against it, sending shivers down my spine.

"Well, it just so happens I've been wondering the same thing about you." He drags an index finger across my bare shoulder, and his teeth nip at my earlobe as his gravelly, deep voice whispers, "Especially in this sexy dress of yours."

Panties have disintegrated. I repeat. Panties. Have. *Disintegrated.*

And we all know what that means: Sarah's lady parts are bursting free from the gates—like those old movies where the school bell rings for dismissal on the last day of class and everyone rushes out the front doors in mayhem, desperate to be free. That's exactly what my lady parts did. They burst free and practically pulled a Julie Andrews's move, dancing around merrily and singing, "We're aliiiiiiive and readyyyyyyy, Jack!"

Things got weird for you just then, didn't they? Well, brace yourself because that's pretty much me.

Allllll the time.

I make the decision while he's whispering in my ear in that panty-melting voice of his to do it. I turn my head and catch him off guard, our lips meet, and it happens.

It freaking happens!

The fireworks. The heat. The feeling in the pit of my stomach where just a little bit of "magic" mixes in with lust. That's exactly what I'm feeling. We're talking decadent, orgasm-inducing goodness.

With simply one kiss from Jack Westbrook.

CHAPTER TWO

JACK

She's been killing me all night in that fucking dress. The shimmery material is practically begging me to unwrap her like a present on Christmas morning. I'd love to take it off her nice and slowly back at my place and see exactly what's underneath it.

Ever since we met—when Ry and Maggie first became roommates and before they became more, of course—Sarah and I have been tiptoeing around our attraction to one other. I'd been in a pseudo relationship with Brittany, but with her being in Boston and me only making the occasional stop there for work, it never really got off the ground. She's a great woman, and I know she'll find someone more suitable. Not to mention, Brittany never made me feel the way I do just being near Sarah does. Like a match dropped onto dry tinder, my body feels like it's instantly going up in flames.

The moment she turns her head and kisses me is the moment I've been dying for. To see if the ever-present attraction and sexual tension between us—which hinted at the possibility of rocking my world—are valid. And her lips on mine prove it. Vaguely, I register the sound of her small clutch purse dropping to the floor. Her hands slip beneath my suit jacket and glide around to the back of my button-down shirt before they descend to cup my ass and tug me closer. A rough sound erupts from deep in my throat at her boldness. I've never encountered someone like Sarah before.

And I like it. A whole hell of a lot.

I rock my hips against her, allowing her to feel how hard I already am and show her what she's doing to me with just a kiss. She tastes like dark chocolate and champagne, and I can't seem to get enough of her. My hand grazes her side, rising to slide the pad of my thumb across the silky smooth skin atop her luscious breasts, and her breath hitches before releasing a tiny moan against my lips. That sound in and of itself sends more blood rushing to my cock. *Jesus.* There's no way in hell I'll be able to return to the dinner party in the state I'm in.

Which means I've got to even the playing field.

My other hand reaches down to her knees and slips underneath the hem of her dress, sliding up the expanse of the smoothest, silkiest thigh I've ever felt, and makes a beeline for her center.

Fucking hell. She's soaked. Sliding a finger over the dampened fabric of her panties, I break the kiss. My lips descend to the graceful column of her neck, and I whisper, "These are mine now." Her chest rises and falls with slightly staggered breathing. It makes me damn glad I'm not the only one who's turned on. "I *might* give them back." My eyes meet her heavy-lidded ones, and I can't resist a smug grin. "Maybe."

Working them down over her hips, I kneel to tug them off the rest of the way and over the fuck-me heels she's wearing. My jaw clenches at the thought of her in only these heels while fucking her and making her scream my name until she's hoarse. Rising, I bring what must be the tiniest excuse for a thong—blue, of course, to match her dress—dangling from my index fingers. And hell if I can't smell her sweet arousal on them.

My eyes fall closed in a painful wince—if I thought I was hard as nails a moment ago, that's nothing compared to right now. Something about this woman just gets to me like no other.

"You always go around stealing women's underwear?"

Goddamn. That voice of hers, the sound of it—slightly husky and heady—and the way her eyes are watching me, as though she'd let me take her right here, right now…

"Actually, I don't." My lips quirk upward. "You're the first." And damn it, I shouldn't be doing this at Ry's engagement dinner party. He's my best friend, for fuck's sake. But when I get around Sarah, all bets are off.

She matches my slight smile. "I'm honored."

Footsteps sound down the small corridor, and her entire body jolts in alarm at the clicking of firm heels upon the stone floor. Abruptly shoving her underwear into my pants pocket, I grab her purse from the floor and reach out to tuck the few stray strands of her hair behind her ear.

"Debauchery time is over." Her whispered words and the underlying tone of disappointment are at odds with the way her eyes crinkle at the corners in humor.

Dipping my head to dust a kiss over her lips, I murmur, "Until later."

"Sarah?"

Her eyes widen at hearing Maggie call out for her. Stepping back where I'm still safely out of sight in the small storage alcove, I place my index finger to my lips and tip my head toward the corridor, gesturing for her to go. With a brief nod, she brushes past me.

But in typical Sarah style, it isn't without a hitch. She allows her palm to brazenly graze my dick.

"I'm here, Maggie." She steps out, and her heels clatter as she walks. "I was just checking out the architecture of this place. But now I've got a really good feel for things."

Nicely done. My lips quirk at her play on words.

I listen for the sounds of their heels to fade before adjusting myself and willing my hard-on to ease.

I had no idea my best friend's engagement party would be this much fun; not to mention I might have a chance with the beautiful blond, soon-to-be maid of honor.

~

Two hours later

Max Londons restaurant

Sweet Jesus. If this woman leans her ass into my crotch one more damn time, I can't guarantee I won't toss her up on the lacquered bar top, part those smooth thighs, and fuck her in front of everyone here. Just the knowledge that her pussy is bare beneath that dress is more than I can handle right now.

I dip my head closer to Sarah's ear and mutter, "You're playing with fire."

It's noisy and crowded here, which is why the handful of us who decided to walk to Max Londons and have a few drinks are standing around the bar, shooting the shit. Actually, "crowded" is a polite way of putting it; packed in like sardines is more like it. On any other day, I'd call it a night and head out. Tonight, though, the overcrowding works in my favor.

Her head turns, gaze locking with mine in the bar's mirrored wall, and a wicked smile toys at her lips. And that's all it takes. Because I refuse to let her one-up me.

Continuing to carry on a conversation with one of Ry's cousins about my business, I casually shift the arm I've been resting on the small portion of available bar space. Using the space beneath the bar top to hide my actions, I slip my hand underneath the back of the short hem of Sarah's dress. Her body stiffens immediately, and I can see the tiny goose bumps popping up on her bare shoulders and arms. Before she can think to react further, I slide my middle finger between her thighs.

And into hot, soaking wet heaven.

The pulse point at the side of her neck is going crazy, and I would give anything to nip at it. Slowly pumping my finger in and out of her, I decide to get even braver—thanks in part to her reaction and probably the number of drinks I've had—and add another finger. It just so happens it's at the exact time she decides to take a sip of her white wine. She sputters and coughs slightly.

Withdrawing my fingers, I pat her on the back, genuinely concerned. She turns to face me fully with ire in her eyes.

"You." She points her slim index finger at the center of my chest.

"Me...?" I raise my eyebrows expectantly.

Crooking her finger at me to lean in closer, I comply. Her cerulean blue eyes meet mine. "You need to decide whether you're taking me home with you or not." There's a brief pause. "Right n—"

"I am." I hold her gaze, not caring that I'm acting like an overeager teen who's about to get laid for the first time in his life. Something about Sarah makes me revert to the painfully nerdy kid I was back in the day.

A wicked gleam shines in her eyes. "Let me say my good-byes, and I'll meet you out on the sidewalk."

"Deal."

She shifts to move away, but I snag her wrist at the last second. Her eyes lift, meeting mine curiously, and I dip my head, bringing my lips to her ear.

"Don't plan on going to the gym tomorrow. You'll be getting more than your fair share of cardio tonight."

Spinning around, I begin bidding my farewells in haste, knowing how I'll be ending my night.

Between Sarah Matthews's thighs.

CHAPTER THREE

SARAH

Goldilocks and the Three Bears. That's what I feel like I'm about to embark on. You know, our girl, "Little G" as I like to refer to her, busts on into that house —one that's *not* hers, by the way, so that warrants an instant, "Girl, you crazy!"—and tries out all the different things: porridge, chairs, and finally beds until she finds one that's *just* right.

I feel like I've been doing that all along; except in my case, it was with penises. *Waaaait*. Now, bear with me on this one, okay? Penises. If you've only seen or been with one, plug your ears because I'll probably send you into some deep, dark depression, and I can't have that on my conscience. Otherwise, stick around for a moment.

Here's the thing. While I wouldn't classify myself as slutty, I've been with my share of men. And each of them had a different "penis story." One guy—many moons ago—was tall and had huge feet. I thought for sure he'd be well hung. *Ohhhh*, no siree. I actually had to ask him, "Are you in yet?"

Go ahead and gasp at my misfortune—and his. It's not like I have a super-sized hoo-ha that could double as some sort of deep abyss or anything. But, right hand to God, there's not a chance in hell I could've told you if his erect penis had delved into my lady cave or not.

Another guy had one of those skinny, pretzel rod penises. It had no girth whatsoever, and while I love me some pretzels (now I'm craving one, damn it!), I sure as hell don't want a guy's appendage to resemble a snack food.

Another one had a curved penis. Yes, I said it. *Curved*. Talk about interesting. I was continuously trying to determine which way I'd have to swivel to get him to hit the right spot.

So you see, I've not had that final "Goldilocks moment." But I have faith Jack's going to change that. I mean, I copped a good feel to see what I'd be working with. Because let's be honest. I've done some "hard time"—pun intended—in "bad penis penitentiary" and deserve to be released from that prison once and for all. I hope I'm finally embarking on my own *"Goldilocks, this one's just right"* penis moment.

And tonight, my friends, is the night.

"You're heading home?" Maggie asks just as I near where she and Ry are chatting with his parents.

"Yes." My smug smile is ridiculously wide and cheesy, and my best friend instantly picks up on it.

Her eyes dart around the room before returning to me. She leans in. "You're not going home alone, are you?"

My smile stretches even wider. "Nope."

Her expression grows troubled. "You need to be careful. I don't want—"

I hold up a hand to stop her. "Maggie, chill. It's all good."

She steps closer, laying a hand on my arm in concern. "But I don't want anyone to get hurt."

"I'm not going to get hurt."

She gives a halfhearted laugh. "It's not you I'm worried about. It's Jack."

Rearing back in surprise, I stare at her. "You're worried about him?"

She lifts a shoulder. She looks awesome in her white halter-style dress with a black lace overlay. "I just get the feeling he's not quite as tough as he seems. And you're..."

"I'm...?" I raise my eyebrows expectantly, but I'm sure I already know what she's about to say. That I'm a ballbuster or tough or something to that extent. Which isn't far from the truth.

It doesn't, however, mean I'm at any less risk for being hurt than the next girl.

"I just don't want things to be weird for the four of us, okay?" The look Maggie gives me has me tugging her close for a hug.

"You know I love you, right?" I say as we embrace. She nods before we break apart. "Then don't worry. We're both adults. It'll be fine."

I receive another skeptical look from Maggie before I hug Ry goodbye and make my way out onto the sidewalk. Although it's August and the temperatures reflect that, I still tug on my thin cardigan, braving the slight chill in the night air since downtown is much like a wind tunnel.

The moment I spot Jack leaning casually against the large black light post with a soft, easy smile playing at his lips, my lady parts officially speak up, practically hollering, "*Put me in, Coach!*"

Ohhh, yeah. Tonight's going to be the night when Jack rounds all my bases before sliding home.

~

Have you ever seen that old show on HBO called *Taxicab Confessions*? If not, go and Google that shit right now. Now. *Doitdoitdoitdoit*. I'm talking hidden cameras, talking freely about anything and everything sexually related, and individuals getting freaky in the back of the cabs, horny as hell after a night of clubbing or doing God knows what.

Well, Jack and I are teetering on the edge of a could-be episode because he's got some serious Roman hands and Russian fingers, if you get my meaning. Naughty Jack Westbrook is fast becoming my favorite.

On a quiet gasp, I tear my lips from his and press them to the cords of his neck to feel his rapidly beating pulse. "You're killing me." My words sound breathless, mixed with his own slightly ragged breathing.

The hand which has been encroaching on my "homeland" territory flexes, and I feel the slight rumble of laughter run through him. "Ah, but I'm pretty sure you're the one who's killing me, gorgeous."

I raise my head just as he turns his own to peer at me with a heavy-lidded gaze. Taking my hand, he guides it to cup his hardness pressing firmly against his slacks and smirks. "But what a way to go, right?" I catch a spark of naughtiness in his eyes before his head descends, and his lips catch mine, his tongue delving deep inside to war with my own.

I'm greeted with mixed feelings when the cab driver pulls up to his place because holy hellaciousness. I don't want Jack to stop, but at the same time, I don't want our cab driver to catch sight of my goods. Nuh-uh. No bueno.

Managing to throw the door of the cab open after Jack pays the fare, we exit quickly, and I practically drag him up the sidewalk so he can punch in his code and unlock the doors to his building. Once inside, we catch an empty elevator, and I shove him against the wall as it ascends.

Making out with Jack Westbrook could be added to my list of things I love. Holy moly. He kisses with just the right amount of tongue. Another Goldilocks moment for me. Not too much tongue, not too little. *Just* right.

You know those kisses you feel all the way to your toes? The ones that make you shiver in the most delicious way? The kisses that make you feel like you've been kiss-starved and need more and more and more?

Jack's kisses have me feeling that right now.

Finally, we exit the elevator and arrive at his door. He aims his key toward the lock, and I cop numerous feels, distracting him until he finally manages to unlock the door and shove it open.

Boom! Once we're locked inside, I press my palms against Jack's muscled chest, backing him against the door. If I thought our kisses in the elevator moments ago were hot, I was sorely mistaken. Because when our mouths fuse again, it's a kiss hot enough to melt off my panties.

If I still had them on, that is.

My hands frantically unbutton his suit jacket, and he breaks the kiss to peer down, those dark blue eyes watching me with a mixture of amusement and barely restrained lust.

"In a bit of a hurry, are we?"

Without responding, I move on to tackle his belt and quickly unfasten his pants enough to allow me to reach inside his black boxer briefs and feel what I've been hoping to get my hands on.

Jackpot, baby. Jack-freaking-pot. Jack Jr. gets my stamp of approval already, simply by judging his size and girth. *Ohhhh, yeah.*

Shifting with the intention of dropping down to get "better acquainted" with JJ—yes, I've already nicknamed Jack Jr.—Jack's firm grip on my upper arms draws me to a stop. My eyes dart up to his in question, and I find him watching me with the slightest smirk playing on his lips. His eyes are slightly glassy from the number of drinks we've had tonight, but he still seems alert and "in the game."

"Not yet." God, that sexy smirk combined with the deep, rich sound of his voice sends tingles straight down to my core, making me squeeze my legs together to ease the pressure.

Abruptly, he rids himself of his sharp black dress shoes and kicks off his pants, standing before me in his suit jacket, button-down shirt, and boxer briefs, and I swear to you, my ovaries are practically chanting his name. *Jack, Jack, Jack.* Suddenly, I'm scooped up in his arms.

When is the last time I had a guy pick me up like I weighed next to nothing—no groaning or anything—to carry me off for sexy times? Hmmm, let me think about that.

The answer is *never*. Which makes this even more memorable.

"Pulling out all the stops tonight, aren't you?" My voice is breathless, and I loop my arms around his neck as he carries me to the bedroom. Soft shards of moonlight are streaming through the small slats of the venetian blinds, casting an ethereal glow upon the room.

Setting me on my feet beside the bed, he turns me around, gliding his hands over my cardigan and tossing it aside. Once he removes the clips from my hair, his fingers drape my hair over one shoulder, pressing a light kiss to the nape of my neck. He caresses my bare shoulders before tracing a finger down the middle of my back and sliding down the zipper of my dress. The fabric gives way and falls in a heap at my feet, leaving me clad in only my bra and heels.

He releases a long exhale, and his hot breath washes over my skin. "Your ass"—he slips a hand down, fingertips grazing my skin—"is so fucking hot."

I'm startled at the sudden nip on my shoulder, but he immediately soothes it with his tongue and lips. Another hand slips around to cup the fullness of my right breast, his thumb dipping into my bra to slide across a pebbled nipple. "I can't wait to put my mouth on these." The feel of the slightly calloused pad of his thumb elicits a gasp, and I arch into his touch.

Spinning around, I make quick work of tugging off his suit jacket before tackling the buttons of his shirt with much less grace than I'd like to admit, but time is of the essence here. This man needs to be naked, and I need his skin on mine—stat.

Gazing up into his eyes, heavy-lidded with arousal, I whisper, "You won't need to go to the gym tomorrow morning, either, buddy."

CHAPTER FOUR

JACK

S arah's practically shredding my shirt in her haste to remove it, and if it were under any other circumstance, I'd be pissed since it's Armani and cost an arm and a leg. However, I want to be rid of my clothes just as badly—if not more—as she does. The urge to feel her silky soft flesh against mine without the barrier of clothing is excruciatingly fierce.

Tossing my shirt aside, I reach around to find the clasp of her bra and let it drop at our feet. Nothing could prevent me from taking those luscious breasts in my hands, cupping their weight, and dipping my head to take one nipple in my mouth. I suckle it before laving it with my tongue.

Sarah's hands tug at the waistband of my boxer briefs, dragging them down, and I kick them off to the side. The second my dick is released from its constraints, and her petite hand grasps it, it takes everything in my power not to come right then. Her soft palm grips me, gliding up and down in slow, steady strokes before she slides the pad of her thumb over the tip, gathering the moisture there.

But that's not what has me nearly losing my mind. What makes my entire body shudder in anticipation of those lips wrapping around my cock is when she brings her thumb to her lips and sucks it clean.

Gripping her waist, I steady her as she steps out of her heels. I lift her, and she settles onto the bed. Her blond hair fans against the pillow, and her chest rises and falls likely with the same anticipation I feel.

Joining her, I prop myself up on my forearms, and the instant my flesh meets hers, neither of us can resist the low hiss that escapes our lips. I feel singed by the contact, the heat radiating through my body. When I capture her mouth, the way she returns the kiss with such passionate abandon sends shards of gratification through me. As I rock my hips slightly, the tip of my cock rubs against her clit, and the tiny groan in the back of her throat urges me on.

I tear my lips from hers and slip down her body, dropping kisses along the beautiful landscape of curves and softness until I'm between her slim thighs and my hands press her legs wider. Placing my mouth over her, I slip my tongue inside, and my cock jerks at the first taste of her.

My tongue darts and retreats, and her hips begin to move in response. She works herself against my mouth, her fingers entwining in my hair. As her whispered moans and the tightening of her firm thighs indicate she's nearing her orgasm, I slide up her body. I have to be inside her.

Now.

Pressing a gentle kiss to her lips, I gaze down into her eyes. With my hands framing her face, I skim my thumbs across her cheekbones. And I can't help but be a bit awed by the fact that I've put that hunger in her eyes. I'm the cause for the light catch in her breath.

"You'd better be about to grab a condom." Her words are breathless and belie the demanding tone—the typical, no-nonsense Sarah I've come to know.

Grinning down at her, I can't resist teasing her. "I'm actually kind of hung—" My words are cut off when she tugs me closer, and it throws me a bit off-balance.

Damn. Maybe I shouldn't have had that last drink at Max Londons.

"Condom," she murmurs huskily. "Now."

The fact that she's resorting to brief, staccato commands spurs me on. Reaching over to my bedside table, I pluck a condom packet and quickly sheath myself. I'm at the precipice of pain with how hard I am right now. Pressing my tip to her entrance, I lock my gaze with hers, and something I can't decipher flashes in her eyes.

Sliding my thumb across her cheekbone, I whisper, "You're beautiful."

A soft smile plays at her lips. "Quit stalling, Westbrook." Her smile widens saucily. "I've been waiting a long time for you."

I've been waiting a long time for you. Her words rattle around my mind before they slide down, leaving a trail of warmth behind.

The thick head of my cock nudges against her opening, and I shift my hips, watching as her eyes fall closed. Her thighs tighten around my waist, and her responsiveness emboldens me further. Just as I press firmly, sliding my length inside her inch by inch, her lips part on an inaudible gasp. I duck my head and give into my urge at the same moment her inner muscles clench around me.

My teeth sink into the side of her neck as I work my cock in a little deeper. Then she's suddenly shoving me away, her palms pressing insistently against my chest.

I lift to brace my weight above her and peer down with concern. She moves a hand to her neck, staring up at me with eyes wide with shock. "What the hell was that?"

Shit. What did I do?

"What was what?" Jesus. Is it just dark in here or is my vision becoming hazy?

24

"Dude. You *bit* me." Her tone holds a mixture of disbelief and accusation. "Hard."

"Sorry," I offer with a sheepish smile. "I guess I got a little carried away." I swear, I read in *Cosmo* or *Glamour* that women got off on biting. Maybe I did it too hard?

Her lips quirk up at the corners. "Tone it down on the biting, Westbrook." She wraps a hand around the base of my neck, drawing me down for a kiss, and I slip farther inside, both of our moans muffled by our joined lips.

Once I'm buried deep inside her, I work my hips, thrusting in and out slowly before quickening my pace. She breaks the kiss, and her lips part as she throws her head back on the pillow.

She is the most gorgeous sight I've ever seen.

Judging by the way her inner muscles tighten around me and the way her breathing has become staggered and harsh, much like my own, I know she's about to find her release. I anticipate feeling her pussy spasm all around me and can't resist trailing kisses down the column of her neck down to her collarbone. An idea hits me, and as I hike up one of her legs and bend it at the knee, I look forward to seeing how wild she'll get.

"Who's my naughty girl?" I ask, spanking the side of her hip.

"*Jesus!*" She shoves me even harder than before—hard enough that I land beside her. Her hand flies to the side of her hip to gingerly rub the area I just spanked.

"That hurt." She stares at me incredulously before scrambling off the bed, grabbing my shirt, and pulling it on quickly before tossing over her shoulder, "I have to...use the restroom."

With a frustrated groan, I fling an arm over my eyes. *Fuck.* I really thought she'd like that. Sarah seems like the type of woman who'd be on board with it. Obviously, an awkward as hell nerd can grow up and discover contact lenses and better clothing, but when it comes to women, it's the same old story.

Clueless as hell.

Damn it. Removing my arm from my face, I peer down at my dick. I've never been so hard before in my life. And judging by the way she sprinted off to the bathroom, I'm guessing I'm in for a horrendous case of blue balls.

After tossing the condom in the waste bin by my bed, I roll onto my side and tug the pillow closer, breathing in the faint scent lingering from her hair. When my eyesight grows fuzzy and the room begins to sway slightly, my eyes fall closed to ward off the dizziness.

"Shit," I exhale on a sigh in the silence of the bedroom. I hope I can talk to her and somehow save face when she returns from the bathroom.

That's the last thing I remember.

CHAPTER FIVE

SARAH

What is this? Fifty Shades of Westbrook?

Sweet baby Jesus in swaddling clothes, that freaking hurt like hell! My sensitive skin will surely have welts tomorrow, not to mention there's a good chance my collarbone will be bruised from his bite.

Shoving Jack away, I quickly grab his shirt and tug it on, and—discreetly grabbing my cell phone—excuse myself to the safe haven of his en suite bathroom.

Closing myself inside, I breathe a sigh of relief and lean with my back against the door. I can't call Maggie since she's celebrating her special night, so my fingers fly over my phone, preparing a text message to the only other person who might be able to rescue me.

Clint.

Me: 911, now. NOW. Please. For the love of ALL THAT'S HOLY.

I stare at my phone, willing it to light up. Because every woman knows the code I just pulled with Clint, my coworker. And being a Prada-loving gay man, Clint will know what's what and see it for the definitive *Get me out of this situation, please* text. It's a cry for help.

A glaringly loud one.

Flushing the toilet for good measure and then washing my hands, I swear I'm practically channeling my inner Jedi mind tricks to get Clint to respond to my text.

Finally—*fi-na-lly*—the screen of my phone lights up and rings as I'm drying my hands.

"Oh my gosh! Are you okay? What happened?" I exclaim loudly, not bothering to wait for Clint's greeting.

"You'd better take me to brunch with endless mimosas tomorrow, beotch," he responds dryly. Then he utters in monotone, "Come and rescue me, honey."

"I'll be right there."

Rushing out of the bathroom, I practically skid across the hardwood floor of Jack's bedroom in my haste to collect the rest of my clothes.

Only to find him dead asleep.

Guess I phoned a friend for nothing.

Once I'm fully clothed, I tiptoe around so as not to rouse him in any way and take one last glance at the handsome man lying on the bed before me. An arm is flung out into the space where I had been lying only moments ago, his chest rising and falling steadily with each breath. His lips are parted slightly, and a small lock of hair has shifted over his forehead.

I carefully pull the covers up over him and can't resist a slight smile at how boyish he appears right now. Quite the contrast to Mr. *I'm going to bite and spank you*—hard—from mere minutes earlier.

Spying his cell phone lying on the nightstand, I can't resist the temptation to screw with him. Once I quickly tap a few keys, I return it to its place on the dark mahogany wood.

"Sarah." My head whips around at Jack's low murmur. His eyes are closed. *Is he awake?* "I could really picture us together..." He trails off, his voice heavy with sleep. "...could be my wife."

At his words, my entire body freezes. He's obviously talking in his sleep, but *whoa*. This isn't what I signed up for. I don't need him getting any ideas like that—because I'm definitely not interested in something serious.

Quickly exiting the apartment, I hurry down to slip into the cab.

The entire ride home, I stare blankly out the window and can't help but wonder what might have been.

And his sleep-whispered words continue to haunt me.

~

"It's not that funny! It really hurt!"

My best friend is officially dead to me. She's currently doubled over in laughter, nearly falling off the couch after listening to me tell her what happened last night.

"I'm...sorry." Maggie attempts to smother her laughter and promptly fails.

"Yeah. You're so incredibly sorry. I can totally feel the sincerity in your words," I mutter dryly, leaning back into the corner of the couch to wait until she gets herself under control.

Finally, Maggie's giggles subside, and she reaches over to the laptop resting on the coffee table and pulls it on her lap. "We're going to have to research this."

"What's to research?"

Maggie pulls up Google and types in "biting," "spanking," and "fetishes." She turns and peers at me closely. "Did he draw blood?"

I barely resist a shudder at the thought. "No, thank God." My fingers move to my left collarbone subconsciously. "I have a bit of a bruise, though."

Her eyebrows rise, and she gasps. "What if he watched those *Twilight* movies too many times?"

"Wouldn't explain the spanking thing."

Maggie's face falls. "Oh. Right."

"Unless he's trying to combine the whole vampire thing with…"

"Light BDSM?" she offers.

I cover my face with my hands with a loud groan. "I don't even want to think about this." Releasing another groan, I blow out a long breath. "It's like the universe is trying to tell me something."

"Like you're not cut out for sadomasochism?" Maggie offers helpfully.

Pulling my hands away from my face, I shoot her a dirty look. "It was going so great, Maggie." I tug one of the throw pillows to my chest, hugging it tightly. "And then *bam!* He put me on the express train to crazy town." I let out a sigh. "That's not the worst part, though."

"What could be worse than getting bruised from being bitten and a welt from being spanked?"

My lips twist wryly. "Getting lady blue balls from the whole experience."

"Sarah." Maggie rolls her eyes at me. "You did not get lady blue balls."

"I did!" I protest, standing up and pacing back and forth in the living room. "He had me so freaking close. So close, Maggie."

She curls her legs up beneath her on the couch, resting her head against the cushion and watching me with interest. "And it was good before…?"

"Before he pulled me into Fifty Shades of Westbrook? Yesssss." My breath comes out in a slow hiss. "It was so. Freaking. Good." I pause. "And he still packed another whammy with his sleep talking."

Maggie gives me a look. "I think that was sweet."

I make a face like I'm about to be ill. "Sweet? Not even."

Dropping onto the couch in a heap, I stare up at the ceiling and brace for the reaction I know is coming. "By the way, I've decided to take the job."

Maggie's quiet for a moment. "Which job?"

I grimace at the wary softness in her tone. "The travel nursing job."

"You're leaving?"

"I think it's a good decision. Not only that, but it'll also be a great experience." I say this with a sigh because I'm going to miss my best friend something fierce. "I've always wanted to try out travel nursing. And who knows?" I shrug, trying to pass my words off as casual. "I might end up finding someone who's normal in the bedroom."

After restructuring and cutbacks at the hospital where I'd been employed twenty minutes away in nearby Ballston Spa, I'd gotten in touch with my contact offering a travel nursing position. The job starts with a three-month stint in California, and then more scheduled positions follow in other locations along the West Coast.

"Where's the first position?"

"San Diego."

Maggie's features depict both surprise and dismay. "San Diego?" Her shoulders slump. "That's so far away."

"I know." God, this sucks. "I'm going to drive there, so I have to leave Tuesday. But we can Skype and everything while I'm gone. It'll be fine." The forced cheerfulness in my tone is obvious.

"But...you'll be back in time for the wedding, right?"

The hesitation in her voice bothers me. Lightly gripping her shoulders, I offer my bravest smile. I know it's weak at best, but I try. "Maggie. You know I wouldn't miss it for the world." Pulling her in for a hug, I hold tight. "I'll miss you."

"I'll miss you, too," she whispers back softly. We embrace for longer than normal because I know it'll be a while before I see her again.

Maybe it's selfish, but I want to take advantage of this opportunity to bounce around and get great work experience.

It doesn't escape me that I'll also be leaving behind the memory of the handsome man who ended our night in the worst way possible.

~

The day I left Saratoga Springs to head to San Diego

Jack: Hey, I've been trying to get a hold of you, but you're not answering your phone. I wanted to say blue balls for everything the other night.

Jack: Wait. I'm trying to say blue balls.

Jack: Christ. I'm trying to apologize, but every time I try to say blue balls, it says blue balls.

Me: Maybe your phone is trying to tell you something…

Jack: Did you do this to my phone?

Jack: What am I asking? Of course, you did this to my phone.

Me: You have yet to apologize to me, Westbrook. Keep trying. Wait. Do you hear that? That's the sound of my maniacal laughter.

~

Three months later

Jack: Roses are red,
Violets are blue,
Blue balls
For falling asleep on you.

Me: Why have you not changed it back? Seriously, Jack? I know you're smarter than this.

Jack: It got you to respond after you went radio silent on me for a few months. I call that a win.

Me: Need I remind you of the fact you fell asleep AFTER you bit and spanked me? And both were WAY too hard.

Jack: Would it be insensitive to mention that wasn't all that was hard that night?

Me: It wouldn't have made a difference if your penis had been like a freaking windsock. You still bit and spanked me.

Jack: Blue balls.

Me: I know you are.

~

Six months later

Jack: Just checking in. Heard that Justin Bieber song a minute ago, and he says something like "Is it too late now to say blue balls?"

Jack: Well, he obviously doesn't say blue balls. You know what I mean.

Me: Would you stop already? Just change your damn phone settings back!

Jack: But this is so much fun. When I have to apologize and say blue balls.

Jack: By the way, I was listening to that eighties song by Chicago, "Hard to Say I'm blue balls."

Jack: Well, you know the song.

Me: Jack. Stop.

Jack: It got you to talk to me again. I miss our text messages. They're so chock full of warmth and goodness.

Me: I've been working my ass off. I eat, sleep, and breathe work.

Jack: Oh, blue balls to hear that. So blue balls, Sarah.

Me: OMG, Jack. I swear, I'm going to block your number.

Jack: Why would you do that? And stop all this fun? Just think of the stories we'll tell our children about how things first started with their mom and dad. Or, more importantly, how their mom wooed their dad.

Me: First, there aren't going to be any children. Second, we sure as hell won't be telling them about how we were both left with blue balls.

Jack: You wouldn't tell the children that part. But the part about how you wooed me... Surely, you'd mention that.

Me: There will be NO stories because there will be NO children!

Jack: What?! But children love stories! Would you really deny the children the story of how our love first began?! YOU CAN'T DENY THE CHILDREN!

Thirty minutes later

Jack: You can only ignore me for so long.

~

Nine months later

Jack: Word on the street is that you'll be returning home to Saratoga Springs soon. Maybe we can get together in person so I can say blue balls.

Me: Seriously, Jack. Stop. It.

Jack: What can I say? I'm nothing if not persistent.

Me: Or annoying.

Jack: Admit it. You miss me.

Me: Please stop. Please.

Jack: Prepare yourself. I might even sing you Chicago's hit song, "Hard to Say I'm blue balls." Unless you'd prefer that Bieber one...

Me: Gah! Stop it!!

Me: Wait a minute... Your body is freaking amazing, you dress really well, AND you love eighties music and know a Bieber song. You're either gay...

Jack: I'm not gay.

Me: Or you're a unicorn amongst the male species.

Jack: I'm a unicorn.

Jack: A really manly unicorn, though. With really big hooves. And a MASSIVE horn.

Me: I'm done here.

Jack: See you soon. Maybe if you're a good girl, you can go for a ride...

Me: Westbrook. Don't.

Jack: Ah, but I've missed you. Messing with you via text isn't the same.

Me: Good night, Jack.

Jack: Sweet dreams, Sarah. Sweet dreams.

CHAPTER SIX

SARAH

Back in Saratoga Springs, New York

T here's something to be said for running from your problems.

Or rather running from the man who came so close to making you scream his name only to send you fleeing from his biting and spanking. And we won't give mention to the other words he sleep-mumbled that night.

Of course, I hadn't been able to completely distance myself from what I'd left behind in Saratoga. The first text had come in the day I'd been packing up to start my drive to San Diego.

Yeah, well... I *may* have programmed Jack's phone to replace the word "sorry" with "blue balls," but I refuse to feel bad about it. It could be worse. *Much* worse. Especially considering the fact that during the "debacle," I'd been on the brink of orgasming before he'd spanked me.

The only consolation is the knowledge that Jack was just as painfully aroused that night.

I hadn't disclosed to him in those text messages that I'd

accepted an out of town job, packed up my car, and was intent on leaving everything behind in Saratoga Springs for nearly a year. I'd let him find out through Maggie and Ry.

A cop-out, for sure, but my damn collarbone hurt for *days*. That damn bruise took forever to fade, and I had to be sure to cover that sucker up, fearing people would think I was either a battered spouse or into some freaky shit.

Did what happened with Jack make me consider sinking down into a hot bath, chugging champagne straight from the bottle while listening to a compilation of the saddest—and depressing as hell—Adele songs? To mourn the fact that the delectably gorgeous man I'd been lusting over apparently preferred to channel his inner freak-ho?

Nope. Not at all.

Okay, *yes*. But that stays between us. Because we all know that's a cry for help. I can't help that when it comes to Jack, my brain never really tends to be my ally.

I'd exchanged a few text messages here and there with Jack, and obviously, he's tried to apologize. The thing about horny vaginas, though? They never forget. They remember everything—especially when they're halted on the brink of an orgasm. And they hold grudges. *Big* time. My vagina is still scarred even now. If she could talk, she'd be like, "Honey-child, don't you ever bring me close to that man again, ya hear?"

I probably should've mentioned that my vagina's voice resembles a version of Aunt Jemima, shouldn't I? Mmm, my bad.

But seriously. She was scarred from the "incident" with Jack, and I'm telling you, she kept repeating, "What the hell just happened?" on the cab ride home that night.

Also, I should have disclosed the fact that my vagina speaks to me. Try to ignore how strange that is.

Now that I'm back in Saratoga Springs, though, I must admit that it feels good to be here. It really does...for a moment. For an extremely *brief* moment. Because after that moment's up, I recall why I'm back and what I'll soon have to face—the sole reason I couldn't muster up much excitement or interest in any other guy during my travel nursing stint. The one person I was unable to get off my mind; the man who seemed to cast some crazy spell over me, ruining me for other men.

Jack Westbrook.

Maggie and Ry's wedding is fast approaching, and me as her maid of honor and Jack as the best man, we're going to be thrust together once again. I have to fortify myself so I'm fully prepared to face him; the man I'm not entirely sure I'm looking forward to encountering after that god-awful debacle.

"Are you sure you'll be able to make it down to the dress shop to have your final measurements taken?" Maggie asks me for what I calculate to be the sixth time. I'm not annoyed, though—I've noticed that tiny crease between her eyebrows. I don't want her to fret and doubt her and Ry's special day will be anything but perfect.

"Yes, sweetie. I promise I'll be there." I hold up my cell phone. "I even programmed a reminder an hour beforehand." Reaching down from where I'm seated on their couch, I grab my purse. "I'm going to head home and..." I catch a silent exchange between Maggie and Ry. "What was that?"

Maggie's expression is one of utter innocence. "What was what?"

My eyes narrow in suspicion as I gesture between them. "That little look you two had just now."

"It was—"

"We just—"

They both start and stop abruptly before Maggie finally lets out a long sigh, fixing an expectant look upon me. "We hoped you and Jack could try to move past what happened and help us with everything for the wedding."

Biting the inside of my cheek before answering, I attempt to school my expression. "Sure thing."

And fail because best friends...yep. Best friends are all-knowing.

"Sarah." My name is spoken on an exhale. And I know what's coming next. "Please." Maggie's expression is pleading, hopeful. "Can you do this for me?"

Damn it. I'll have to willingly be in the company of the man who left me high and dry in the worst way possible.

Mr. Blue Balls, here I come.

CHAPTER SEVEN

JACK

She's back.

A shard of excitement and anticipation rushes through me. Sarah's back in Saratoga Springs from her travel nursing stint.

"She's still pretty weirded out about what happened with you."

Scratch that. My excitement and anticipation have officially begun to ebb at Ry's statement.

Scrubbing a hand over my face, I slump against a locker in our gym's locker room, waiting for him to tie his shoes. We've just finished playing racquetball, and I swear, being in love, engaged, and preparing to get married has made him cross over into the superhero stage of a racquetball opponent. He kicked my ass out on that damn court.

With a sigh, I stare at the row of lockers across from me. "Yeah, I know."

He grins. "What the hell happened? I only got the bare bones version from Sarah, which was that you took"—he hooks his fingers in air quotes—"a bite out of her collarbone, and if that wasn't enough, you also spanked her hard." There's a pause, and he presses his lips thin as if to restrain a smile and laughter. "Please tell me you didn't go all snuff porn on her."

With a groan, I softly thud my head back against the metal locker. "It's fucking hilarious, I know," I remark dryly.

I hadn't wanted to talk to Ry about what went down between me and Sarah because it was too damn embarrassing. Luckily, he and Maggie hadn't badgered me about it. But, now, with Sarah returning home …

"Did you make her call you Sir?" His eyes widen, lighting up with laughter. "Or maybe you collared her? Poured hot wax on her?" He's not even trying to resist a widening grin as his white teeth nearly blind me now. "Tell me the truth. You had her call you Big Daddy, didn't you?"

Barely a beat of silence passes before my best friend doubles over on the wooden bench, and his entire body shakes with laughter at my expense.

Once it dies down to soft chuckles, Ry clears his throat. "So what happened. For real?" He rests his elbows on his knees, watching me.

Running a hand through my hair, I exhale, staring up at the ceiling of the locker room. "I'm still the nerd—the mega geek. I've always been, even after all these years. Maybe I traded my glasses for contacts, finally have a decent haircut, and clothes that actually fit and are in style, but deep down—"

"You're still the same nerd around a woman you're interested in," Ry finishes for me.

Pushing off the locker, I wave a hand in gesture. "Dude. I read articles about what women like or want. And those *Fifty Shades* books and movies are so popular, so I thought…" I trail off.

"You thought she'd be on board with it." Ry offers a small smile. "I get it, man. I do, but," he breaks off with a chuckle, "it's still pretty damn funny."

"Yeah," I deadpan. "Hilarious."

"One thing's certain." He rises from the bench, slinging his gym bag over one shoulder. "You need to figure out how to break the ice in order to get through all this wedding stuff."

"Hey, now. What's with the doubt? I exchanged a few text messages with her while she was away. Plus, you know how charming I can be. It's in the bag."

My best friend simply shakes his head at me and mutters, "We'll see."

I don't want to admit that I might just have that same niggling doubt.

~

Be at the Tux and Bridal Boutique at 10AM sharp, please. ☺

That's the text message I received from Maggie yesterday after I got home from racquetball with Ry.

Don't be a weirdo to Sarah. Smooth things over, cupcake.

The message that followed was from Ry, and his use of the old nickname I'd given him doesn't slip past me. I'd nicknamed him that while he pretended to be my gay lover in order to get closer to Maggie while she'd been firmly set in her anti-dating stage. Nor does it escape me that my best friend still has no faith in me. Which means I have to bring my A-game.

Time to woo the hell out of the sexy, sassy spitfire of a blonde and get back in her good graces.

~

I'm dead in the water. Crash and burn style.

Nothing is working on Sarah, but I'm not giving up. I didn't become a successful business consultant by being a quitter.

"What about this one? I, for one, think you should exchange the bridesmaid dress Maggie picked for this one."

I'm holding up what must be the gaudiest bridesmaid dress I've ever laid eyes on. It's from the eighties, that much is certain. Gaudy as shit and looks like some preteen bedazzled the hell out of it.

Oh, and it's hot pink.

The look she gives me says she's not amused, but I'm not one to give up easily. Luckily, I don't care about looking like a fool, so I hold the heinous excuse for a dress up to my front and start swaying back and forth while I softly sing Madonna's "Like A Virgin."

Just when I'm really getting into it, closing my eyes and going so far as to run my hand through my hair and down my neck dramatically, I suddenly feel her palms on my chest. Opening my eyes, I peer down, and that's when I see it.

Jackpot, baby. The corners of those beautiful lips of hers are quivering, and I know I've got her. "Jack, please. Stop."

With exaggerated seriousness, I pout. "But I was just getting started. Next was my all-time favorite song." Then I let out a breathy, whimsical sigh. "Girls Just Wanna Have Fun."

Her chin drops to her chest, and she shakes her head, shoulders shaking slightly, and I know it. She's weakening...

Abruptly, her head snaps up, and she shoves me. Giving me that squinty-eyed look, she hisses, "Stop making me laugh. I'm supposed to be mad at you, you jerk!"

Neither the fire in her eyes nor the fierceness of her scowl can detract from her beauty as I gaze down at her. Maybe I'm a glutton for punishment, but I love how feisty she is.

"And anyway"—she steps back—"I already have a dress. They have to take my final measurements to be sure everything fits as it should since I haven't tried it on yet."

An older woman comes out holding the designated bridesmaid dress and gestures for Sarah to follow her to the women's section of the dressing rooms near the back of the store. Quickly, I replace the gaudy excuse for a dress on the rack and trail behind the two women.

Taking a seat in one of the plush chairs, I wait for Sarah to change. The moment she steps out for the woman to take her measurements, my breath catches in my throat, and I can't help but stare. The dress is a soft shade of lavender, strapless, knee-length, and it hugs every curve like it was made for her.

"Wow." Yeah. That's all I've got. No one would know that I graduated magna cum laude from college—both undergrad and grad school.

Sarah tosses a sharp look in my direction. "Is that a good wow or a bad wow?"

"Good. Definitely good." *Jesus, Westbrook.* I sound like a freaking numbnuts.

The woman moves around Sarah, taking measurements as she goes. "I'd suggest taking this in a bit in this area here." She pinches the fabric of the inside seam directly beneath Sarah's underarm area, pinning it. "You want it to be a little snugger across your breasts."

Sarah darts a quick glance in my direction, and I can't resist a smug grin, wiggling my eyebrows at her. The woman finishes pinning the dress and directs her to undress before rushing off to see another customer.

Wanting to catch her before she can head back to the room, I step up on the carpeted area behind her. She regards her reflection in the mirror, and I swear I detect a tinge of uncertainty in her eyes. It's as though she might be doubting —or be unaware of—how magnificent she looks. And that just won't do.

Smoothing her silky hair back to bare one shoulder, I lock my gaze with hers in the mirror. I lower my head, bringing my lips close to her ear, and they brush against the shell as I speak. "You just might give Maggie a run for her money."

"Stop trying to sweet talk me." Her pulse point is beating

rapidly, and combined with the slight breathlessness in her voice, it gives her away.

"We're supposed to have a truce," I whisper softly. "For Maggie and Ry." She eyes me warily. Holding her gaze in the mirror, I tip my head to the side with a quizzical expression on my face. "Do you feel that?"

Squinting at me with suspicion, she asks slowly, "Feel what?"

I widen my eyes in excitement. "I feel a hug coming on."

Her eyes narrow, and she steps away, intent on making her way to the changing room. "You should feel it dissipate. That's what you should feel, Westbrook."

"Is that any way to talk to the best man?" I watch as she walks away, body encased in lavender, and her ass beckons me. She mutters something before shutting the door behind her, and my eyes drop to the only visible part of her body— her sleek, muscled calves and delicate feet, her toes painted a soft pink.

Shit. I discreetly adjust myself. Clearly, I've sunk to an all new low by letting a woman's lower legs and feet arouse me. What kind of a fucking weirdo is she turning me into?

"Mr. Westbrook?" At the sound of the tailor's voice, I turn and find him watching me with an apologetic expression. "I'm sorry for the wait. Your tux was accidentally misplaced."

He looks nervous as hell, and it's probably because the abundance of wealthy people in this area believe that having money means you don't need good manners or have to be kind to others.

Offering an easy smile, I wave him off. "Don't worry about it..." I quickly scan his nametag. "Allen. I'm not in a hurry today."

The relief on his face is palpable. "Thank you, sir. We'll get you to a changing room over here and then ensure your measurements are accurate."

Following him to the men's fitting room on the other side

of the boutique, I quickly disrobe and pull on the tux. As often as I wear a suit for meetings with new or potential clients, you'd think I'd be accustomed to it. Even so, I still prefer casual clothes any day. But, hey, this is for my best friend's wedding. I'd do just about anything for the guy.

Fastening the buttons of the white shirt, I tug on the jacket and pants. Allen wants confirmation that everything fits properly, so I step out of the dressing room door. Automatically, my eyes seek out Sarah, and when I watch her turn from perusing a display of fancy looking purses and other accessories, her gaze snags mine, and she appears to falter slightly at the sight of me.

Allen appears pleased with the fit—aside from my inseam, apparently. I give him a sharp look when his hands get a little too "neighborly" with my crotch. He skitters away, muttering that my tux will be ready in time for the wedding. I guess I can't blame the guy for wanting to get handsy with me. Plus, I realize it's karma for pretending to be Ry's gay lover for a year.

Raising my eyes from the elevated steps where I stand, I can see the top of Sarah's blond head in the shoe section. Evasion. I know she liked the sight of me—know she still feels that fierce tug of attraction whenever we're in the same vicinity. Which is likely why she took advantage of Allen's handsy moment and my subsequent distraction to move farther away.

"Oh, Sunshine," I call out to her. I watch as she ducks down, trying to hide. Chuckling softly, I return to the dressing room to change.

You can run, but you can't hide.

CHAPTER EIGHT

SARAH

It's confirmed. I'm in love.

I'm seriously in honest to goodness love. It might be one-sided, but I swear it's the real thing. I have the sweaty palms, the shortness of breath, the dry mouth—the whole nine yards.

"If it were possible to be sexually attracted to an object, this would be it," I murmur softly to myself, coveting the sparkly heels in my hands.

"Then get them."

The sudden sound of Jack's voice behind me causes me to physically jerk. My lips tip down at him suddenly homing in on my special moment. And trust me, it was special. It was just me and these spectacular heels beautiful enough to remind me of something Cinderella would wear to a ball.

Minus the asshole prince who doesn't remember what she looks like when she's not wearing a face full of makeup and a pretty dress, of course. Because, yeah. Talk about a douche of epic proportions.

Scrunching my face, I give him my best side-eye. "I can't do that."

"Sure, you can." He says it just like that. Like it's easy peasy.

With a long sigh, I stare at him.

He simply waves a hand at me. "Don't look at me like I just confessed to sharing responsibility for kidnapping the Lindbergh baby or something."

Huffing out a short laugh, I return my eyes to the shoes as I place them back in their box on the shelf.

"Get them, Sunshine."

I'm ignoring his new—and obviously snarky—nickname for me because I don't want to get into it with him. "I can't do that."

"Why not?"

"Because"—I purse my lips—"I'm a nurse, and I don't... have anywhere to wear them. Aside from the rare occurrence of a wedding."

"Or out to a nice dinner one night."

I peer at him skeptically. "A nice dinner?"

"Yeah. A nice dinner out where you dress to the nines and splurge a little on food that's delicious and packed with calories. And"—he leans in with exaggerated emphasis—"you even get dessert." He covers his mouth with his hand, eyes going wide as if what he just said was scandalous.

And it kind of is.

"I don't...know..." I'm hesitant. He's planted the seed, and can you hear that? That sound?

Damn it. The roots have already begun to grow.

But, no! Nooooo. It wouldn't be practical. It wouldn't be—

Jack abruptly grabs the box with the heels I've been coveting and walks down the aisle toward the counter.

Sputtering, I give chase. "But wait! You can't—"

He stops suddenly, causing me to nearly barrel into him, but I catch myself just in time. "I can." He pauses. "Are these your size?"

I can only manage to nod numbly.

His expression softens. "You're one of the hardest working people I know, Sarah. You deserve this." With a shake of his head, he adds, "Actually, you deserve far more than this."

Just as he turns back, I blurt, "And who's going to take me out to this fancy dinner you speak of?"

Meeting my eyes again, he steps closer and his word is low and husky.

"Me."

~

Two and a half hours have passed, and Jack and I have taken care of the final fittings, checked on the deliveries for the wedding cake, and chosen our personal gifts for Maggie and Ry.

Now, we're in floral hell trying to choose centerpieces because neither Maggie nor Ry can decide—or care—about any of the floral arrangements.

"What about plain roses? Then we can have the DJ play the Tango." Jack plucks a long-stemmed rose from a nearby bucket filled with dozens upon dozens of the fragrant flowers and places it between his teeth. His fingers encircle my wrist, and I'm tugged against the firm wall of his chest. Quickly setting the shopping bag with the heels he insisted on purchasing for me aside, he nudges it beneath the nearby display table. One of his hands settles at my waist while the other grasps my hand.

And he freaking leads me into a Tango-like walk down the main aisle of the flower shop.

Before I can escape his clutches, he dips me, and my hair flies back. He has that stupid rose still secured between his perfect teeth with his lips curved into a smile. His dark blue eyes are dancing in amusement, and I can't resist a little laugh at his antics.

He lets the rose drop soundlessly to the floor, and his

features change, eyes darkening, as they flicker between my lips and my eyes. My breath catches with the anticipation that he'll close the distance between us and kiss me. What's worse is I want him to. Badly. Even after what happened.

Traitorous lips. Traitorous hormones. Traitorous—

"Hey, you two!"

At the sound of the shop owner's voice, I jerk with a start, causing Jack to nearly lose his grip on me. Thankfully, he rights us swiftly enough that I'm certain my hair whipped forward so fast I've given my own cheeks brush burn.

Smoothing down the fabric of my sleeveless blouse, I attempt to compose myself and do everything in my power to avoid meeting Jack's gaze. It feels like I've blasted back in time to the fifth grade when I lied to my teacher about being allowed to wear lipstick. Totally failed at looking Mrs. Frost (and she lived up to her last name, in case you're wondering) in the eye back then and can't look Jack in the eye right now.

At least I learned to leave bright fuchsia lipstick a memory. Turns out that's far easier to leave in my past than Jack Westbrook.

"Hi, Ms. Paisley! So great to see you!"

Shit! Why do I sound like a peppy cheerleader? Maybe I should just break out the old back handspring and end it with one of those little spirit finger waves, too, while I'm at it.

Kill me now.

The weight of Jack's eyes on me is heavy, but do I look over? Nope, nope, nope. Not going to happen. I'm staying strong here, people.

Ms. Paisley's eyes dart curiously back and forth between me and Jack. The older woman is in her late sixties, not to mention the kindest lady around, and has owned this floral shop for ages. She donates arrangements to terminally ill patients in our hospital and is also well known throughout our community as an active city council member. Ms. Paisley is one of those people who makes it a point to get to know everyone who crosses her path.

"What are you up to today?" she asks sweetly.

"Oh—" I start to answer, but I'm cut off.

By the new official bane of my existence.

"Nothing much, Ms. P. Just trying to make out with Little Miss Sunshine here," Jack interrupts, playfully nudging the older woman.

My death glare is fierce, and let's get something clear. I've perfected this glare since I've had to use it on a few pretentious doctors I've dealt with over the years as well as some asswipe patients who think they've watched enough *Grey's Anatomy* to know what's what. This particular glare has quieted burly men who look like they'd just gotten off the set of the movie *Deliverance*. I like to think it has the same power as Darth Vader's little Jedi move where he squeezes people's throats simply by *thinking* it. My glare is paralyzing.

Or so I thought. Because, yep, you guessed it. Jack Westbrook is not only immune to it, but he has the audacity to *smile* at me. No, scratch that. He's grinning smugly because he knows it pisses me off.

Yet I still want him. I'd even go so far as to consider giving up the last, jumbo chocolate-covered strawberry from Sweets 'N' Treats—and those suckers are like manna from heaven, I tell you—on Valentine's Day just to let him have his wicked way with me.

Minus the biting and spanking thing, obviously.

Jack continues sweet-talking Ms. Paisley, telling her all about Maggie and Ry's wedding and asking for her input since she knows the couple as well. I stand back, not so discreetly watching the two interact. Or more aptly, watching the way Jack interacts with the older woman. His side profile with that straight nose and strong square jawline with just the right amount of dark scruff to send him over the line of the

"*Wow, he's sexy*" category and into the "*He needs to get me naked NOW*" territory gets me feeling swoony.

Damn it.

My eyes drift up to his hair, and I recall how soft it felt that night I gripped it while he put his mouth all over me. My gaze trails down the dark gray shirt stretched over his firmly muscled torso, and I falter at his jeans. Sweet Jesus, those jeans. My vagina lurched a little when I caught sight of him earlier. I swear I felt it move as if it were practically trying to flag him down like, "Jack!! Over heeerrrrrreeee!!"

Whoa. That was weird. Plus, directionally speaking, it should be "down here," shouldn't it?

Oh. My. God! Why am I having an internal conversation about my vagina waving at a guy? I blame it all on Jack. He's making me crazy. As if that's not bad enough, my eyes are locked on his jeans and the way they hug him in all the right places. Specifically, over his ass and crotch. Over that really nice—

The sound of Jack clearing his throat is jarring, yanking me from my inner turmoil. When I meet his gaze, those blue eyes crinkle at the corners and one eyebrow rises. It's clear what he's silently saying. *Checking out my package, huh, Sunshine?*

Gah. I totally hear his voice in my head, too! I need an escape. *NOW*.

"I'll be just a moment." Turning, I rush out the shop's door; the tiny bell sounding at my exit as I practically spill out onto the sidewalk.

CHAPTER NINE

JACK

That wasn't *quite* the reaction I expected.

"Now, Jack. Are you giving that poor girl a tough time?"

Turning back to see Ms. Paisley peering up at me with that lopsided smile, the only sign of her stroke a few years back, I see her eyes sparkle with humor. I can't help but grin back at her.

"Me?" My expression is one of faux innocence as I place a palm over my heart. "Why, I would never!"

She giggles, swatting at me before her expression sobers. "I may be old, but I still have this"—she taps her finger to her temple—"and I can tell you've messed things up with her."

With a curious look, I have to ask, "How's that?"

She scoffs at me, turning to head back to the front counter when the phone rings. "By being a typical man, of course."

"Huh. Of course," I mutter to myself before snagging Sarah's bag and heading outside the shop in search of her.

She's not difficult to find, standing next door by the bakery window; her blond hair tousles slightly with the intermittent, soft breeze. Warmth spreads through me, and it's as though my brain nearly stutters. Because it's here at this moment that I have an intense yearning for her to turn to me and smile. And it wouldn't be one of those polite smiles, but a bright smile that grows wider and wider at the sight of me.

Instead, when her eyes meet mine, I receive what must be the wariest and least encouraging look.

Shoving my hands in my pockets, I shrug slightly. "So I'm thinking lilies. Something simple but still classy. What do you think?"

This is the most pathetic attempt at an "olive branch," but it's all I've got to work with at this point. Damn Maggie and Ry for being so indecisive in choosing floral centerpieces for their wedding...and meddling. Because I know for a fact they could've easily asked Ms. Paisley to choose the flowers for them instead of asking Sarah and me to do it.

"Sure. That sounds great." Her words sound forced and rushed, and she nods quickly, her eyes darting to where I'm still grasping her bag containing those sparkly heels she'd lusted over. I'd never be caught dead spending more than a hundred bucks on a pair of shoes that had next to nothing but a heel and straps because, hey, I'm a guy, but apparently, Jimmy Choo knows his stuff.

When I hand over the bag, her slim fingers wrap around the handles, and she hesitates briefly. Her blue eyes dart to mine, lips parting.

"I can...pay you back for these." Uncertainty lines her features, and the combination of that, along with her words, pisses me off.

"I don't want your money, Sarah." My tone has a bite to it, and I run a frustrated hand through my hair before turning toward Ms. Paisley's store. I'm not worried about the damn money. I just want...*her*. "Let's get in there and get the flowers straightened out."

Before I reach the door to the floral shop, Sarah calls out. "Jack."

Something in her tone has my shoulders relaxing infinitesimally, and I turn to look at her.

"Thank you for the shoes." She worries the edge of her bottom lip with her teeth. "And for saying I deserve them."

Not wanting to screw up our tentative truce, I simply nod and walk inside.

And I feel the weight of Sarah's gaze on me the entire time.

~

"Well, I have to say we've been pretty damn productive today."

I've officially resorted to pleasantries boiling over with awkwardness. Damn it, I feel like I'm back in high school all over again.

"Ready for our final stop?"

"Final stop?" I hear the hesitation in her response, but I don't care. I'm pushing past it.

"Yep," I answer with much more confidence than I feel. "We deserve a good lunch after all these errands."

Sarah holds up her hands, two shopping bags dangling from her fingers and an amused expression on her face. "Somehow, I ended up with more gifts today, simply by running errands with you."

I'd insisted on a small clutch purse to match her shoes after I'd noticed it had snagged her attention, sitting in a display window. By the look on her face, I knew she had to have it.

Her brows furrow as she peers curiously at the small bag of my own, nodding toward it in gesture. "You never did mention what you got from Ms. Paisley's shop."

Grinning smugly, I lead her toward a nearby bench along the sidewalk. I retrieve a small white box out of the bag and hand it to her. When she grasps it, her fingertips brush against mine, instantly sending an electric-like charge rushing through me.

Her eyes dart up to me as she holds the small, rectangular box in her hands.

"Go on. Open it."

I feel like crossing my fingers that she's okay with this gift...of sorts. My breathing slows as she slides a finger through the thin strip of tape securing the lid, releasing the top of the box and lifting it open.

At the sight of the blue flowers inside, the confusion lining her features is clear. Because these particular flowers aren't anything to write home about in the least. In fact, they're pretty plain.

Leaning in, I say softly, "They're globularia cordifolia. Or more relatably called..." I pause, waiting for her eyes to lock onto mine to finish.

"Blue balls."

CHAPTER TEN

SARAH

I don't know whether to laugh or punch him in the junk right now. Because let's be honest, what woman has been given flowers with the name of "blue balls" from a guy who's inflicted the syndrome of the same name on them both?

Lifting my gaze, I find him watching me with a guarded expression, and I swear, he appears almost boyish and shy. Which is ridiculous since the guy is well over six feet tall and one hundred percent man. A man who also happens to have a really thick—

Whoa, whoa, whoooaaa. Who suddenly jumped on the horny train and has damp panties?

Oh, just this girl right here. The one who's holding blue balls in a box.

I couldn't make this shit up if I tried. Seriously. Only me. I'm a magnet for ridiculousness.

"Think of these as a peace offering of sorts."

Twisting my lips, I hedge. "It's an...odd peace offering."

"What?" His face is a mask of innocence. "You mean every woman doesn't dream of receiving these as a gift? Especially such fragrant ones?"

Pinching the bridge of my nose, I close my eyes and mutter, "These are the moments I have to remind myself it's not worth the jail time."

"This is a moment, Sarah. We're having a moment. It's special. Don't ruin it." His voice is dripping with amusement. He's enjoying this.

"It's not a special moment." I open my eyes, squinting up at him.

"What would you call it then?"

My response is instant. "A migraine."

He throws his head back in laughter. "I think you're interested. In fact, I'd go so far as to say you want me." He leans in close. "Still." His smile spreads across his face, wide and cocky.

Patting him on the chest placatingly, I wear an expression of faux concern. "What you don't realize is that I have a superpower. It's called, 'I don't care what you think.'"

Jack's eyes sparkle in amusement. "If that's what you want to believe, Sunshine. Just remember what they say..." He gestures for me to walk with him to where his car is parked a few feet away along the main street. "Denial ain't just a river in Egypt."

At the sound of my grumbling, he laughs, and God, it's the kind that makes a smile tug at your own lips. It's infectious and makes warmth unfurl deep within you.

He playfully tugs at the bottom hem of my blouse and winks. "What do you feel like doing for lunch?"

What do I feel like? I feel like seeing if your penis feels as good inside me as it did that night. I bet it would slide right in and—

Wait, what?

My lips clamp shut, my eyes widening in fear that I just spoke my thoughts aloud. Luckily, Jack simply flashes me an odd look, still waiting for me to respond to his question like a normal person.

Which I'm clearly not. *No surprise there.*

"How about…"

Crap! My mind goes blank. We are literally standing on the sidewalk in downtown Saratoga Springs, amidst dozens of restaurants and shops, and I can't think of one. This should be classified with my other not so brilliant moments, ranking up there with the whole "push" versus "pull" for doors. I mean, really. I'm intelligent and have a college education, yet I still struggle with opening doors, for God's sake.

I won't even go into the whole I'm looking for my phone and panic when I can't find it only to realize I'm TALKING on it.

Now, it seems I'm also struggling to maintain brain power around Jack.

Luckily, he must sense my struggle because he offers, "How about we take a ride up to Limoncello?"

I pull one of my favorite chocolates from my purse and unwrap it. Not biting off a piece like usual, I pop the entire thing in my mouth after reading the message on the inside foil.

I'm totally stalling. Because, *nuh-uh*. Nope. Not happening. Limoncello is one of those romantic joints. It doesn't matter if you go in there for brunch, lunch, or dinner because the restaurant is practically dripping in passion with its low lighting and cozy atmosphere.

Don't believe me? Imagine combining old Richard Marx ballads with flickering candlelight and tables meant for two. *That* would be Limoncello.

Of course, my stomach chooses this moment to grumble so loudly I wouldn't be surprised if people three counties over heard it. Crap. I'm starving, but I need to play it safe. Just as I begin to scramble for a response, I'm saved.

"Sweet cheeks!" a loud, exuberant male voice calls out from behind me suddenly. Before I can spin around to see him, I'm practically tackle-hugged. Thick, tanned arms wrap around me, lifting me up in a bouncy backward hug.

Finally, Clint releases me, turning me to face him, and his perfectly straight, blindingly white smile fixes on me. "Have you missed me? You've missed me, haven't you?"

Before I can respond, he catches sight of Jack, instantly doing his open appraisal. "Well, *helllllloooo*, tall, dark, and handsome." Clint thrusts out a hand, and his smile turns brighter. "Name's Clint. Like Eastwood."

"Jack Westbrook." Jack's blue eyes crinkle with amusement. "Nothing impressive about my name." With a shrug, he smiles in self-deprecation. "Just Jack."

"Well, I beg to differ, Just Jack." Clint reaches over to flick the collar of Jack's button-down shirt. "There's nothing 'just' about you."

I tug Clint's wrist, flashing him a stern look that says, *"Back off, buddy."*

He gives me one in return that asks, *"He's yours?"*

And then I falter. Not only because we're having some sort of weird silent conversation with looks alone—creepy, right?—but because my initial thought would be *yes*. *Yes, he's mine.*

Cue my inner tantrum. You know, the one where you wish you could throw yourself on the ground with flailing arms and legs while screaming or yelling in complete and utter frustration. That one. I wish I could do that right now. Because, gah! I'm clearly still hung up on Jack.

I need to put a stop to this madness right now. I. Have. To.

Instead, I end up going to lunch with Jack and Clint. At Limoncello.

Kill me now.

~

"Gluten is considered Satan's tool to bring on death and destruction in epic gastric proportions around Saratoga. You know what I say to that?" Clint asks us in a loud whisper.

When Jack and I shake our heads, he answers, "Pass the breadsticks and pasta my way, baby."

"I'm going to request that my ashes be spread over their shrubs when I pass away." I pat my stomach with a sigh of contentment. I just ate my weight in pasta and regret absolutely nothing. Lunch was *that* good.

"Honey. I'm right there with you." Clint pats the top of my hand before expelling a long sigh of his own.

Jack looks amused. "Already planning for the end, are we?"

I lean toward the table, and before I realize it, my words spill out. "If this were my last night on earth, what a way to go." I wave a hand toward my nearly empty plate of homemade cheese ravioli in cream sauce.

"That's it?" Jack props his forearms upon the table, drawing my attention to the slight play of the muscles and the light sprinkling of dark hair on them. He offers an easy smile. "A good plate of pasta is all it takes, and then you're good to go?"

"Well, ideally, it'd take more than that."

Oh, shit. What the hell am I saying? Word vomit is happening again. Not to mention, my tone was *seriously* flirty. And not only with the *"Aren't you just the most handsome guy around?"* flirty. Nope. It was the *"If I were a cartoon character, my tongue would be hanging out of my mouth limply with saliva dripping from it"* crossed with a sexy Catwoman version of *"I'm going to crawl across this table lithely and seductively until I get to you, and you'll be dazed by my sexual prowess."*

"Really? Do tell." Jack leans in with obvious interest.

"Yes, do tell." Clint wiggles his eyebrows. He rests his chin in his hand, gazing at me expectantly. "I'm all ears."

Right now, I'm blaming the damn ravioli. *Damn you, ravioli! You got me into this mess!*

I know, I know. You're shaking your head at me in disgust right now because I refuse to take responsibility like an adult.

"Well, it'd take this ravioli and maybe a little make-out session." I lift a shoulder in a half shrug, picking up my fork and toying with it to avoid any eye contact.

And I continue to dig myself deeper.

"You know, I'd even be cool with some middle school, over-the-clothes type of action."

OH. MY. GOD. I did not just say that.

Please tell me I didn't say that out loud. Please. *Tellllllll meeeeeee.*

Horrified, my eyes fly up and meet Clint's gaze first—he's doing the whole silent, shoulders shaking, "I'm dying with laughter" thing. And Jack? Well, the expression on Jack's face says it all. It's clear he's trying not to laugh, those full lips pressed together but tugging up at the corners.

Dropping my face into my hands, I let out a tiny groan. Maybe I'll drown myself in the leftover cream sauce. Because let's be real here. That's a hell of a way to go. I can imagine the news reports now.

"We're live from Limoncello in Saratoga Springs where reports have a young woman drowning herself in the restaurant's decadent cream sauce to escape mortification from the man who seems to be her greatest weakness. The same man who inflicted a blue balls condition upon them both. We'll keep you posted on further developments."

Here's the moment where, if Jack and Clint were decent human beings, they'd laugh it off and let my word vomit slide, chalking it up to the slight food coma I'm in. Wait for it. Wait for iiiiiiiiiiiitttt…

"So what you're saying is you'd be interested in some middle school, over-the-clothes action, huh?" Clint's tapping a finger to his lips as if he's considering taking part.

Damn smartass. He's gay, which means I'm about as appealing to him as Vegemite is to a chocolate connoisseur.

"Should I put a rush on the check?" Jack offers.

Great. I'm stuck at lunch with two friggin' comedians. My

fingertips massage my temples, and my eyes drift closed in an attempt to shut them out.

"What do you think?" Clint says in a loud whisper. "Maybe I can be on top?"

Oh my God.

Jack whispers back, "I don't know, man. She looks like she's getting a"—he pauses, and I open my eyes to barely a squint and see him using air quotes—"headache."

"Nah. I have faith she'll rally for Eastwood Junior here."

Leaning back in my chair, I cross my arms as my eyes flit back and forth between the two men who clearly don't need me to carry on this conversation.

"However," Clint says with a pointed look at Jack, "you need to hold off on the blue balls if you plan to get lucky with me."

Raising my hand in the air, I attempt to flag our waiter for the check.

"Speaking of which." Clint rests his forearms on the table and fixes his eyes on Jack. "You planning on more episodes like the last one I heard so much about?"

Jack's eyes flicker over to me, shining with a mixture of dismay and amusement before returning to Clint. "She mentioned that, did she?"

Clint flashes a gleeful smile. "Oh, yes." Leaning back, he folds his arms across his chest. "As far as I'm concerned, you'll be referred to as Mr. Blue Balls for years to come."

"Great." Jack chuckles, shaking his head.

"You can remedy this by bringing out your A-game," Clint suggests before leaning over to me and speaking in a loud whisper. "And maybe *you* can liven things up a bit—"

I interrupt, wagging a finger. "You of all people should know that most men are simple creatures. I mean, really." I give them a pointed look. "A guy would do me even if I had chips in my hair."

Jack throws his head back on a husky laugh whereas Clint stares at me, appearing thoughtful.

"What kind of chips, though?" my friend asks. "If we're talking salt and vinegar, sure thing, but sour cream and onion"—he makes a face—"are game changers."

My hand shoots up in the air. "Check, please."

CHAPTER ELEVEN

JACK

I have no idea how I managed it, but it seems that Sarah's giving me another chance. Our late lunch was...interesting, to say the least, especially with her friend, Clint. He was fun and served as a bit of an icebreaker, and I finally feel like Sarah and I fell back to the Sarah and Jack we were before...well, before the initial "incident."

As we walk up to the new apartment where she's lived since returning to Saratoga, she flashes me a sexy smirk over her shoulder. Then turning the key in the lock, Sarah opens her door. "You ready, then?"

"Ready for wh—" My words are cut off as she tugs my wrist, pulling us inside and kicking the door closed behind us. I'm suddenly pressed back against the wall of the entryway, her palms braced on my chest.

Rising on her toes, she holds my gaze with lips so close to mine I can feel her hot breath wash against my skin. "Ready for this." Pressing a kiss to my lips, she then toys gently with my bottom lip, and a soft moan escapes me.

Leaning away slightly, she whispers, "Was that a moan?" Without waiting for my answer, she trails soft kisses along the side of my neck and nips at my earlobe. I swear, if she gets me much harder, my dick will bust through these jeans.

Gripping her waist, I slide my thumbs beneath her filmy blouse to skim her hipbones. I steer her against the opposite wall, caging her in, and she presses herself into my touch, her mouth finding mine again instantly. With my body flush against hers, I angle my head, deepening the kiss and sweeping my tongue inside.

I taste the slightest hint of chocolate, and when her tongue darts against my own, a deep rumble of a moan is pulled from me. Her hands are everywhere; fingers thread through my hair, palms sweep over my jawline to rasp against my scruff and glide down to cup my ass. I embrace the rise and fall of her breasts against my chest and the fact she's experiencing the same reaction as I am to our kiss.

Trailing a line of kisses down her throat, I gently nip at the rapidly beating pulse, and I murmur against her hot skin, "How firm are you on this whole over-the-clothes-only rule?"

A breathless laugh escapes her. "There's a chance I could be persuaded."

Backing away, I glide my palms down to cup the weight of her breasts. The way she arches into my touch, as her heavy-lidded gaze locks with mine, sends a rush of arousal through me. Lowering my head, I place my mouth over the outline of a hardened nipple, tonguing it through the layers of the thin fabric of her blouse and bra. Sarah's hands move to my head, her fingers sinking into my hair, and tightening slightly as if to prevent me from moving away.

Sucking hard, I reach between her thighs, rubbing her over the soft denim of her jeans to create friction. Her moans are the most erotic sound, pushing me to the brink of painful arousal. Unfastening her jeans, I slip my hand inside, over the thin fabric of her panties. I continue to draw circles over her clit, my cock hardening further at the feel of the damp fabric at my fingertips.

Sarah's body arches, hips moving of their own accord. Her eyes are closed, lips parted, and her breathing is ragged. "Jack…" She's so fucking close, and I'd give anything to slide my tongue deep inside her.

Fuck that. I'd give anything to sink deep inside her and have her come all over my cock.

When I slip my hand inside her panties, about to delve into her, thinking I'll get to watch this beautiful woman fall apart in my arms, there's a loud knocking at the door.

We both stare in disbelief in the direction of said door, and our agitated, breathless voices speak in unison.

"You've got to be fucking kidding me."

~

I'd sell a goddamn kidney for an opportunity to finish what Sarah and I started in that entryway.

Instead, I'm braced behind the kitchen counter in her apartment, hiding a near crippling hard-on while Maggie and Ry sit on the couch, exchanging humorous glances and making small talk.

"So Sarah spilled something on her shirt, huh?" Maggie asks innocently before furrowing her brow in faux concern. "Only right here?" She circles a finger, gesturing to her left breast. "So interesting."

"Mags," Ry admonishes playfully. "Quit with the sexy gestures." Turning back to me with a shit-eating grin, he adds, "Let's leave the sex talk to the kids. Isn't that right, cupcake?"

Instead of answering, I call out down the hallway to where Sarah's changing her shirt. "Sunshine! Please hurry."

It's bad enough I have to put up with Ry, but when he and Maggie get together, it's like Frick and Frack multiplied exponentially.

Both Maggie and Ry's eyebrows rise to nearly meet their hairline before turning to one another, mouthing, "Sunshine?"

I ignore them. I've got bigger fish to fry, as becomes evident when my best friend rises from the couch. He strolls over to the counter where I've since placed the flower box I'd given Sarah earlier. The corner of the box is slightly dented from being dropped in our haste to go at each other before the rude and untimely interruption.

Ry tosses me a curious look before opening the box, promptly frowning down at the blue flowers. "What the hell is this?" Then his gaze is back on me, worry edging into it. "Please tell me you didn't choose this god-awful flower for our centerpieces."

I roll my eyes in exasperation. "Relax, would you? No way in hell would I choose flowers named blue balls for your wedding centerpieces. Give me some credit."

He visibly relaxes. "Thank God."

"Wait a minute," Maggie begins slowly. "That flower is actually named—"

"Blue balls," I finish for her.

"And you gave it to…" Ry trails off expectantly. Like he doesn't already know the answer. I mean, come on. We're standing in Sarah's place.

"Sarah." My tone is dull.

I need a stiff drink. Speaking of stiff, I really need to do something about this…

Maggie and Ry exchange another one of those looks before dissolving into laughter. Attempting to speak between their schoolgirl giggling, Maggie asks, "You gave the blue balls to her just before we—"

"Gave you guys blue balls," Ry assists when she falters, holding her sides. He braces a hand on the kitchen counter separating the living room and kitchen, laughing so hard he's nearly wheezing.

Crossing my arms, I stare at the pair. "So glad you're enjoying our discomfort."

And I call these people my friends.

CHAPTER TWELVE

SARAH

I t's been a few weeks since I've seen Jack after our second, uh, "episode," courtesy of our best friends.

After that day with the flowers, we'd watched a movie with Maggie and Ry until the three of them had to leave. Jack had early conference calls the following morning, but our kiss goodbye had hinted at the promise of more time spent together.

Upon returning to Saratoga and accepting the position at the local hospital, I've been working like crazy. It's good money, but it's exhausting as hell. The other day, I'd sent Jack a text at one in the morning after my shift ended—far later than expected, mind you—to see if he wanted to grab some sushi if he was still awake. I know that he sometimes pulls late hours for his business, which is why I didn't think anything of it when I'd sent that message.

Until the following Monday evening, that is, when I stop over at Maggie and Ry's place to help her decide table assignments. We're tasked with keeping Ry's aunt, who tends to get handsy when she drinks, away from some of Ry's college-aged cousins, and another uncle, who likes to tell offensive jokes, away from Ry's other super-conservative aunt.

As soon as I knock on their door, it opens, and I'm faced with the man who's been on my mind, lips curving into an easy smile.

"Hey, Jack." I step inside, and he closes the door behind me. Before I'm able to move farther down the hall, he corners me, backing me against the wall, his head dipping low.

"Were you sexting me?" His quiet, raspy voice wraps around me, enveloping me in a daze of warmth and instant arousal.

Until his words sink in.

"Wait, what?" My head rears back in surprise.

His lips dust gently over mine. "You texted me one word: sushi." Another brush of his lips. "At one a.m., Sarah. That's code, right?"

"Noooo." Stunned, I can't help but stare back at him. "I was asking if you wanted to get sushi at Liquid since they stay open until three a.m. on the weekends."

"Riiiiiight." He drags out the word, tone full of disbelief. His smile is far too wicked and sexy; it makes me want to jump into his lap.

Or just jump him. Either way sounds great to me.

His head descends, bringing those perfect lips and piercing blue eyes closer. I feel transfixed, mesmerized by the way he's watching me right now.

"The next time you text me at early hours of the morning, it'd better not be about eating"—he pauses, the corners of his mouth tilting up naughtily—"*food*." His wicked insinuation hangs between us.

And that's it. That's the moment it happens.

Boom. Impregnation.

I swear to you; my ovaries gave an honest to God lurch with the divinity of immaculate impregnation.

"Want to get together sometime this week?" he whispers against my lips, one hand gently cupping the side of my face, his thumb brushing my cheek.

Let's get one thing straight. "Want to get together some-time this week?" from Jack Westbrook is much like the whole snake in the Bible who taunts Eve about the delicious apple. Or the time my so-called best friend in college taunted me about trying the weird smelling brownies at a party. Of course, she proceeded to make fun of me afterward because I decided to channel my inner Jamaican the remainder of the night.

Ya, mon. Took me forever to live that one down.

"Maybe," I whisper back. "As long as there are no more of those…episodes."

He chuckles softly, pressing a kiss to my lips. "I'll do my best." Another soft kiss. "Plus, I might have a surprise for you."

"I hate surprises."

He stares at me in disbelief. "You can't hate surprises."

"I hate surprises," I reaffirm. Then a thought hits me. "Except for"—I lean closer to whisper—"surprise fellatio. That's one I definitely don't hate."

Jack tosses his head back on a laugh before settling his gaze on me, eyes sparkling with humor. "Consider that noted."

"Jack? Is Sarah here?" Maggie calls out.

"Yes, she's busy molesting me against your wall," he calls out, smirking when I swat at him. "I keep telling her I'm not that kind of guy."

Shoving against his chest, he relents only after another kiss, whispering, "Until later, Sunshine."

Then he walks to the door, laying his hand over the handle. "Bye, Maggie; later, Ry!" With a quick wink at me, he exits the apartment.

And I'd be lying if I said my lady parts weren't figura-tively trailing quickly after him.

CHAPTER THIRTEEN

JACK

It's eleven thirty on a Thursday night, and I'm still at work. My eyes are bleary from drawing up plans for one of my newest clients. Pushing back from my desk, I release a tired sigh and scrub a hand over my face. With a glance around my office, I determine I've logged more than enough hours for today.

My grumbling stomach reminds me I've been so focused that I worked through dinner and haven't had more than a granola bar. I can't keep up with Sarah's schedule at the hospital. She's been so busy, and I went out of town to meet with some clients, so we haven't seen each other in a few weeks. I figure it can't hurt to send a quick text and see if she feels like grabbing something to eat if she's pulling a late shift.

Me: Sushi?

Sarah: Ha-ha. Very funny.

My lips curve upward at her response. She clearly thinks I'm messing with her, referencing her text which had the same one word question to me a few weeks ago.

Me: Is that a yes or a no?

Sarah: Depends. Are you talking about food or…?

Me: Depends. Which one are you down for? Sushi? Or "code sushi"?

Sarah: Imagining you, me, and "code sushi" made my panties grow damp.

Hell. Now I'm shifting in my desk chair to ease the start of a hard-on at the thought of going down on her.

Sarah: My stomach just voted. Loudly. And she overrules.

Me: Want to meet up at Liquid in about twenty minutes?

My phone lights up with an incoming call from her. Swiping my thumb across the bottom, I answer. "Hey, Sunshine."

"Hey, Jack." God, her voice is…everything. Silky smooth, it wraps around me.

Tonight, however, she sounds bone-deep tired. "Rough shift at work?"

Sarah lets out a long exhale. "It's a full moon and that *always* brings out the crazies." There's a pause. "Anyway, I'm going to shower and change clothes but…"

"But?" I prompt.

"Well." She sighs. "I really don't feel like putting on a face full of makeup and doing my hair so late. If you're cool with me looking like a scrub with damp hair and little makeup, then I'll definitely meet you."

"Sunshine, you're beautiful regardless. Bring yourself down whenever you're ready. I'll be waiting."

"See you soon."

CHAPTER FOURTEEN

SARAH

After a cheap, five-dollar cab ride over to Liquid—
I'm far too exhausted to drive and don't want to
walk it alone this late at night—I enter the dimly lit
sushi restaurant. Spotting the back of Jack's dark head above
the high-backed chair he's sitting in, I rush over and place my
hands over his eyes.

"Hey, handsome. Guess who's wearing sexy lace
pantieeeees?" I draw out the last word mischievously.

"Well, I sure as hell hope it's you and not him, Sunshine."
This remark comes from a voice behind me. Jack's voice.

I repeat. That sounded from *behind* me.

Jerking my hands away from the man's eyes—the man
who is decidedly *not* Jack—I find him turning to me with an
avid interest in his gaze.

"I'd definitely be interested in hearing more about those
panties." The man grins at me with what have to be the most
stereotypical nicotine-yellowed teeth.

"Mmm, yeah." I back away slowly. "Sorry. I thought you
were someone else."

"I can be whoever—"

"No." I hold up a hand, interrupting his nonsense. "You

actually can't. Trust me." Forcing an overly bright smile, I wish him a good night before spinning around. Jack's watching me, looking mighty entertained by my little mistaken identity episode.

"Ready to eat?" I ask nonchalantly, as though I'm not secretly wishing the floor would open and swallow me this instant.

His grin widens. "Definitely." With a hand at the small of my back, he leads me to the correct booth. "Then you can tell me more about these panties of yours, you little dirty talker, you."

"Ha-ha." I roll my eyes. "A true gentleman wouldn't draw more attention to a lady's embarrassing moment."

We take our seats on opposite sides of the booth, and Jack's lip quirks upward, his eyes gleaming with humor. "Ah, but it was a classic moment, Sunshine." He tips his head to the side. "Reminds me of one of those chocolates you like with the messages.

"Embrace the shenanigans."

⁓

Jack stares at me, features contorted in disgust and shock. "She had a bottle stuck where?"

I've been regaling him with some crazy hospital stories and patients I've had to put under so the doctors could undo their often awkward and disturbing mishaps.

After I finish chewing, I answer, leaning across the table of our booth, and lower my voice. "In her ass. And"—I gesture with my chopsticks—"she claimed she was gardening, kneeled down to pick up weeds, and didn't see the bottle. Then *whoops!*" I break off with a laugh. "The bottle made its way where it shouldn't have."

Jack shakes his head slowly. "That doesn't even seem plausible."

I raise a shoulder in a half shrug. "Trust me; they don't care if it's plausible or not. They simply refuse to give the honest story. Happens all the time."

"It seriously happens that often?"

"Oh, yes." I release a sigh. "There was a guy who came in with his penis stuck inside a shampoo bottle."

Jack's hand stills, chopsticks halting in midair with a piece of sushi squeezed between. "Inside?"

"Yes. The part where the top screws on. Inside that hole."

He frowns. "But that's really small—"

"Exactly." I finish my last piece of sushi before continuing. "It's a really small space. And somehow he fit inside." I take a sip of my water. "Awkward for the guy because everyone had to witness it and," I emphasize while I raise my eyebrows meaningfully, "that meant his stuff was small enough to fit inside it."

"How did you…?" Jack trails off in question.

"Well, it turns out that part of the plastic bottle is so hard and difficult to cut. We couldn't manage to do anything with him being a nervous wreck and squirming, so we sedated him and carefully cut it off him."

He shakes his head in disbelief. "Wow. I really can't wrap my mind around that."

With a laugh, I lean back in my seat. "The things that come through the doors of that hospital…" I chuckle.

Taking in the sight of the man sitting across from me in the booth, I allow my eyes to drift over him appreciatively. He's wearing a dark gray button-down shirt with the sleeves rolled up and cuffed just below his elbows.

In a suit, Jack's hot as hell. Out of a suit jacket, though, with those shirt sleeves rolled up for my viewing pleasure, I have a front row seat to forearm porn. Because, let me tell you, those veins and corded muscles are *magnificent*.

"Pulling a late night, too?" I nod toward him.

With a weary sigh, he runs a hand down his face. "I've

been approached by some new companies." His lips twist. "It's great—don't get me wrong—but I feel like I'm fast approaching the point when I'll have to turn away potential clients." His blue eyes are tired, lacking the light and luster I'm used to seeing.

"Hey." I reach across the table to cover his hand with mine. "It's not the end of the world if you have to turn some people away. You're only one man. Don't spread yourself too thin."

Jack nods, and we fall silent for a moment before I notice his eyes drifting over me. He turns his hand over and links our fingers together.

"You look great."

Let's get something straight here. I'm clad in jeans and a sweater, light makeup, and hair now air dried from my earlier shower. I do *not* look great.

Passable for a female? Sure. Great? Not a chance.

Flashing him a dubious look, I raise one eyebrow. "Don't lie. I look like crap."

Jack gives our joined hands a little tug before raising them to his lips. Holding my gaze, he presses a soft kiss to my hand. "I never lie, Sunshine."

His nickname for me, when he utters it in that husky, intimate way, just does something. Besides dampen my panties, of course. This is what happens when one is a horndog of epic proportions.

Okay, so that's not the only thing that happens. I feel my stomach give a little, teeny tiny flip, which is...nice, I guess. But I don't do the emotions that go along with stomach flips. Stomach flips mean feelings, and feelings like that lead to relationships. And that is *not* my territory.

Ick. Simply thinking of the dreaded "R" word makes me feel like I'm one Adele song away from overeating myself to death on Dunkin' Donuts. Which means it's time to change the subject.

"So about my panties," I begin, giving him a saucy wink.

He grins at me. "Do tell."

"Well, I know it's tough to tell beneath this elegant exterior"—I wave a hand, in a sarcastic gesture, toward my attire—"but I pulled out all the stops with my undergarments in hopes…" I trail off, grinning.

"Why, Sunshine"—his smile widens—"are you hoping to get lucky tonight?"

I let out a long, breathy sigh. "Yep."

Jack throws his head back on a laugh before pulling out his wallet. "Then let's head home."

CHAPTER FIFTEEN

JACK

Kissing Sarah is unlike anything I've ever experienced before. Not only does she taste decadent, often with the faint flavor of those chocolates she always carries around, but there's something else. When our lips meet, something uniquely intoxicating sets her apart from anyone else I've ever kissed.

I love that she allows me to see her with slightly damp hair and minimal makeup; I feel like maybe she's letting me in, letting me slip past those carefully guarded walls of hers.

It's no secret Sarah doesn't exactly do relationships, and I'm guessing much of the reason has stemmed from her job and simultaneously tackling school and her certification. But now, I can't help but wonder if maybe she's ready to take the plunge and possibly embark on something new.

With me.

Breaking our kiss, I trail my lips along the graceful column of her neck, and I note with pride that her chest is heaving ever so slightly. We seem to have a trend of barely getting inside the door before attacking each other.

"What is it about you," she murmurs softly, "that makes

me want to be at your beck and call? I mean, not serving you bacon, eggs, and pancakes—"

She breaks off with a sharp intake of breath when I abruptly slide her sweater up to tug the cup of her lacy blue bra down, baring a rosy nipple. Latching my lips around it, I suckle her puckered flesh. "But," she manages to continue breathlessly, "to serve you sexually."

Chuckling softly, I murmur against her skin. "Sounds good to me."

Her palms press against me, giving me pause. Light blue eyes meet mine. "Bedroom, Westbrook."

Taking my hand in hers, she leads me down the hallway to her small bedroom, the nearby streetlights casting a soft glow upon the room through the small slats of the blinds.

Once we're inside the room, she makes quick work of the buttons on my shirt, and I shed it, letting it fall to the floor. I tug her sweater off, dropping it to join my shirt. Sarah backs away to remove her jeans while I rid myself of my socks and suit pants, leaving me in my black boxer briefs and her clad in only her bra and panties.

And she wasn't kidding when she talked about her panties earlier. They're lacy and a vivid shade of blue, matching her bra. She's a sight wet dreams are made of; on par with the scene in the old eighties movie, *Weird Science*, where the two computer nerds create their dream woman.

Fucking gorgeous.

My fingers slip beneath the lace at her hips, tugging the fabric down her legs before she kicks them off. Rising, I reach around to unfasten the clasp of her bra at her back. When she shrugs out of it, my hands immediately cup her breasts, skimming the pads of my thumbs over her nipples. My mouth takes hers again, swallowing her tiny moan. I continue to toy with one hardened tip while my other hand slips down her body in a caress until I reach the apex of her thighs.

Sarah automatically widens her stance for me, and I slide a finger inside her, finding her wet and ready for me.

So fucking ready for me.

Adding another finger, I thrust in and out of her, and her hands grasp my shoulders. She moans into my mouth, warring with my tongue. Breaking the kiss, I take in the sight of her standing before me, flushed with arousal, eyes heavy-lidded, and nipples beautifully hardened peaks.

I catch sight of her suddenly trying to stifle a yawn. "Am I putting you to sleep, Sunshine?"

A sheepish look crosses her face. "Sorry. It's been a long day."

Walking her back until her knees hit the mattress, my gaze locks with hers. "Let's see if this wakes you up."

Gripping her waist, I set her on the bed, guiding her to lie back as I spread her legs while I stand at the edge of the bed. Gazing down at her, I have to adjust myself slightly, the head of my cock now jutting up past the waistband of my briefs.

Lowering myself, I trace the seam of her entrance with my tongue while my hands grip her upper thighs, feeling her muscles tense. When she breathes my name softly, it spurs me on. Fastening my mouth over her, I taste her thoroughly, fucking her with my tongue.

Her hands fly to my head, fingers threading through my short hair as her body writhes, giving in to primal urges as she works herself against my mouth. Releasing my hold on one of her thighs, I move a hand to her clit and press my thumb to it. I apply just enough pressure, moving in circles, until her body tightens and her muscles become rigid. I can feel the tiny jolts of her inner muscles around my tongue, knowing she's fast approaching an orgasm.

I quicken my tongue thrusts, continuing to work her clit with my thumb, and then it happens. Her body jerks just before she floods me with the taste of her release, muscles clenching and releasing, her grip on my hair borderline painful.

But it's worth it.

Once the shudders subside and her body falls lax, I trail kisses up along her smooth stomach, past the center of her chest and up to her lips.

"Beautiful," I murmur against her mouth.

Her eyes are still closed, a languid, satisfied smile playing at her lips. "Mmm, I might have to keep you around."

You can keep me around for more than just that, Sunshine.

As my lips part to respond, I notice the evenness of her breathing, and it gives me pause.

"You really just fell asleep on me, didn't you?" I'm not sure why I'm voicing this question when I already know the answer. Guess I'm a bit stunned.

This is a new one. Certainly can't say that I've ever put a woman to sleep via oral sex before.

The corners of my lips tip up. "Guess there's a first time for everything, huh, Sunshine?" Backing away, I carefully pull down the covers and shift her fully beneath them. Tucking her in, I press a soft kiss to her lips. "Sweet dreams."

Quietly, I lock up behind me as I exit her apartment, huffing out a small laugh.

Guess I'll be the only one with a case of blue balls tonight.

CHAPTER SIXTEEN

SARAH

"You did *not!*" Clint stops abruptly, nearly causing a pileup on the sidewalk. Some give us dirty looks while others glance at us in question.

We met at the little family-owned Italian joint downtown to get some gelato and decided to walk around and window shop while we partake in our treat.

He holds up a palm. "Girl, no. Just *no.*"

Throwing up my hands, my tone is full of exasperation. "I didn't plan for it to happen, for God's sake. I was exhausted."

He fixes me with a stare. "You fell asleep on the man." With a pause for added emphasis, he arches an eyebrow. "After he provided such excellent fellatio, nonetheless."

"It's not like I meant to fall asleep after he went to town on my vagina."

A loud gasp draws our attention.

My head turns in the direction of the gasp, and instant mortification hits me. "*Shit!* Oh, holy sh- Sorry!" I cringe as I stumble over my words. Because I'm face to face with a nun.

A freaking nun.

Crap. I'm going to hell for combining the words freaking and nun, aren't I?

"Sorry, uh..." I wave a hand nervously and end up doing some sort of awkward bow. "Sister."

She frowns hard as if God himself is communicating with her and determining my fate as a sinner on Earth.

Also, I just *bowed* to a nun. As if she were royalty. Could the sidewalk open and swallow me? Please?

Clint, of course, is doubled over, snort-laughing, and his cup of gelato slips, tipping slightly, sending drops of the rich chocolate dripping onto the paved sidewalk.

The nun dismisses me with a disgusted huff and a glare before striding away from us as if the devil is at her heels.

"You...just...bowed"—Clint's words are choppy, spoken through near wheezing laughter—"to a nun." He swipes at his cheeks, which are now glistening with tears.

"I panicked!" I run a hand through my hair, agitation running through me. "I didn't know what to do!"

"And your go-to was to bow?" Clint stares at me incredulously. "Who does that? She's a nun, not the Queen of England, Matthews."

I wave him off. "Eat your gelato before it melts." We resume walking, but Clint continues to chuckle softly.

Pausing intermittently to browse at a few shop windows, we finish our dessert and toss our trash in a nearby bin.

"Are you planning to see Jack tonight?"

"No. I'm meeting Maggie for dinner." We wait for the crosswalk light to indicate we have the right of way. Once it lights up, we cross over South Broadway and head down Phila Street toward my apartment building.

"You and Jack are even now."

My eyes dart over to him. "What do you mean we're even?"

He shrugs. "He fell asleep on you, and now you've fallen asleep on him." Another shrug. "Even."

I consider it a moment. "Mmm, but I only fell asleep on him once. He fell asleep on me *and* bit and spanked me."

"Surely, you can forgive the man. Especially after he went to town and got the VIP tour of your cave of wonders."

I stare at him. "Cave of wonders?"

He laughs, nudging my shoulder with his. "Would you prefer I say he got a first-class ticket to fly through your love tunnel?"

"Clint," I warn dangerously. Which does absolutely nothing, of course.

"You should try to make it up to him," he offers suddenly. "Because any guy who sent you on your way to 'O' town without receiving so much as a thank you in return deserves to have some reciprocation."

He's right. I really do feel bad about falling asleep on Jack.

I just need to decide the best way to make it up to him.

~

"Thanks for the dinner date." I smile at my best friend.

Maggie had asked me if I'd wanted to have a girls' dinner night. Of course, I jumped all over her offer because I love to hang out with her one on one, and I also love sushi.

It's a win-win in my book.

"I don't know how you eat that super spicy stuff." Maggie points her chopsticks in the direction of my spicy tuna roll topped with a spicy sauce I'm currently adding wasabi to. "I'd want to claw at my own tongue because it burned so badly."

I shrug. "I love this stuff."

"So"—she sets her chopsticks aside to take a sip of water —"you're planning to make the whole falling asleep after oral thing up to Jack?" I nod. "How exactly are you going to do that?"

"Well"—I tip my head to the side in thought—"I thought I'd show up at his place or at his office—whichever he happens to be at after we finish up here." I lean in closer, lowering my voice. "And then, I plan to *really* make up for the other night."

Maggie smiles. "You know, Jack's a good guy. He probably doesn't care about any of that. He simply likes you."

The way she's looking at me is unsettling. This is her motherly look, the one where she knows something I don't. And that makes me nervous.

Averting my eyes, I eat my last bit of sushi. "He can like me all he wants. Doesn't mean anything's going to happen."

"Mmmhmm," my best friend responds noncommittally. Which means one thing.

She thinks I'm full of shit.

~

Me: Paging Mr. Blue Balls…

Jack: I think you have the wrong number.

Me: Where are you?

Jack: Why? Are you bringing me food?

Me: Do you want me to bring food?

Jack: Ah, Sunshine, you should know by now the only food I want from you is…well, you.

Me: Are you trying to sext me, Westbrook?

Jack: Is it working? Because I've never sexted in my life.

His response gives me pause. *He's never sexted before?* Something akin to pride runs through me at the knowledge that I'm his first sexting recipient.

Me: I can show up with that version of "food" if you like? Are you home or at the office?

Jack: Still at the office, finishing up some things.

Me: I can be there in about ten minutes.

Jack: The special code is to knock three times, rapid staccato, and call out, "Housekeeping!"

Me: Ha-ha. See you soon.

Jack: Looking forward to it, Sunshine.

∿

Ten minutes later, I knock on Jack's office door before turning the handle.

Poking my head in, I school my expression to be one of extreme seriousness. "I'm looking for a hot guy in a suit who goes by the last name of Westbrook. Know where I might find him?"

His soft rumble of laughter floods my senses as his dark blue eyes meet mine, the slight upward curve of his lips displaying his pleasure at seeing me. "I might know where you could find him. Why don't you come a little closer?"

With a laugh, I shake my head before shutting and locking the door behind me. "Don't you sound like the big bad wolf now?"

He slides his rolling desk chair back to stand, his eyes flicking over me in a smooth caress before his voice drops to something low and husky. "You look beautiful."

Closing the distance between us, I stop once I'm a foot away, gazing up at him. "You, smooth talker, you. You're just saying that because I have this." I hold up the bag of sushi I brought for him before setting it off to the side of his desk.

His eyes flicker with something I can't decipher. "Thank you." Then he does something that sends shivers scattering down my spine. He cups my face in his hands, eyes studying me reverently as if I'm a precious artifact he's grateful to hold. "Even if you hadn't brought me food, I still would've said that." He pauses, his gaze searching. "Because it's the truth, Sunshine."

His lips press to mine in a kiss vastly different from our previous kisses. This one feels like it has more emotion behind it, so ripe with affection, caring, and ...

No. *No.* We are not going there.

With a desperate need to change the mood, to shift the path he's attempting to set us on, I skim my hands down the hard wall of his chest, one palm sweeping over his cock and the other sliding around to cup his ass.

He breaks the kiss, though his lips still brush against mine as he speaks. "Someone's certainly not beating around the bush."

I smile against his lips, walking him back to his desk chair while my hands make quick work of his belt. Shoving his pants and boxer briefs down over his hips, I guide him to sit down in his chair.

With a smug grin playing at my lips, I kneel before him, grasping his cock in my hand, and stroke him slowly. His eyes grow heavy-lidded with arousal, and his cock hardens further in my grasp. Slowly, I slide my mouth down, taking him as deep as I can possibly go, and begin to work his length using my lips and tongue to create a light suction. When his fingers tighten their hold on my hair, I know I'm on the right track.

His hips begin shifting slightly as if a part of him is trying to urge me on, to take him deeper, yet he still maintains some restraint so as not to gag me, and I know he's getting close.

I speed up my motions, my saliva coating his hard shaft, and have a steady rhythm in place when he suddenly jerks away, causing me to stumble.

"Holy shit!" He peers down, gripping his cock, as his face distorts in extreme discomfort.

Panic rushes through me. "What? What's wrong?"

"It burns!" He jumps up from the chair, nearly toppling over since his underwear and suit pants are at his ankles. Managing to right himself, he disappears into the small bathroom in the far left corner of his office. I hear a frantic swooshing of water until finally, he returns after a few minutes, having now refastened his pants.

"Sunshine…" I'm relieved to see he appears slightly amused. "Did you eat something spicy earlier?"

"N—" I literally feel all the blood drain from my face.

Oh shit. *Ohshitohshitohshit!*

Cringing, I cover my eyes with my hands. "A spicy tuna roll with spicy sauce and extra wasabi." My tone is faint, flat, and dejected.

Because let's be real here. In my efforts to make up for falling asleep on him, I'd single-handedly attempted to singe his freaking penis.

With. My. Mouth.

I mean, really. Who *does* that?! Or even better, who does that happen to?

No one. Except me, of course.

CHAPTER SEVENTEEN

JACK

"Well"—my lips curl up into a small smile —"that was definitely...*hot*." I'm attempting to put Sarah at ease because it's obvious she's mortified at what just happened.

Dropping her hands from her eyes, she exhales a long breath, blue eyes apologetic. Her lips twist into a weak smile. "That's one way of putting it."

"One might even say it got a little *heated*."

With a sound of dismay, she shoves at me playfully. "I think you've driven that point home, Jack."

"What do you say we head out?" I pull on my suit jacket and grab the bag of takeout along with my keys. With a soft smile, I tip my head. "I could use a shower to get rid of the lingering spiciness." I raise my eyebrows in jest on that last part, and it causes a deep flush to spread across her cheeks.

"The least I can do is bring you back to my place. You can shower there, and we can watch a movie." She offers this with a hopeful expression, the depths of her blue eyes nearly entrancing me.

"Can we watch *The Princess Bride*?"

She lets out a tiny laugh. "As you wish."

~

"She's trying her hand at dating."

The ball whizzes past my cheek, nearly sideswiping me, I'm so caught off guard with Ry's admission. It bounces wildly off the walls of the enclosed gym court.

"What the hell?" I glare at him.

"What?" He flashes me an exasperated look, getting ready to serve again. "You're the one who didn't swing at it."

As if I can concentrate on our racquetball game now when the idea of Sarah dating is fresh in my mind.

Returning his serve with a grunt, I ask, "What do you mean she's trying her hand at dating again?" The idea of Sarah seeking out other men is beyond troubling, and a panic sweeps over me.

"Mags also told me Sarah's been considering this app where you swipe in different directions on things you either love, hate, dislike, or like, and it matches you up with people who have similar tastes."

"Sounds ridiculous."

Ry bounces the ball a few times before tossing out casually, "Or useful. Because, really, if you hate shag carpeting and flannel shirts, how can someone truly get past that and fall in love?"

Oh Jesus.

Finally, he grins and bounces the ball a few more times. "Word has it she's meeting a guy at The Tavern at around seven tonight after she finishes her shift." Then he winks. "But you didn't hear that from me." Two more bounces of the ball. "Now are you going to get your head out of your ass and into the game or what?"

"Bring it on."

~

"Jack? What are you doing here?"

Sarah's clearly caught off guard as I stop in front of the booth where she's seated, waiting on the guy she's meeting tonight.

"Just happened to be around and thought I'd stop by for a drink. Saw you and had to say hi," I explain cheerfully.

"Hi." She waves as her eyes quickly dart past me, checking to see if her date's arrived.

"Oh, Sunshine." I pout dramatically. "You're just going to discard me like that? Without a backward glance?"

"Yes." Her response is quick; the corners of her lips quirk up with the barest hint of humor. The sparkle in her eyes is proof that she loves our back and forth banter as much as I do.

"Do you know what I think?"

She lets out a dramatic sigh. "I've been on the edge of my seat wondering that."

Leaning down, I brace a hand on the table in front of her and revel in her sharp intake of breath at my closeness. "I think you wanted me to show up tonight." Her lips part, but before she can respond, I move closer. "I think you hoped Ry would tell me you were meeting another guy because you wanted to see how I would react."

Moving my mouth to her ear, I speak softly. "To see if I'd show up here and tell you I want you to come home with me tonight. That I want you to be thinking about me and not some other guy. That I want you to think of the way my tongue and lips felt when I tasted your sweet pussy the other night."

Her breath hitches, and I push on. "I want you to think of the way it'll feel when I sink my cock deep inside you."

Drawing away slowly, I take in the sight of her parted lips, eyes hazy with lust. With a wink, I straighten, and rap my knuckles softly on the table. "Have a nice night, Sunshine."

I head on over to the bar, sliding up on the worn leather

seat, and order a beer. God knows I'm going to need a drink to help me get over the fact Sarah's on a date tonight.

~

I've been fucking played. And by my own best friend, no less.

Their laughter rolls over me as I sit at the bar a few feet away like a fucking stalker as Sarah giggles again.

Date, my ass. Damn Ry made me think she would be on a date—not simply meeting her friend, Clint.

Staring down into my glass, I shuffle the ice cubes around. Before I can decide whether I should call it a night and head home or have another drink, there's a nudge at my elbow.

"Hey, Just Jack." Clint's smiling at me with those perfect teeth of his, his blond hair perfectly coiffed. "You know you could've joined us."

With a humorless laugh, I shake my head. "I wasn't aware I was welcome."

He nudges me. "Ah, now. You're not going to sit and wait around for an invitation, are you? Come on. I didn't have you pegged as that kind of guy." He tips his head to the side with a small laugh. "You know, if someone had bitten me hard enough to leave a bruise and spanked me, I might have enjoyed it." He falls silent for a beat before grinning. "Actually, that's a lie. I'm not one for pain. But at least now you know what she doesn't like."

"Except for the part where she doesn't seem to want the same things I do."

His eyebrows rise. "Ah. You want the prospect of a relationship, do you?" Nodding slowly, as if mulling it over, he lays a hand on my shoulder. "Jacky, Jacky, Jacky. You have your work cut out for you. But"—he leans in, lowering his voice—"facts are facts. And the fact is, that woman wants you so bad it's making her crazy."

"With an emphasis on the crazy part, I suppose."

"I'm just saying don't give up. I think you need to be firm and show her who's boss." He winks. "And tonight is the perfect night since she's had two drinks and is feeling relaxed. I'll leave the rest up to you."

He strolls back over to Sarah, and I catch sight of them saying goodbye in my peripheral vision. Tossing money down on the bar to cover my tab, I walk past their booth and wait for her on the sidewalk.

Once she exits the bar, I sidle up to her.

"Hey, Sunshine?"

"Yes?" She pulls a foil-wrapped chocolate from her purse and unwraps it. As is her routine, she reads the message written on the inside before taking a small bite.

"When I stand next to you, I can't feel my face."

She stares at me. "You're communicating using song titles, now? Really, Jack?"

Well, at least she noticed it was The Weeknd's hit song "Can't Feel My Face." That should count for something.

She tips her face up to the night sky, lips twitching in her attempt to refrain from smiling. Then she swats at my chest. "Seriously, Jack? You can't be—"

Swiftly, I reach out, cupping her nape while my other hand slips to her waist, and I tug her to me, dipping my head.

And my mouth cuts off her words.

CHAPTER EIGHTEEN

SARAH

I'm convinced Jack's kisses are magical and have some super-secret power because I'm barely aware he's steering me back beneath the awning and against the door of a nearby closed shop. All I care about is the fact he's kissing me again. And let me tell you, his kisses are unique and something to savor. He doesn't slobber all over your face or practically eat it off. He's gentle, and he uses the perfect amount of tongue.

Speaking of tongue… *God in heaven above*. When his tongue slides against mine, I feel a jolt all the way down to my toes. The taste of my chocolate and Jack combined is beyond decadent.

When we finally break the kiss, our breathing is labored, and I exhale loudly. "Your kisses…" I shake my head; my eyes still transfixed on Jack's lips. "They have some sort of strange magic—"

"Like voodoo magic?"

"And I feel it all the way down deep in my—"

"Lady parts?"

I make a face. "I would say toes."

"Oh." He offers a look of exaggerated disappointment.

Grinning suddenly, I wink. "I'm kidding." Leaning in, I brush my lips against his as I softly whisper, "I feel it all the way down deep in my lady parts." My teeth gently toy with his full bottom lip before I add, "And then some."

A low growl erupts from his throat, and I'm immediately caged in by his firm, broad chest at my front and the hard brick building at my back. His muscular body presses against me as he cradles the back of my head in his hand. When his mouth slants over mine, taking it in an even hotter, more passionate kiss, every fiber within me feels electrified. Every slide of his tongue against my own sends another delicious shiver through my body, and I'm certain my nipples couldn't be harder than they are now.

When we come up for air, I press my palms against his chest. Our gazes lock as I whisper against his lips, "If you want to continue this, then you'd better come home with me now."

Instantly, Jack's fingers link through mine, and we're rushing along the sidewalk to the corner to flag a cab for the short ride over to my place.

～

Masturbation is one of the best activities in the world. Some days, I'd go so far as to consider it *the* number one best.

Here's the deal. I have the sex drive of a teenage boy. I'll let you decide whether that's a blessing or a curse. No, seriously. I really do. Here are some examples.

When I finish having sex—good sex, like the kind where I actually have an orgasm—and then the guy and I are lying there, trying to catch our breath, the guy is usually thinking about a nap or a beer or whatever else. But me? I'm ready to go again. I need zero recuperation time. I'm all systems go.

Next example—I love masturbating. If I could get paid to do that, I'd totally jump on that opportunity. Not to mention,

I'm convinced I'd make *millions*. I can masturbate multiple times in one sitting—or more aptly, lying. I think my top number is sixteen times in a row. Yeah, I was a little sore afterward, but it was absolutely worth it.

Go ahead, say I'm a weirdo and tell me how much help I need, but I can claim with complete honesty that I once had someone say, "Teach me, Obi-Wan Kenobi." But I will say this: there's a price. Because, honest to God, I burn up the motor in at least one vibrator quarterly. And have to replace the rechargeable batteries twice a year. The Subscribe and Save option Amazon has? That sucker is perfect because, *thank you, masturbation gods*, they allow me to save money and automatically send me a new vibrator quarterly. Just in time for the old one to kick the bucket.

The issue I have is men who aren't confident enough to allow my vibrator to come out and play during our sexy times. They act like I've somehow insulted them and say something like, "That's weird."

Um, you know what's weird? When guys don't care to think outside the box when it comes to pleasing their woman. That's what's weird, people.

You're probably wondering where I'm going with this. I'm going to make Jack run the gauntlet; as in, I'm going to introduce him to my vibrator. If he accepts it, he'll pass with flying colors. If not, it's going to be the old, *Sorry 'bout ya luck.*

You're hoping he doesn't pass, an inner voice whispers. He makes you uneasy because you know he wants more than you're willing to give.

Mentally shaking off those errant thoughts, I tug Jack inside my apartment and barely manage to close and lock the door behind us before we start tearing at each other's clothing, leaving a trail down the hallway leading to my bedroom.

When I shove him back on my bed, I can't help but give myself a mental high five at managing to get over six feet of manly goodness in his naked glory atop my covers. Shifting to straddle him, I reach over to tug open the small drawer on my nightstand, my fingers wrapping around a familiar object before withdrawing it.

My eyes meet his with a challenge. "Get ready, Westbrook."

His heavy-lidded gaze flicks over my naked body before coming back to rest on the toy in my hand. Reaching for it, he thumbs the wheel, adjusting it to the highest speed. Pressing the tip against my clit, I jerk at the contact, adjusting my perch over him. The feel of his further hardening cock right beneath my spread legs combined with the way he moves the vibrator over my clit sends delicious shivers down my spine.

His other hand slides up my body, a palm cupping the swell of one breast while the calloused pad of his thumb skims over the tip of my hardened nipple. Arching into his touch, I rock my hips slightly, silently urging him on as my eyes fall closed.

"Fuck, Sarah." He lets out a harsh breath. "So damn wet." He continues his ministrations on my clit, driving me closer to orgasm while toying with my nipple, plucking at it. I can feel the way I'm coating the tip of his cock with my wetness. God, I need him inside me again.

"Jack," I whimper, rocking myself over him. "Don't stop."

I'm so close. So freaking close. My toes curl, my muscles tighten in anticipation, and I feel the start of the first spasm of my inner muscles—

"Aaaaah!" I rear back, scrambling off him so frantically, I end up tumbling over the side of the bed and toppling onto the floor. The impact knocks the breath out of me, and I lie here, naked on my back on my bedroom floor, stunned.

"What the hell was that?" I hiss quietly, staring up at the ceiling.

Jack hovers over me worriedly. "Are you okay?"

"What happened?" My eyes are wide in shock and horror.

My hand rubs gingerly over my lady parts which just received a shock—literally.

"Uh, I think there was…" he trails off as if unsure how to tell me, "some sort of short-circuit in the vibrator?" His expression hovers between shock and mirth.

Throwing an arm over my eyes, I groan, muttering to myself, "Did I seriously come close to searing my own vagina tonight? Brilliant, Sarah. Just brilliant."

"Seared pussy is probably a delicacy in some parts of the world."

Moving my arm, I shoot him a glare, but I can't hold it for long because he's grinning down at me playfully. That small lock of hair comes loose again and falls over his forehead. Reaching up to smooth it back, I leave my hand there and gaze up into his blue eyes, letting his soft smile wash over me.

With a sigh, I huff out a tiny laugh. "Want to play it safe and veg out and watch *The Princess Bride* with me?"

His lips lift at the corners, and he stands, holding out a hand to help me up.

"As you wish."

CHAPTER NINETEEN

JACK

The credits are rolling on the screen of Sarah's television, marking the end of the movie, and she releases a sigh that sounds far more whimsical than I'm used to. Gazing down at where she's curled up at my side, I raise an eyebrow in question. "Sad that it's over?"

She sighs again before she shifts my way, her expression thoughtful. "It's the same every time I watch it." Her eyes dart away, and she shrugs. "I always wonder what guy would go through all that for a woman. A woman who basically didn't give him the time of day until way late in the game." Her gaze locks with mine. "Then I wonder what it would be like to have a guy who never gave up—a guy who would never willingly leave me."

She falls silent for a beat before averting her eyes and gives a forced laugh. "Look at me, getting all maudlin." Rising off the couch, she grabs the large bowl from the coffee table, which contains only a few remaining kernels from the popcorn we'd devoured earlier.

My eyes track her movements as she walks around the corner, heading toward the kitchen before she disappears from my sight. And her words linger.

"I always wonder what guy would go through all that for a woman. A woman who basically didn't give him the time of day until way late in the game."

A part of me can't help but wonder if those words ring true for me and Sarah.

The sudden vibration of my phone against the glass surface of Sarah's coffee table draws me from my thoughts. Reaching for it, I dismiss the calendar reminder, alerting me of what I know will be an intense conference call early in the morning for a company primarily focusing on linguistics software based in Moscow.

One of the guys I'd met while working on my MBA in college had transferred to the company's headquarters there. He'd reached out to me to see if I would pitch my thoughts to them. I'd agreed because, if I gained them as a client, it would be a huge account and would also give an even larger boost to my career and reputation.

"Heading out?"

My eyes snap up to find Sarah leaning against the wall, watching me. She looks tired, and though I have an early morning tomorrow, my hesitation to leave weighs heavily on me.

Hell, if I'm being honest, I always hate leaving her. Sarah's become my one addiction. Like those tiny chocolates she keeps handy, she's my own sweet craving—I always want more time with her.

Releasing a long sigh, I rise from the couch and tuck my phone in my pants pocket. I step up to her, drawing to a stop, and let my hands rest lightly on her waist.

"I have an early call in the morning, and I need to bring my A-game."

The obvious regret in my tone is further proof that I don't want to leave. And I swear a hint of something in her expression gives me the feeling she might be experiencing the same disappointment that our night is coming to an end.

One thing's for certain, I couldn't have predicted the events of this evening—as crazy as they were—yet I wouldn't go back and undo it if given the chance. Because it got us here, at this moment, and I think it's pretty damn perfect.

"Night, Sunshine." I dust my lips softly across hers, knowing I have to resist deepening the kiss. I have to maintain restraint since I plan to go over my business proposal tonight to ensure I'll be ready in the morning.

As I leave her place, her soft-spoken goodbye trails after me like the most delicate caress enveloping me. And I realize the real challenge I'm faced with.

I need Sarah as addicted to me as she is to those damn chocolates.

CHAPTER TWENTY

SARAH

"You got zapped by your own vibrator?" Maggie's already repeated this five times. "How does that even happen?" she muses yet again.

"Are you done yet?"

"Guess you could say that what you and Jack have is"—she pauses for emphasis—"electric." She makes zapping noises before dissolving into laughter.

"Glad I could serve as comedic relief for you."

"You have to admit..." Her smile widens. "It's pretty damn funny."

"Hilarious," I respond dryly. Settling on her couch, I release a long sigh.

"Maybe the universe is trying to tell me something," I muse. "Like maybe I really should give that new dating app a try."

Maggie makes a dismissive sound. "Sarah. That app is ridiculous. They include stuff like whether you hate paying extra for guacamole or not."

"Well, it *is* kind of a downer..." I trail off playfully. She rolls her eyes at me. "I should just give up on men and put all my energy into growing my window basil."

"Seriously?" She stares. "Do you hear yourself right now?" She wrinkles her nose. "Besides, your window basil is pathetic."

I blow out a heavy breath. "Yeah. Chalk that up to yet another Pinterest fail." I reach for my cell phone and pull up the dating app. "Get over here and let's see if I can find a guy who won't channel his inner Dom."

Maggie slides closer to me, peering at the screen of my phone. "You should also make sure he likes to snuggle on the couch and watch classics like *The Breakfast Club*, *Pretty in Pink*, or, oh, I don't know"—she lifts a shoulder in a half shrug —"maybe *The Princess Bride*."

Her ploy at being nonchalant is pathetic at best. I eye her, but her gaze remains on my phone's display.

"Subtle, Maggie. Real subtle."

Finally, her eyes lift and meet mine. Her lips curve upward in a sly smile. "Just sayin'. You're not going to find a guy like that"—she nods toward my phone—"there."

With a huff, I toss my cell aside, and it lands softly on the couch cushion beside me. Reaching into the pocket of my hooded sweatshirt, I withdraw one of my chocolates and unwrap it.

And hell if the message written on the inside foil wrapper doesn't stop me in my tracks.

Stop searching for what's right in front of you.

~

"He's a cutie. You could totally bag him."

I shove Clint around the corner of the nurses' station, hissing at him. "You can't be serious right now."

He smirks. "He seems like he'd be a ton of fun, Sarah."

My glare is hard. "He came in with an English cucumber stuck in his ass, Clint."

His smirk widens, eyes dancing with delight. "Like I said,

he'd be a ton of fun." His expression sobers suddenly, and he appears concerned. "You'll have to keep him away from the produce section in the grocery store, though." He purses his lips thoughtfully. "That might be far too much temptation for him."

With a frustrated sound, I turn my attention back to the patient's chart, purposely ignoring him. "Clint," I growl softly in warning.

"Yes, Sunshine?"

My head whips around to stare at him, and he offers a knowing look. "Don't worry. I know that's the special nickname Jack gave you. I just wanted to see if it still worked its magic. Especially since you've been avoiding him lately."

"I'm not—"

"You are," Clint interrupts me calmly.

I toss my hands up in exasperation. "How do you even know this?"

He folds his arms against his chest. "Because we talk, Sarah. We may not be close enough to, oh, I don't know, share little episodes of spanking, biting, and electrical shocks to the vajayjay, but Jack and I've become friends."

I attempt to ignore him as I turn and look over the schedule.

"Haven't found anyone on that app yet, have you?" The whispered words in my ear make my jaw clench tight.

"I never said that."

"You didn't have to. Your dry panties say it all."

Whirling around on Clint, I poke a finger at his chest, hissing quietly. "You'd better stop now, or I'll file a complaint."

He merely wiggles his eyebrows, pulls out his cell phone, and backs away with a gleeful grin. "As if anyone would believe that I, Nurse of the Month, could be anything other than charming." There's a millisecond pause. "Plus, I'm on break right now, so I figure I'll head over to the cafeteria and text my new BFF the news about someone's horribly dry undergarments."

"Cli—"

"Later, Sunshine." He strolls away, leaving me glaring at his back.

~

"What's the deal with you and Jack?"

Pushing the door to the dishwasher closed, I press the start button and lean back against the kitchen counter. "No deal, really." I shrug. "I mean, I'm convinced the universe is against us. But it's also no secret that I think he's so hot someone could drown in my panties when he's nearby."

Maggie's eyebrows shoot up, eyes going wide. "Whoa. O-kay, then."

"I heard the word panties, so count me in." Ry strolls into the kitchen with a wide smile. He slings an arm around Maggie's shoulders and whispers something that makes her cheeks flush before dropping a quick kiss to her temple.

"Ugh." I wave a hand at them as if shooing them away. "Couples in love."

In truth, I adore them and the fact they're deliriously in love thrills me. Is it slightly nauseating how perfect they are for one another? Yes. Does it also make me throw up a bit in my mouth at their little, obviously naughty, whispers? Double yes. But I deal because that's what best friends do.

Grabbing a bottle of water from the fridge, Ry turns and eyes me curiously as he uncaps it. "So what's this about panties?" He smirks and takes a swig of water.

Maggie turns to him. "Sarah mentioned something about how Jack's so hot someone could drown in her panties."

Ry sprays water everywhere, practically showering poor Maggie. Sent into a coughing fit of laughter, he covers his mouth, attempting to regain control of himself. I grab a dishtowel and toss it to Maggie so she can mop up the mess.

"I don't think it warranted a reaction like that," I remark to Ry.

Maggie tosses the towel back onto the counter and announces she's going to change her shirt.

"Sorry, Mags," Ry calls out as she disappears down the hallway. Turning his attention back to me, he shakes his head with a smirk. "Sarah, Sarah, Sarah. Still keeping me on my toes, I see."

I shrug and offer a smug smile. "You asked."

He glances down the hall and then back at me. "You and Jack are back on better terms, I take it? I mean, especially if you're talking about"—he falters for a moment, and I can't help but find his discomfort amusing—"panties and, uh, drowning."

"Kind of." I shrug again. "Aside from the crazy incidents that seem to always happen when we're together."

Sobering, Ry falls silent for a moment and tosses another glance down the hall where Maggie retreated. Returning his attention to me, he waves me closer before lowering his voice. If I didn't know any better, I'd be concerned. Except his eyes are sparkling with mischief, so I know he's up to no good.

"While she's back there," he says softly, "tell me this." One eyebrow raises slightly. "Has Mags ever mentioned me inducing her 'panty-drowning' effect?"

Schooling my expression, I shake my head with faux sadness. "Dry as the Sahara, Ry," I answer, releasing a long, mournful sigh to add more emphasis.

He stares at me for a moment, eyes studying me, and I do my best to maintain a straight face.

Finally, his lips curve into a wide grin, and he hooks an arm around my shoulder, holding me in a headlock. Pulling me in close, he uses his other hand to give me noogies, ruffling my hair as though I'm a small child.

"Ry!"

"You lie!" I can hear the laughter in his voice while I struggle to break free from his hold. "Admit it! Admit to the panty drowning!"

"Fine!" I toss back, continuing to struggle. "Always! She always says that!"

Instantly, I'm released and blow out a huff of breath. Attempting to smooth down my hair, I toss a hard glare at Ry. Before I can scold him, we hear Maggie mutter, "I really don't think that warranted a headlock, Ry." She's standing with her arms crossed, watching us with barely banked amusement.

"Ah, but a man's gotta do what a man's gotta do, Mags." Ry tugs her close and skims his lips over her forehead before leaning back to flash a cocky smile. "Especially when it comes to panty drowning."

CHAPTER TWENTY-ONE

SARAH

I'm sitting in our favorite Thai restaurant with Maggie, Ry, and Jack, who arrived late because of a work meeting.

To say that Jack looks utterly delectable in his charcoal suit would be a vast understatement. This man can irrevocably wear the hell out of a suit. I can't lie and say I'm not fantasizing about crawling onto his lap and ridding him of those layers of tailored fabric.

Instead, I lean over and say in a hushed voice, so as not to let our friends overhear, "I was thinking... Maybe after we finish up with dinner, we can go have some fun. *Downtown*."

Yep. I said it. Downtown. I'm shamelessly implying that we can have some "oral" fun later.

Jack stares back at me with an odd look. "I don't really feel like going there, Sarah." He focuses on stabbing at a piece of shrimp in his pad thai. "It's actually pretty gross."

I'm sorry, *what*? Since when does he find going down *there* so unappealing?

"I don't get it. You seemed like you'd be all for it, judging from past"—I dart a glance at our friends who are now tuned in and glued to my and Jack's conversation—"experiences."

While I practically disclose everything to my best friend, I'm not sure I want Ry to overhear this conversation. But I don't really get a say in the matter because Jack speaks loud enough for Maggie and Ry to hear.

His expression turns a bit queasy. "It's just…sticky." He shudders. "Disgusting."

What the hell is he talking about? Sticky? Disgusting?

He goes on. "I mean, not only is it sticky but it's also a compact, crowded space."

My lips part, gaping at him slightly. "A compact, crowded space?" I repeat, absolutely appalled.

Jack keeps going. "I honestly don't feel comfortable down there." Forking a piece of shrimp into his mouth, he chews and swallows. "Unless I've had a few drinks to numb my senses a bit and not make it so…"

Vaguely, I register the sound of choked laughter coming from Maggie and Ry. But I don't acknowledge it because it seems I've got bigger issues here.

Not to mention, I'm still stuck on the whole "sticky" complaint. No pun intended.

"Then there's the smell," Jack adds, his face scrunching in distaste. "I mean, you can tell that cleaning might've taken place, but the smell seems to linger. And it's a putrid smell. Like rotten tacos or something."

Aghast, I stare at him. "*WHAT?*" My head snaps over to Maggie and Ry, thinking at least my best friend would jump in and defend me. Nope. She and Ry are leaning against one another, shoulders shaking, heads bowed as if they're attempting to hide their facial expressions.

Snapping back, I focus on Jack, and my eyes narrow dangerously. "I beg your pardon! It does *not* smell like rotten tacos!"

"Look, Sarah," Jack says with a sigh. "I get that it might sound like fun to you, but it's not for me. Not at all. I mean"—his features brighten slightly as if thoughtful

—"maybe if there were a way to give it a makeover and a deep cleaning or something. Really get in there and scrub it down thoroughly. Get that smell and all the dust out of there."

I can't.

I. Just. CAN'T.

"It's…" He furrows his brow. "It's hard to get past the appearance of it."

My eyebrows shoot up, nearly hitting my hairline. "The appearance?"

"Yeah. I mean, someone needs to work on the exterior and make it more welcoming. It's pretty drab looking as it is."

Drab looking? "Are you serious, right now, Westbrook?" I'm pissed. No two ways about it.

"Look," Jack replies calmly, "I get that you and Maggie might enjoy it, but it doesn't do anything for me or Ry."

Before I can manage to utter a response, Ry interrupts, holding up his hands. "Whoa, whoa. Hold up for a second." He looks like he's attempting to hold back a smile. "I think there's a chance you're both talking about two entirely different things."

Jack and I stare at Ry before we turn back to one another and he frowns, confusion lining his features. "You weren't talking about the old bar, Downtown?"

Oh.

My.

God.

He's been talking about the bar a few blocks away which operates under the generic name of Downtown.

A bar. A freaking bar. *Not* my vagina.

My lips press together in a thin line, embarrassment rushing to the forefront of my emotions. "Uh, not exactly," I reply slowly.

He stares at me for a beat before his face transforms into a near-blinding smile, laughter booming.

"Oh, Sunshine..." He laughs, shaking his head. Sliding an arm across the back of my chair, he leans in, bringing his mouth close to my ear. "You should know I'm always game for that kind of downtown." His lips dust against my earlobe, eliciting a slight shiver, and goose bumps rise on my skin. "And I'll be sure not to eat anything spicy with extra wasabi beforehand, too."

It takes a moment for my brain to register his words; to break through the fog of Jack's deep, husky voice and the seductive quality practically holding me in rapture.

But when his words finally sink in, my eyes snap up to lock with his laughing ones. His wide smile makes it impossible to hold my stern expression, and I shake my head at him.

"Play nice, Westbrook," I admonish and nudge him playfully with my elbow.

In return, he merely tugs me closer. Pressing a soft kiss to my temple, he whispers, "I always play nice with my Sunshine."

The four of us return to our dinner, and the laughter, good-natured teasing, and storytelling are as entertaining as ever. Yet I'm slightly distracted by Jack's whispered words. Or, more importantly, two of them.

He'd said, *"I always play nice with my Sunshine."*

My Sunshine.

I'd be lying if I said those two words, in particular, didn't make an infinitesimal part of me yearn for that to be true.

For me to actually be Jack's Sunshine.

CHAPTER TWENTY-TWO

JACK

"You're not upset that we're not hanging out Downtown?" I wink at Sarah, who merely shakes her head with a laugh.

She and I decided to head over to Max Londons after we finished dinner with Maggie and Ry. We've been sitting at the bar of the crowded restaurant, chatting and people watching. She's sipping a glass of their house special, a white wine sangria, while I enjoy a Saratoga lager.

I nudge her shoulder playfully. "You should have known better." Leaning close, I bring my lips close to her ear to ensure she hears me over the bustling noise of the restaurant. "I love everything about you." I pause briefly, my voice growing a bit hoarse at the mere thought of her body beneath mine. "Especially tasting you."

Drawing back, she turns slightly, her blue eyes hazy with lust. "You're dangerous."

"How so?"

The tip of her tongue darts out to wet her lips before she leans in closer. "You make me want to do things that could get me in trouble." She runs a palm over my thigh, and it seems innocent enough but then she grazes over my cock before retreating.

Instantly hardening, that brief graze makes me ache for more of her touch. "Sunshine." I shake my head, my gaze locked with hers. "You're playing with fire."

With a wicked smile, she reaches into her purse for what I've come to think of as one of "her" chocolates. Unwrapping it, she reads the small message on the inside of the wrapper before taking a tiny bite. Just as she's about to put the remaining chocolate back in the foil wrapper, I lay my hand on her thigh, my fingers slipping beneath the hem of her skirt to stroke her inner thigh.

"You're not going to offer me any?"

Her eyes dart to mine, hesitating a moment before she lifts the chocolate to my lips. I wrap my lips around her fingers, the tip of my tongue touching a fingertip. Her lips part, pupils dilating slightly, and her breathing quickens. I can't restrain the satisfied look that spreads across my face.

Dipping my head, I dust a soft kiss on her lips, murmuring against them, "Feel like heading back to my pla—"

"Yes." Her immediate response sends anticipation strumming through me. But it's the way her hand easily—readily—slips into mine when I offer to help her down from the barstool that resonates. A flood of possessiveness rushes through me as we exit the restaurant, hand in hand, and all I hear in my head is the echo of one word.

Mine.

~

"You have too many clothes on."

Sarah's whispered complaint makes my lips curve upward. She frantically tugs at the buttons on my shirt as we make our way to my bedroom. She'd stripped me of my suit jacket the instant we were inside my apartment.

"Same goes for you." My hands slip around to the back of her skirt, finding the small zipper and drawing it down until the fabric drops, pooling at her feet.

It doesn't matter how many times I see this woman undressed. The sight of her still manages to rob me of my breath. Gently gripping her waist, I brush my thumbs against the tiny waistband of her panties.

"Off." Sarah tugs at my shirt, and I slip it off each arm while she directs her attention to my belt, tugging at it as if she's being timed and has to unfasten it in thirty seconds or less.

"Sunshine." My tone is laced with amusement, and her eyes flick up to mine in question. "There's no rush here."

"Wrong." Her response is immediate, and I can't resist the small laugh it elicits. "I'm in a serious rush, Jack." Those blue eyes appear to darken further with lust, and she worries the bottom edge of her lip before her voice turns husky. "If you feel me, you'll understand why I'm in such a rush."

Fuck me. This woman… Never have I been with someone so confident, so unafraid of expressing herself and her desires.

Slipping her panties down over her hips, she shimmies out of them while simultaneously loosening my pants and shoving them down along with my boxer briefs. Without any hesitation, my hand dips between her thighs and two of my fingers easily slip inside her wetness.

Her soft gasp drifts over me, and I watch as her eyes flutter closed, her hips canting slightly.

My head descends, bringing my lips to brush against hers with each whispered word. "You're so wet, Sunshine. For me?"

"Yes," she whispers hoarsely.

"Open your eyes," I command, backing away slightly. My

gaze briefly flickers down to where I drag my fingers out of her, finding her eyes locked onto the view of my fingers just as I plunge them back inside her. Her heavy-lidded eyes watch, transfixed, as my fingers continue their ministrations, coated in her arousal. I jerk at the feel of her soft palm wrapping around my thick cock and feel myself harden further at her touch.

"You're coating my fingers." Moisture gathers at my tip as she begins to stroke my length while I simultaneously thrust in and out of her. Frantic, I grasp the hem of her loose-fitting blouse and lift it over her head. Releasing me briefly to pull her arms from it, she hurriedly rids herself of her bra before taking my cock in her hand once again.

"Sunshine." My voice sounds ragged and harsh to my own ears. "Not sure how much more I can take."

When she relinquishes her grasp, moving to lie back on my bed, her smile is wicked. "Then you'd better do something about it."

Reaching for a condom, I tear open the packet with more urgency than I think I've ever felt before and slide it on. Moving to join her on the bed, I brace myself on my forearms above her as my tip presses against her entrance.

Softly pressing a kiss to her lips, I whisper, "You're beautiful." Inching inside her, our combined moans sound in the silence of the room. Continuing to press deeper, I'm nearly buried to the hilt, only a little farther...

BEEP-BEEP-BEEP!

Both of us jerk with a start at the blaring sound of the fire alarm. Rolling off her quickly, I hand her clothes to her and attempt to pull on my own as fast as possible. Once we're dressed, I take her hand, and we rush down the stairs to exit the building.

We huddle together with the other tenants standing near the street curb, curiously discussing what might have happened as there was no sign of a fire nor billowing smoke.

~

We finally learned that one of the tenant's preteens pulled the fire alarm "on a dare." Once the fire department secured the building, they'd allowed us back inside.

"Jack Westbrook," Sarah murmurs as she prepares to leave my apartment. "I feel like your penis and my vagina are determined to maintain a standoff with one another. As in no mutual orgasms." Her smile is halfhearted at best. "Like a royal decree has been declared." She deepens her voice dramatically. "Your penis and my vagina. Never shall the two climax together."

"It'll happen, Sunshine." I brush my lips against hers before deepening the kiss, my tongue twining with hers.

I know she has an early shift tomorrow, which is why she has to leave now, but I can't help it. I have to taste her one final time. Her Uber will be here soon, and I don't want her to miss it. I just need another taste...

She backs away slightly, ducking her head to press a soft kiss to the base of my throat. "I have to go."

"I know. I wish you didn't."

Her lips tip up. "Me, too." Kissing me one last time, she opens the door and steps into the hallway. "Good night, Jack."

"Night, Sunshine." I pause. "Text me when you get home safely." She nods with a soft smile and disappears down the hallway, heading to the elevator. And it fucking sucks to watch her leave. Part of me wants to chase after her and get one more kiss. Just one more taste...

Screw it.

I jog down the carpeted hallway, my shoeless feet sound-less, and approach her right as she steps into the elevator. My hand slips around to stop the doors from closing, and her startled eyes lock with mine.

"One more kiss?"

Her features soften, and she steps forward to briefly press her lips against mine. Backing away, she gives me a smile I know I will store in my memories. Tender, intimate, affectionate.

"Bye, Jack."

I step back, allowing the elevator doors to close, and stand here for far longer than I'd care to acknowledge.

I don't care how much of a pussy it makes me to admit it, but I fucking hate saying goodbye to her.

If I had my way, I'd do everything in my power to ensure I'd never have to.

CHAPTER TWENTY-THREE

SARAH

After a long weekend filled with crazy hours and, in some cases, equally crazy patients and their family members, I have plans to go home and enjoy some one-on-one time with myself.

In case you're wondering, yes, I got a new vibrator and new batteries. I'm not about to worry about round two of what felt like electricity zapping my clitoris. Nuh-uh. No siree.

I need some stress relief, and since I'm off for the next four days, what better way to set the tone than masturbation? Not only does it relieve stress but, according to some medical studies, it can also help to boost the immune system—post-orgasm, of course. So, ultimately, I'm doing a great service to my body in more ways than one. Considering I work in a high-stress environment and am constantly around sick people, this is a brilliant life choice.

Okay, so I'm probably laying it on a bit thick, but you have to admit I'm bringing up some valid points right now.

My game plan is to head home, read some hot romance novel, and break my new vibrator in. Oh, and I'm going to order some takeout—pad thai from the place two blocks away. I know, I know. I sound like some perverted frat boy, don't I? I can't help it.

I settle on my bed, propped up slightly on my pillows, and then start my vibrator. Thumbing the keys on my phone, I pull up the Kindle app, so I can get back to the hot scene in the latest book I'd been reading.

Except something goes terribly awry and, as I adjust the vibrator's placement against my clit, I glance over to start reading and don't see a page of the book.

I see Jack's face staring back at me.

"Oh shit!" I'm trying to cover the screen but lose my grip and my phone lands right over my freaking vagina.

My vagina is officially FaceTiming Jack.

That slut.

"Jesus, Mary, and Joseph!" *Oh my God.* I'm never showing my face again. I'm taking a nursing job in Nairobi next.

Grabbing the phone and tugging it from where it's nestled between my thighs, I rush to shut off the obvious sound of my vibrator. With a wince, I bring the phone up to my face.

"Hello, Sunshine." Without opening my eyes, I can hear the humor in his tone. "I certainly hope that's not how you greet everyone on FaceTime. Not that I'm complaining, of course."

I open my eyes to squint at him. "A gentleman wouldn't mention that to a lady."

A smile stretches his handsome face. "Never claimed to be a gentleman, now, did I?"

"*Jack.*" I draw out his name, my tone one of warning.

"Sunshine," he counters playfully. "So I guess I know what your plans are for the night, huh?"

He's enjoying this far too much.

"And I must say, I'm quite impressed with your recent wax job."

Seriously?

"Maybe I can come over and check it out in person."

"Jack Westbrook." I stare at him grinning back at me. "Do you really expect that to work with me?"

He offers me a sheepish grin. "Not really." His smile dims slightly, and his voice drops, sounding huskier. "You should know by now that I love teasing you."

I release a tiny sigh. "Since I'm clearly not going to molest myself right now, do you maybe want to come over for some pad thai and to watch a movie?"

His eyes narrow playfully. "Depends. Are we watching your favorite movie *The Princess Bride*?"

I roll my eyes with a smile. "As you wish."

"I'll be over in a few." He winks at me. "Put some clothes on, Buttercup."

~

"As many times as I watch this movie—and I never tire of it—I still think she should have been nicer to him and admitted her feelings."

"Women are sometimes slow to realize a guy likes them." Jack's pointed gaze is telling.

"Ah." I nudge him with my shoulder. "Touché, West-brook." Rising from the couch, I head into my small kitchen to put my container of pad thai in the refrigerator. They always give such large portions, so I'll be eating on that for a day or so.

"I think I'm going to head home."

Jack's subdued tone makes me turn to find him leaning against the wall in my kitchen, watching me. Something unreadable flickers in his eyes, and I can't deny a part of me wants to ask him to stay. But another part of me is afraid. Because every single time we get together in a sexual way, it's trouble. Mayhem ensues. And I'd really like to end our evening on a good note and not tempt the universe to throw us another major curveball.

"I'll walk you out," I say softly.

As we head over to my door, I wait for him to put his shoes on and pull on the hooded sweatshirt to ward off the slight chill in the night air. He steps closer, his eyes warm, a soft smile playing at his lips, and he slips a hand to the small of my back.

Dipping his head, he dusts a gentle kiss on my lips. "Thanks for having me over, Sunshine."

"You're welcome," I whisper back.

He releases me, backing away to pull open the door, and bids me good night. When he steps over the threshold, I stop him before he can pull the door closed behind him.

"Wait." I detect the urgency in my tone and catch his worried look when he turns back. Reaching my hands out to hook in the pockets of his hooded sweatshirt, I tug him toward me, lifting to my toes and pressing my lips to his.

As if he had been anticipating my move, one of his hands cups the back of my head, slanting his mouth to deepen our kiss. His other hand lands on my hip, tugging me closer. I'm not certain how long we kiss until a door down the hall sounds, the light slam startling us.

Breaking the kiss, he looks down at me tenderly before pressing his lips to mine one final time. "Good night, Sunshine."

"Night, Jack."

CHAPTER TWENTY-FOUR

SARAH

I'm having one of those rare nights when I feel pretty. You know, the ones where your makeup—specifically an attempt at creating smoky eyes—doesn't actually look like a toddler loopy on Benadryl applied it to your face. I haven't had any unfortunate wardrobe malfunctions to speak of, either, so that's a total win in my book.

Not to mention, these shoes. *Sigh*. The shoes Jack bought for me along with the tiny clutch purse are the icing on the cake.

I'd also like to point out that I deserve a huge pat on the back along with a double high five for not being *that* girl with her cell phone out, glancing every two point five seconds to see if *the* guy has messaged her.

But it did cross my mind. Once or twice.

Ooookaaay, fine. Maybe a hundred times, but who's counting?

Tonight, we're barhopping as Maggie completes her bachelorette party scavenger hunt assigned to her by Ry's twin step-cousins, Molly and Masey.

Oh, wait. They're his step-cousins but "twice removed,"

whatever the hell that even means. In my book, either you're a cousin, or you're not; there's no in-between.

I can also confirm that by my second drink (I'm such a sad lightweight when it comes to drinking), I've given up on trying to tell them apart and have begun to call them "M" individually and together "M and M." Luckily, they think it's cute. Judging by the number of feather boas they have draped around their necks (five each, in case you were wondering because "no one can ever wear too many boas"), the way the corners of their eyes are, in fact, bedazzled, combined with their favorite conversation topics of Perez Hilton and what he'll report on next, the "on the edge of your seat" debate topic of whether One Direction will ever reunite, and their recently "learned" benefits of swallowing semen, I'm ready to put my beverage straw to good use and gouge myself in the eyes—and possibly eardrums, as well—within an hour.

Maggie's far too sweet and tries to partake in their conversation a bit. All seems fine and dandy—*dun, dun, dunnnnnn*—until M and M have a few too many buttery nipple shots and miraculously scrounge up a "legit stripper" named "Magic Mikey."

Right. And I'm a legit porn star named Jenna Jamestown.

Magic Mikey proceeds to try to display his skills, jiggling his leather-clad ass all around where we're seated before hovering over Maggie's lap. It's all fun and games at first until he contorts himself in a way which brings his crotch far too close to my best friend's face.

"Okay, thanks! Um, that's enough." Maggie carefully backs her chair away from the man.

Unfortunately, he suffers a syndrome some guys tend to have around women in bars or dance clubs in which they have total delusions of grandeur. These delusions are triggered when a woman offers a polite denial to any of the following, which, in turn, is interpreted as the woman playing hard to get:

a) They offer to buy you a drink.

b) They insert themselves suddenly—and rudely—into your conversation with your friends.

c) They invade your personal space on the dance floor and proceed to grind their junk all over you like an animal in heat.

Then they take it as a sign to try harder and continue with their above actions. This is what clearly plagues Magic Mikey.

"Yo, Mikey." I pinch the guy's ear between my finger and thumb and yank hard enough to get him to move in the direction I want—away from the vicinity of my best friend's face. "Thanks for the dance, but my friend has reached her maximum crotch-to-face quota for the evening." My sugary sweet smile along with finally releasing his ear gets through to him.

Rubbing his ear, he eyes me warily before his gaze flits over to the M and M twins. "Think they'd be up for some fun?"

"Probably. No, scratch that. *Definitely*. Just woo them with talk about Harry Styles or bedazzling or—wait for it—how healthy they'll be after swallowing your semen tonight."

Just kidding. I didn't really say that to him. But I reeeeeallly wanted to. Instead, I told him he'd have to ask them.

Yeah, I know. I went the responsible adult route. And it was painful as hell.

Within thirty seconds flat, as I confer with Maggie about heading to the next bar, M and M swarm us.

"OH. EM. GEE!" one of them exclaims.

In case you're thinking I'm making this up, nope. Not even.

"You'll never guess what just happened!" The two of them squeal the way teenage girls do over Justin Bieber.

I gasp melodramatically. "I'm dying to know, girls!"

Maggie elbows me, trying to mask her snicker which the twins, thankfully, don't pick up on.

"Magic Mikey asked us to go home with him toniiiiight," they answer in unison with their high-pitched, sing-song voices. "And he lives with, like, five other guys!"

My head snaps to look at Maggie with wide eyes. "Did you hear that, my friend? You know what this occasion calls for, don't you?"

Maggie stares at me warily. "Um, no…"

Abruptly, I hold up both hands, wiggling my fingers and turning to the twins. "Spirit fingers!! Woohoo!" The twins totally dig this move and mimic it.

I think it's safe to say they *love* me.

"We hate to leave you on your special night, Maggie, but—"

"But Magic Mikey's semen is calling." I don't know how I say this without laughing. It will remain one of life's biggest mysteries, I'm certain.

Flashing a pleading look at my best friend, I add, "Surely, you understand the urgency of this matter."

Maggie covers her mouth with her hand, and I instantly react, putting my arm around her shoulders and tugging her close to me. "Go," I tell the twins, patting Maggie's back as if I'm comforting her, "I've got this, girls."

As soon as they disappear in the crowded wine bar, I give a final pat on her back. "All clear."

Maggie lifts her head, wiping tears of laughter from the corners of her eyes. "Sarah!"

"What?" I smile innocently. "They're going to have the best night of their lives, thanks to me."

She shakes her head at me and checks her phone. "Ry and the others are at the whiskey bar two blocks over." Raising her eyes to mine, she arches an eyebrow. "Feel like crashing their party?"

"Is the Pope Catholic?"

CHAPTER TWENTY-FIVE

JACK

There must be some crazy beacon when a group of guys heads out to a bar. Women immediately approach us to ask if we're out for a bachelor party and take it as some sort of challenge to see if they can seduce the groom.

Well, joke's on them since Ry's so far gone over Maggie, it's not even remotely funny. We've barhopped and are at our final stop while the girls are off on their own little excursion for the evening.

And I don't want to admit how much distaste I have at the idea of Sarah being around strippers. Maggie's never been the type to be into that kind of thing, but who knows what goes on at bachelorette parties. I'm sure they're having fun and enjoying a lot of laughs. Hell, I feel a smile tug at my own lips, imagining the way Sarah's face lights up with laughter and the way her blue eyes sparkle.

"What's with you two?" I turn to find Ry's quieter cousin, Aaron, eyeing me curiously. "Well, I get him"—he waves toward Ry, who's currently regaling the small group of women with stories about his early days with Maggie, before turning his attention back to me—"but you've got a similar sappy-ass grin on your face."

Startled, I run a hand over my face, scrambling to come up with something, an excuse of some sort.

Instead, I come up with absolutely nothing.

"Shit," I mutter under my breath. Because, yeah, I've got it bad. She's got me sporting a stupid smile like some lovesick fool who'd do just about anything for her...

Except, it's true. I would.

"Ah, so that's the way it is, huh?" Aaron leans back in the plush chair of the classy whiskey bar we're in. His smug expression says it all. "You just had the revelation I take it?"

It figures that I'd attract the married cousin who apparently takes pleasure in harassing other single guys.

Taking a swig of my whiskey, I attempt to ignore him, but my lack of response serves as no deterrent. Aaron simply continues. "Tell me about her." My sharp look only causes him to smile. "What's she like?"

Knowing the likelihood of him letting this go is slim to none, I heave out a breath, staring into my glass. While I try to think of what to say about Sarah, I feel the upward tip of my lips.

"She's mouthy, sassy, and funny." Peering down at my glass of whiskey, I swirl it slightly. "Smart as hell, too."

"And gorgeous, I assume?" he asks, humor lacing his tone. "With blond hair, blue eyes, and long legs."

"Yeah," I say with a sigh. Fuck if I don't miss her like hell right now.

God, I'm a sad excuse for a best man tonight.

"And when she looks at you, it's like you're the only guy who exists?"

Something in Aaron's tone draws my attention from my glass of whiskey to him. "Exactly." Except he's not looking at me but gazing over my shoulder with an amused smile.

A second later, two delicately soft hands cover my eyes

and a voice whispers in my ear, her hot breath washing over my skin. "Guess who?"

"Amber! I'm so glad you made it!" I can't help but tease her.

Sarah lets out a huff, her teeth nipping lightly at my earlobe before dropping her hands from my eyes. "Amber," she mutters with playful disgust. As she rounds my chair, intent on claiming the available one across from me, I snag her wrist and give a gentle tug, causing her to spill onto my lap.

Her blond hair is loose and falls forward like a silky curtain. Reaching up to slide it back and tuck it behind her ear, I drink in the sight of her. She's wearing a cute little fitted blue dress that accentuates her narrow waist. The dress has long sleeves which have embroidery and some beads adorning the cuffs with the neckline dipping into a sharp V.

Her eye makeup is heavier than normal, but it makes her blue eyes much more pronounced, and her lips are a subtle shade of red. Her eyes crinkle slightly at the corners. "Hey, Jack."

"Hey, Sunshine."

She reaches into her small clutch, diverting my attention, and when I look down to see her extracting a small foil-wrapped chocolate, I can't resist a chuckle. That ends quickly, though, when I catch the sight of something in my peripheral vision, sparkling in the lights of the bar.

My eyes track from the bottom hem of her dress which hits at her knees, traveling down along her long, silky smooth legs to find her wearing the sparkly shoes I bought her that first day we were "assigned" errands for Maggie and Ry's wedding preparation. Smoothing a hand down her leg, I smirk. "These are damn fine shoes."

"Aren't they, though?" she asks smugly. "Some guy bought them for me."

I make a sound of faux dismay. "Some guy?"

Sarah presses a kiss to my cheek before huskily whispering, "He's my favorite guy," before backing away and unwrapping her favorite chocolate. Removing the small candy from the foil, she reads the brief message written on the inside of the wrapper, and her eyes turn soft. Curiously, I turn her hand holding the foil wrapper toward me to read it.

Make love your main adventure.

Meeting her eyes, I catch sight of something indecipherable in the depths. Casually, I toss out, "I'd say we've had a few adventures together so far."

Shit. What the hell am I saying? She's going to think I'm saying we love each other. And she doesn't love me. I mean, I can't... I don't... *Fuck.*

"Yes, we sure have." Her voice draws me from my thoughts. She takes a small bite of the chocolate and then offers it to me. Taking her wrist in my grasp, I bring it to my lips. Biting into it, I brush my lips against her fingers. My eyes lock on hers, and I hear the slight intake of breath, the way her lips part.

"Holy hell. I think I just got pregnant watching that go down."

We turn to find Maggie peering at us, her eyes dancing with mischief. "We're heading home, so you crazy kids be safe." She leans in to hug Sarah goodbye before kissing me on the cheek.

"Thanks, man." Ry slaps a hand on my shoulder, shaking my hand, and then gives Sarah a quick kiss on her cheek. As he backs away, grinning, he nods to Sarah. "Don't let this guy get you into too much trouble."

Slowly but surely, the rest of our group divides up into the *We're calling it a night* or *We're hitting another bar* before bidding their goodbyes. Soon, it's only me and Sarah. When she moves to shift herself off my lap with the intent of taking a seat in the now-available chair beside me, my hand tightens its hold on her hip.

"Stay." I lower my face, nuzzling her neck. "I like you here."

I feel the slight vibrations in her throat from her easy, soft laughter. "I like it, too. But..." She trails off, and I raise my head, meeting her gaze in question. "I'd like to head home."

My stomach plummets while, simultaneously, it feels as though a thousand-pound weight puts immense pressure on my chest because, well... I'd hoped we'd head home together —that we'd end the night together.

That's what I get for being presumptuous.

"Oh. Yeah, of course." I make a show of checking my watch for the time. "It *is* pretty late, now that you mention it. You probably want to—"

"Jack." My eyes meet hers, and she offers a gentle smile. "I meant I'd like to go home, back to my place." There's a brief pause. "With you."

"With me," I repeat like an idiot, a dawning smile spreading my face.

"With you."

And the painful tightness in my chest mysteriously subsides.

CHAPTER TWENTY-SIX

SARAH

"Did you have fun tonight?"

I'm curled up against Jack's side, his arm wrapped around me as we take the short cab ride back to my place. With a laugh, I say, "It was interesting, that's for sure." Once I relay the stories from the wine bar, Jack's still chuckling by the time we pull up outside my apartment.

After we're inside and I've locked up, the mood shifts. Leaning back against opposite walls in my entryway, we remove our shoes. As soon as my second heel drops to the floor, Jack's on me, crowding me in the most delicious way. His palms brace flat against the wall on either side of me. He drags his lips down my cheek, over my jaw, and down my neck before inhaling deeply.

"Are you smelling me, Westbrook?" I try to tease him, but my voice sounds more breathless than anything.

"Stop." I can feel him smile against my skin. "You're ruining the moment." He trails tender kisses along the column of my throat.

I raise my hands, fingers sliding through his hair and gently tug him up to meet my eyes. Staring back at me in the dimly lit apartment, I swear there's a hint of something different in his gaze. Something deeper. Something we haven't embarked on before.

The corners of his lips lift slightly, and he brings the pad of his thumb up to toy with my bottom lip. Still holding my gaze, he whispers, "I missed you tonight, Sunshine."

His hand shifts, his thumb sweeping across my cheekbone as his head descends, giving me what must be the most tender kiss I've ever had. No tongue, just the barest, feather-light touch of his lips to mine.

I swear I can feel it all the way to my heart.

Suddenly, I'm desperate for more. I tug him closer, angle my head to take over the kiss and deepen it, a driving need propelling me with each swipe of my tongue against his. That need increases with each gliding stroke of my hands over his back as I feel the play of his muscles. He presses closer between my legs, rocking against me, and his mouth swallows my moan. My body arches into his as my hands make their way between us to unfasten his pants, reaching inside to grasp his hardening cock.

Taking him firmly in my hand, I stroke him, feeling him grow harder in my palm. When he thrusts into my touch, it sends another surge of heat to my core as I continue to work him with my hand.

One of his palms slaps against the wall beside my head, and he tears his lips from mine, his breathing heavy and ragged as he presses wet kisses along my neck and throat.

"That feels so damn good, Sunshine," he grits out; his breathing becomes more staggered, and I can tell he's close. In fact, the knowledge that he's close to coming makes me so wet; it feels like I've practically flooded my panties.

Oh shit. My entire body goes rigid in alarm. In fear. In mortification.

Breaking the kiss, my eyes grow wide, and I push him

away from me. "Oh shit." I don't want to look down...but I know I have to.

Please let it not be there, please let it not be there, please let it not be there, I mentally chant. Maybe I got lucky.

But when I look down at the knee he'd pressed against me, to the center of my thighs, even in the dim lighting I see it. The tiniest spot of moisture on his pants.

Slapping my hands over my face, I blurt out hurriedly, "Ohmygod I'msosorry!" With a wince, I peek out from between my fingers. "Why don't you go to my laundry room and grab the stain stick while I, uh, do my thing in the restroom real quick." Backing away from him, I practically sprint to my bathroom and lock myself in.

Reaching below the sink for what I need, I quickly strip myself of my panties before taking care of things and decide to toss the poor underwear in the trash. It's not a newer pair, and I really don't want to bother with getting blood stains out.

Cracking the door open before tiptoeing back into my bedroom and rummaging through my dresser drawer for some boyshort panties, a pair of sweatpants, and a T-shirt, I trade out my dress and bra and pull on the comfortable clothing.

Inhaling a fortifying breath, I head down the hall to see if Jack's still here. When I find him sitting on my couch, one arm draped across the back, casual as can be, I'm not sure if I'm happy he's hung around or disappointed he's still here and I have to face him.

His eyes flick over me from head to toe, and it feels like a caress. "That's a decidedly more comfortable look." The corners of his mouth tip up. "It's cute."

Cute. Just what every woman wants to hear. Then again, I practically *Scarlet Letter*'d the poor guy...or you could say I pulled a stunt from the movie *SuperBad.* Either way, mortification is hanging over me like a dark cloud.

"So..." With an overly bright expression, I gesture casually. "Do you happen to know the last time you were about to get your rocks off?" I barely pause before continuing, my words coming out rapid fire. "And oh, you know, the girl's menstrual cycle starts, and she gets a little"—my hands rest on top of my head, and I direct my gaze to my ceiling, my voice faint and weary, trailing to a whimper-like whisper —"blood on your pants?"

The silence hangs between us, awkwardness growing exponentially until he finally speaks.

"Sunshine." I don't move, continuing to stare up at the ceiling as though it's my job. "Look at me."

"I can't. I'm currently attempting to stare a hole into the ceiling because tipping my head at this angle will allow me to survive a bit longer when the full flood of embarrassment comes rushing in to drown me."

I swear I hear him chuckle softly. "Please look at me."

"Did you use the stain stick?" I refuse to move my eyes from the ceiling. In fact, I'm pretty sure I detect the slightest discoloration in that one corner. A sign of water damage, perhaps? I should tell my landlord.

"I don't care about my damn pants, Sarah."

Shit. He's using my name instead of calling me Sunshine. He means business now.

I hear him shift, and before I know it, he scoops me up and carries me over to the couch. Once I'm situated on his lap, he lifts my chin with his finger, directing me to meet his eyes. "Don't hide from me."

With an eye roll, I blow out a breath. "Fine. Quick conversation."

"Okay."

"I say I'm sorry for, uh, marking you, and you say, no worries, it—"

"It's only a pair of jeans and—"

"And I say, hey, would you like to pig out on my 'menstrual snacks' with me, which consists of chocolate and salt and vinegar chips? Not at the same time but definitely partaking in both because that's what I crave during this time and—"

"Salt and vinegar chips are my favorite." His words are spoken so tenderly and sweetly that it gives me pause.

"Really?" I pause for a beat. "You're not just saying that?"

He gives me one of those smiles, and I suddenly realize it's special because it has a different quality to it. It's not the smile he gives Ry or Maggie or the waiter when he thanks them for refilling his water. No, this smile is different.

It's a smile he only gives *me*.

"Really, Sunshine." Pressing a soft kiss to my forehead, he adds, "Now, go get those menstrual snacks."

Slipping off his lap, I make my way to the kitchen, and he calls out to me. "Any chance there might be some 'menstrual snuggling' on the menu tonight, too? 'Cause I might be feeling kinda crampy myself."

Damn smartass.

But I find myself smiling like a fool the entire time I gather the snacks in my kitchen.

CHAPTER TWENTY-SEVEN

SARAH

Two weeks later

I've been spending my day getting all the items on my list to prepare for Maggie and Ry's upcoming nuptials. I swear, I was about to run out of lotion, mascara, foundation, and my favorite eye shadows all at once and, with the chance that my work schedule might throw things off, I decided to take advantage of my day off to get things squared away.

As I'm exiting the final store, I realize I'm standing across the street from the building where Jack rents space for his office.

Hesitating as I peer up at the second floor where his office is located, I waver between wanting to stop by and see him and the uncertainty in doing so because, let's be honest—dropping by unexpectedly and unannounced would be a girlfriend thing to do, and Jack and I are not together in any capacity.

As I shake off the idea, I feel the telltale vibrating in my purse signaling an incoming call. "Please let it not be work calling me in," I mutter to myself. Instead, I see Jack's name on the caller ID.

"I was just thinking about you," I say in greeting.

"Really?" his deep voice questions. "I hope you were thinking good things."

"Actually, I was finishing up some errands and ended up outside Putnam's." Putnam's is known to have the best salads around.

"I was about to order from there. I'm stuck here for a while longer and want to make some more headway before I call it a day." He hesitates. "Why don't you tell me what you want, and I'll call in the order for us? My treat. You can bring it over and keep me company for a bit?"

"Are you sure?"

"Sunshine." His voice drops deeper, huskier. "I wouldn't have asked otherwise."

"Are you sure you're not simply curious whether my vagina will accidentally FaceTime you again?"

A loud gasp sounds from behind me, and I turn to see a nun.

"Oh holy shit!" I clap a hand over my mouth in horror. "I mean, I'm so sorry, ma'am. I mean, Sister!"

Recognition hits, and I realize this is the same nun I saw when I was with Clint. And she's overheard me mentioning something about my vag in public. Yet again.

I'm convinced God has it out for me. This *must be* a sign or something, right?

With a look of pure disgust, she stalks off quickly while Jack laughs in my ear. Staring up at the sky, I groan. "Why me?" Then to Jack, I offer, "Still want to eat dinner with a sinner?"

"Absolutely."

"Call in the goat cheese and walnut salad with raspberry vinaigrette, please."

"On it. See you in a few, Sunshine."

~

"That totally hit the spot." I've made myself comfortable in one of his cushy office chairs. "Thanks for dinner."

"My pleasure." He gathers our plastic containers and disposes of them in the trash bin beside his desk. "So are you all ready for Maggie and Ry's big day?"

"Definitely."

I rise to my feet, really taking the time to peruse his office space. It's on the smaller side but not cramped. A good-sized conference room table is off to one side with a few rolling office chairs pushed in around it. His desk sits on the opposite side of the room, closer to the set of large windows overlooking South Broadway Avenue.

"I like your office." I turn to lean back against the conference table and draw in a sharp breath when I find him in close proximity.

"Yeah?" He dips his head, dusting a soft kiss to the side of my jaw. "I like you in my office." His hands grip my hips, lifting me to sit on the table. He steps between my legs, the flowing fabric of my dress not providing any restriction. A large palm skims up my knee to my upper thigh, causing my breath to hitch.

"This isn't the type of business you normally conduct at this table, is it?" I whisper huskily.

His lips curve against mine. "Sadly, no." He playfully tugs at my bottom lip with his teeth. "But what I can tell you is the only business I'm conducting with you is pleasure."

"Are you sure about—" His hand at my thigh slides over to cup me intimately, cutting off my teasing words.

"Oh, I'm sure," he whispers before his mouth crashes down on mine. His fingers slip beneath my panties, dipping inside to find me already wet.

A groan rumbles deep within his chest as the kiss turns even hotter, our tongues sparring while two of his fingers pump in and out of me. My fingers frantically work at his belt and practically tear at the button and zipper in my desperation to get my hands on him. The moment I slip my hand inside his boxer briefs and his pulsing arousal is in my grasp, I revel in his slight moan against my mouth.

Tearing his lips from mine, he rests his forehead against my shoulder, pressing tiny kisses to my exposed collarbone. "You're so fucking wet." He thrusts his fingers deep, hooking them, and I suck in a ragged breath as my climax nears.

"I want you to come, Sunshine." His breathing is ragged and harsh like my own.

"I want you to come with me."

"I'm close," he whispers against my neck before his tongue darts out to taste me. His pumping fingers combined with the way he's thrusting into my hand pushes me closer to the edge. My inner muscles clench around his fingers, my body tensing right as my orgasm hits.

"Jack, I'm co—"

"Hey, stranger! How's—*Oh shit!*" Jack and I jerk apart just before we hear the door to his office slam closed, a trail of cuss words in its wake.

Jack's still standing between my legs, his pants around his ankles, his arousal still apparent even as he attempts to tuck it back into his underwear with extreme care, wincing slightly.

"Oh boy," I say with a sigh, gazing up at him.

He offers me a weak smile. "Sorry about that. Clients never stop by here unexpectedly, but apparently, my best friend decided to do so." He leans his forehead against mine with a low groan. "Right in the midst of one of the hottest fucking moments of my life."

I can't help but laugh. "Oh, Jack." He lifts his head slightly, and I press my lips to his. "Seems like a trend with us, doesn't it?" He only offers me a weak smile.

"Think maybe the universe is trying to tell us something?"

Before he can answer me, there's a knock on the door

before Ry's voice calls out, "Can I come in? Sorry for barging in. I've never...yeah. Um, are you two decent?"

Jack hurriedly fastens his pants, and I smooth down my dress before slipping off the table and heading over to the chair where my purse and bags sit.

"I'm going to head out. I'll catch up with you later."

Avoiding his eyes, I rush out the door, offering a rushed greeting to Ry as I practically sprint down the hall to the elevators.

CHAPTER TWENTY-EIGHT

JACK

"Well, that was certainly quite the greeting," Ry remarks. "I avoid looking your way when we change in the locker room at the gym, but I've inadvertently caught glimpses here and there. It's definitely not as jarring as catching you with your pants at your ankles while you're with Sarah."

When I don't respond, he continues with, "Which reminds me, I guess since she doesn't have an older brother or dad around that I should officially give you the 'what's what.' Should I call you over for a man-to-man chat and polish my shotgun while we talk?"

I let out a grunt in disbelief. "You don't even own a shotgun, Ry."

He crosses his arms and cocks an eyebrow at me. "Or so you *think*." Then he tips his head to the side in thought. "I could tell you I know people in Little Italy who will break your kneecaps if you hurt her—"

"You don't know anyone in Little Italy, Ry," I interject.

"Or that I know some old Italian Mafia members who will dispose of your body for the small price of a few grand?"

I expel a weary sigh. "Are you done?"

Ry holds up a finger, lips parting, but then appears to think better of it. "Actually, yeah. I think that's all I've got." His expression turns to one of disgust. "How sad is that? I need to up my game if I ever have a daughter."

Looking over at my best friend, I shake my head with a little laugh. "You'll figure it out, man." After a moment, I ask, "You ready to get hitched soon?"

"Hell yes."

His lack of hesitation makes me happy—as does the fact that Maggie's perfect for him.

"So the wedding is the perfect way to get things back on track."

My brow furrows in confusion at his words. "What do you mean?"

He gestures with a hand. "You know, with a wedding, love is in the air, the champagne is flowing, and there's something magical about it." With a wink, he adds, "If you're careful with the execution, it could be the end to the 'plague' you two have been dealing with."

"From your lips to God's ears, man," I murmur, shaking my head. "From your lips to God's ears."

∼

Two days later

I'm lounging on my couch, the TV on with the volume turned low as I channel surf. Finally, I turn it off and toss the remote aside with a groan. I shouldn't stay up late since I have a full day of conference calls tomorrow, but I'm feeling antsy as hell right now.

My cell phone is practically taunting me from where it sits on my coffee table. I want to call her or text her—whichever—but with the odd way things ended between us the other day at my office, I'm left at a loss.

Shit. Running a hand through my hair and tugging at it in frustration, I decide to man up. "Fuck it, I'm calling her."

The exact moment my fingers reach my phone, there's a knock on the door, startling me. It's nine thirty on a Thursday night, and I'm definitely not expecting anyone.

Padding over to the door, I peer through the peephole only to find no one there. Huh. Since I live a few blocks from Skidmore University, I figure it might be a drunk college kid who realized he had the wrong place. Turning to head back down the hall, I hear another knock. This time, when I peer out, I'm caught off guard at the sight of the woman standing there.

Pulling open the door, I know my surprise is apparent.

"Hey," Sarah greets me with tentative wariness in her eyes.

"Hey, Sunshine." Something about the way she shifts her weight from one foot to the other is like she's uncertain whether I'd welcome her. Just as I start to say something, I catch sight of the shadows in her eyes, the way her lips press thin.

"Jack..." She falters, her features drawn, and I catch a glimpse of pain in her eyes. "I don't know why I'm here. Somehow, this is where I ended up." Her face crumples. "I just...need you."

Without a thought, I shove the door open wider with my foot and hold out my arms. Within a split second, she's pressed her body against me with her face burrowed in my chest. I wrap one arm around her securely and close and lock the door behind us. Reaching my other arm to scoop her up and cradle her to me, I walk down the hallway. Noticing the sudden dampness of my T-shirt, I feel the shuddering of her shoulders as she weeps silently.

"Let it all out," I murmur against the top of her head into the softness of her hair. Heading to my bedroom, I go straight to my bathroom and gingerly set her on the edge of the large garden tub that I use once in a blue moon. Adjusting the water temperature, I start filling it and try to comfort her by running my hand over her back and pressing soft kisses to her hair.

Once the tub is filled, I start tugging off her shoes and socks before peeling off her shirt. "I'm going to shift you to stand so I can get your jeans off, okay?" I wait for her tiny nod before I do so.

When her red-rimmed eyes meet mine, it guts me like a swift kick to my solar plexus because my gutsy, ball-busting Sunshine is nowhere to be found right now.

Once I've stripped her of her jeans, she robotically moves to rid herself of her bra and underwear before allowing me to help her step carefully into the tub. The moment I go to release her hand, she tightens her grip, eyes darting up to mine, and there's a hint of desperation in them.

"Please." Her voice sounds delicate, thin. "Will you...get in with me?"

There isn't anything I wouldn't do for you. The thought hits me instantly with such fierce intensity that my chest suddenly has an odd sensation of pressure, tightness.

"Of course."

Quickly, I disrobe and step into the tub behind her, gathering her into my arms once again. She leans back into my chest, our legs tangled together beneath the warmth of the water, and we remain silent as I hold her.

"It never gets easier."

Her words are so faint and softly spoken I nearly miss them.

"They say it's supposed to get easier, that you'll eventually get hardened by it, but it hasn't yet for me." She shakes her head, the ends of her hair swishing in the bath water. "And I don't know that I'd want it to." Her voice cracks, and she pauses as if trying to collect herself. "I don't know that I want to be hardened to it, to not...*feel*."

After a lengthy pause, I'm certain she's finished. But then she says, "I had a nine-year-old girl come in for an appendix rupture." Sarah clears her throat before continuing. "Things were going along smoothly like they should. Until something happened." Her shoulders shake, and I tighten my embrace. "Her body just...shut down, and nothing any of us tried to save her worked."

Shifting in my arms, she repositions herself to the side, her left shoulder flush against my chest, and burrows her face into my neck. This is how we stay until the water grows tepid. As much as I love being able to comfort her, to be the person she turns to at a time like this, it's not what ends up gutting me the most.

It's her tiny, whispered words spoken against my throat.

"Thank you, Jack."

My eyes fall closed as numerous emotions wash over me. I simply relish the feel of her in my arms, of her letting me be the one to hold her, of her choosing *me* tonight.

"Anytime, Sunshine. Anytime."

CHAPTER TWENTY-NINE

SARAH

I have no idea what brought me to Jack's doorstep instead of Maggie's. It makes no sense. Except for the fact that something deep within me ached for him to hold me. A part of me yearned for his touch alone, and a tiny voice inside my head whispered that only he could comfort me and help ease the pain brought on by this night.

"Thank you, Jack."

My whispered words against his throat echo in the silence of the bathroom. I have no idea if he realizes how much his mere touch has soothed me. I'm practically burrowing into him, and he has yet to complain as he simply continues to hold me tightly nestled in his arms.

"Anytime, Sunshine. Anytime." The gentle murmur of his response, with his voice maintaining a slight huskiness, washes over me.

The water grows tepid, and chill bumps begin to spread across my skin. Instantly, Jack shifts us. "I'm going to get towels." He rises from the bathtub, and the water cascades over his muscular physique. Any other time, I'd take a moment to appreciate the sight. Right now, though, I see him as so much more than the handsome face and tight body.

I see him for the man he is on the inside. A man who didn't think twice to hold me, who didn't think twice about allowing me to disrupt his evening. A man who has more heart and compassion than I realized.

After we dry off, he tugs a soft, worn T-shirt over me, the hem falling to mid-thigh. He kneels at my feet with a pair of boxer briefs for me, and I place my hands on his shoulders and place each foot into them. Sliding them up my legs and over my hips, he rolls the waistband down a few times for a better fit.

His concerned gaze locks with mine, and his hands smooth back my hair from my face. As his thumbs dust across my cheekbones, his lips part, and his words absolutely rob me of breath.

"I'm glad you came to me tonight, Sunshine." His Adam's apple bobs as though he, too, is struggling with the cloud of emotion hanging over us tonight. He leans in, presses his lips to my forehead in a feather-soft kiss, and leaves them to linger. Speaking against my skin, he whispers, "I'll always be here for you."

My throat is tight with emotion as he backs away. "Let's get you tucked into bed." He pauses briefly. "Do you have an early shift tomorrow?"

Shaking my head to answer his question, I suddenly feel at a loss. The intimacy of the moment is at odds with my usual MO. I don't make it a habit of opening up to men. I'd learned my lesson early on from my own mother. She never was the same after my dad left, and to this day, she continues to spend her life trying to change herself to please her latest man.

Jack leads me to his bed and peels back the covers. Wordlessly, I crawl into bed only to falter. *Which side should I lie on?* He must sense my hesitation.

"Pick any side you want."

Turning my head, I question, "But you have a specific side, don't you?"

His tender smile causes an unfamiliar feeling to flood through me. "As long as you're next to me, that's all that matters."

I hold his gaze for a beat before nodding and settling on one side. He slips in beside me and pulls the covers over us. He doesn't reach for me, and we lie side by side on our backs surrounded by the silence of the night.

My entire body is on edge, and I feel the urge to fidget. I'm still emotionally raw from this night, and it's late. He's done enough for me as it is, letting me barge in on him unannounced and—

"Get over here and snuggle with me, Sunshine."

My head whips over to stare at his profile in the darkened room; the only light comes in slight shards, peeking through the venetian blinds. For a split second, my second-natured urge to give him sass comes rushing to the forefront, but he stops me before I can get the words out.

"It's okay." He sighs before turning his head on the pillow. "It's okay to be held sometimes, you know." There's a pause and then, "Come here." His voice has a light hint of his usual playfulness, so much to my own surprise, I find myself scooting over and resting my head on his chest.

His arm wraps around me, ensuring I'm wrapped snugly against his firm body, and a blanket of calmness settles over me.

"Night, Sunshine," he murmurs.

"Night, Jack," I whisper, my eyes falling closed as sleep was already pulling me under.

CHAPTER THIRTY

SARAH

One week later

Let's talk nipples, shall we? Mine are unique [weird] in that they overreact to *everything*.

A two-mile-per-hour breeze from the northeast? Nipples get hard. Air conditioning kicks on? Nipples get hard. Someone tickles me? Nipples get hard. Someone innocently massages my shoulders? Nipples get hard. The barista at the coffee shop makes my latte just right? Nipples get hard.

Okay, so I'm kidding about that last one, but you get my point. My nipples are starved for attention. They're like the Kardashians—always trying to be prominently in sight everywhere and anywhere. I have to wear a bra with some sort of padding because, otherwise, I'll be visibly saluting everyone from the mailman to the old lady walking her dog in the morning. I'm not exactly well-endowed, but because of my whorish nipples, I don't ever dare to go braless.

The one semi-plus to this "affliction" is the fact guys tend to love my nipples. My nipples getting hard are interpreted as a visual pat on the back that they're doing something right.

The truth of the matter is, a guy could simply *glance* at my nipples, and they'd get hard.

Jack is the first guy to notice my strange nipple-isms.

"Are they always so responsive?"

He peers curiously over his coffee cup at me. After separate workouts at the gym, we are now showered and sweat-free and decided to grab some coffee on this brisk Friday morning. I'm off work, and he's ensured the day and weekend are clear for Maggie and Ry's wedding festivities on Saturday.

"Pretty much." I shrug. "It's a curse. It's like if you"—I lean toward the table, lowering my voice—"got aroused at the slightest thing at random moments."

"You've just described puberty," he remarks dryly.

Rolling my eyes, I add, "You know what I mean. It continues well past puberty."

"Not that I'm complaining, but I can see how that would be a pain in the ass." He leans in closer, tipping his head to the side with a thoughtful expression. "They're responsive on their own, but I have a question." He glances around before lowering his voice. "Do you especially like extra attention toward them?"

Dark blue eyes watch me intently, waiting for my response. Feeling especially naughty, I smirk and whisper back, "Depends on what exactly the extra attention is."

Reaching into the front zippered pocket of my gym bag, I withdraw one of my chocolates. Unwrapping it carefully, I read the message on the inside, take a small nibble, and am about to place the remaining piece back in the foil when Jack's fingers snag my wrist.

"May I?" His eyes lock with mine, and when I nod, he brings my hand to his mouth; those full lips wrap around the chocolate, and the tip of his tongue barely touches my fingers. He makes it a point to place his lips on my index finger and thumb as if ensuring no remnants of chocolate are left.

Releasing my hand, he leans back to chew, watching me the entire time. Once he swallows and takes a sip of his coffee, he leans his forearms on the table, eyes flashing with heated lust.

Sweet baby Moses in the river. I'm in fear of having perpetually hard nipples and soaked panties around this man. Do they have support groups for this kind of thing? I can hear myself addressing them now. *"Hi, I'm Sarah. My bras have nipple imprints in them, and I could probably supply enough moisture from my panties for a good-sized greenhouse to thrive for a solid year."*

TMI? Yeah, the greenhouse thing totally pushed it overboard, I think. Sorry about that.

"Did that have any effect?" He has the audacity to ask me this. I mean, come on. He's walking, talking sex appeal and can practically catapult me into Orgasm-ville by simply giving me one of *those* looks.

"Oh, I think it's pretty safe to say it did." I frown in faux concern. "But I have to be honest with you. I think you might need to come back to my place and, you know"—I shrug casually—"test things out to be sure."

His eyes sparkle with mischief. "I'm always a supporter of science and research." He tips his head toward the door. "Shall we?"

～

This might be the moment when we get to follow through with everything, and Jack will be able to slide all the way to home plate. To make that winning touchdown. To sink a hole-in-one.

You know things are in dire straits when I start tossing out sports analogies. But seriously. This might finally be it! <mentally bounces up and down like a preteen who scored tickets to a Justin Bieber concert>

We're tearing off each other's clothes the second we get in

the door. We decided to head to my place since it was closer by approximately two minutes per Jack's calculations. And who am I to argue with a business consultant's math?

We stumble against my bedroom door, the cool wood pressing against my naked back while Jack's warm hands cup my breasts, lightly dragging the pads of his thumbs over my hardened nipples.

"Are they reacting to my touch or are they just..." His low, gravelly tone trails off as his lips fasten over my earlobe, sucking gently.

"It's definitely your touch." My voice is breathless and ragged.

Grasping at his broad shoulders, I feel the play of muscles as he shifts slightly, dipping his head to take one hardened peak between his lips. He toys with my nipple, darting the tip of his tongue out and flicking it before fastening his lips around it to create a light suction. Releasing it, he moves to pay homage to the other, and my hands fist in his hair as I arch into his touch.

Abruptly, he straightens and scoops me up, depositing me onto the bed. Standing at the edge of the bed between my spread legs, he proudly displays his arousal, thick and ready for me. Adjusting my legs so my feet are flat on the mattress, his lips curve up in a smirk I won't soon forget. It's mischievous, sexy, intense, and heated all at once.

Lowering to crouch beside the bed, he brings his face closer to my center without breaking eye contact. His hands slide over my legs, spreading my thighs wider, and he lowers his head only to stop once his lips are barely a centimeter away.

"I want you to play with your nipples while I have my way with your pussy." That smirk and the fact he wants me to touch myself, combined with his words, send hot arousal strumming through my body. My only option is to heed his command.

My eyes drift closed, and my head tips back against the mattress the moment his soft lips graze my opening. When the tip of his tongue darts inside to taste me, my hands and fingers move of their own accord, caressing my nipples. Jack slides two fingers inside me and hooks them, the movement causing my inner muscles to clench, anticipating his thick cock in its place.

"Jack," I breathe out, "I need you. Please." I'm unbothered by my begging. All I know is if I don't get him inside me right now, I might die.

But does he listen? *Noooo.* Instead, he chooses to make me suffer even more. Fingers slick with my arousal, he thrusts them in and out, pushing me closer to release while he fastens his lips over my clit and sucks with just enough pressure to send me tumbling over the edge.

I ride his fingers, my hips bucking, inner muscles clenching and releasing in rapid fire, and my nipples are harder than ever. Once my tremors finally subside, my eyes open to peer down at him, watching as he slips his fingers out of me and into his mouth to suck them clean.

"You'd better get up here now," I warn, my voice hoarse.

Shifting, he reaches for a condom on my bedside table and sheaths himself quickly then grips my hips to drag me closer to the edge of the mattress. Leaning over me with his hands braced on either side of my head, he presses his tip to my entrance. Inching inside me slowly, he gazes down at me with a mixture of tenderness and heated lust as one thumb drags along my cheekbone.

"You're so beautiful, Sunshine." He presses his lips tenderly to mine as his cock presses deeper, and I already feel the telltale tightening of my inner muscles. The way he feels inside me; each subsequent thrust from Jack pushes me closer to the edge. As he continues to drive deep, working his hard length in and out of me, my muscles grow taut in anticipation of my release. One more thrust is all it'll take...

"Oh, honey. You've chosen well."

Jack and I both jerk at the sound of the intruding voice, our foreheads smacking together as we attempt to grab something to cover ourselves with.

"Ouch!" I cry out, holding a hand to my forehead before yelling in the direction of the trail of muttering down the hall. "Mother! What are you doing here?!"

Jack has a large red spot on his forehead near his left eyebrow. He's using the comforter to cover himself while I quickly pull on one of the oversized T-shirts I often sleep in.

"Your mother?" he hisses in question.

"She's crazy," I whisper-yell. "She'll be planning our happily ever after." Hiding my face in my hands, I shudder. "God, she saw your freaking ass. While we were…" I drop my hands from my face to gesture with one as I try to find the words.

Jack raises an eyebrow. He's sitting back against my headboard as if he's not at all scarred or perturbed by what's just transpired

"Copulating? Fornicating?" His expression brightens, and he tosses out, "Shagging?" before imitating the Austin Powers's British accent. "But we were just shagging, baby."

"You think this is funny?" The frenzied panic in my voice is evident.

"What's your young man's name?" my mother calls from the kitchen. She's probably rummaging through my pantry and refrigerator, judging me for the takeout containers because of the plastic that hurts the environment or the GMOs that the prepared foods might contain. My mother's a bit—okay, a lot—of a hippie. She's into free-range anything.

"Or should I call him sweet cheeks?" She giggles. "You know, because his butt is so—"

"Jack!" I interject loudly. "His name is Jack!"

Of course, he's sitting here grinning away as if he doesn't

have a care in the world. As if his clothes aren't scattered throughout my apartment willy-nilly.

He shifts to get off the bed, standing and walking over to me. My eyes automatically drop to where he's still visibly hard. Like, *really* hard. Jerking my eyes back up to his, I wince.

"I'm sorry about this and"—I wave a hand toward his obvious arousal—"that. Because I know it's painful and—"

He cuts off my words with a kiss before pressing his forehead to mine. "Sunshine, you forget. We've been here before."

I blow out a heavy breath. "It's getting to be a trend, isn't it?"

His hands cradle my face, gaze searching. "I love being with you." His attention drops to where his thumb softly caresses my cheekbone. "Not only for this."

With a quick kiss on my lips, he backs away and grins. "Now, go get Mr. Sweet Cheeks his clothes so I can meet your mother."

CHAPTER THIRTY-ONE

JACK

Sarah moves at Mach speed, darting down the hallway while I sit on the bed and wait for her to return with my clothes. I hear her release a few soft grunts and picture her frazzled while she scoops up clothing as she goes.

"That key you used was for emergencies only, Mother."

Sarah's mother responds, sounding completely nonplussed at the blatant irritation in her daughter's tone. "Honey, I wanted to surprise you."

Sarah huffs loudly and stomps back down the hallway, muttering, "You certainly succeeded." Entering the bedroom, she tosses our clothing onto the mussed bed and quickly begins sorting through it. Once she's divvied up our clothing, she frantically pulls on her clothes from earlier while I tug on my underwear and pants.

She runs a hand over her hair to smooth it down. "Okay," she says suddenly, "we can say that you have to go to your office because you have some big project at work and—"

"You trying to get rid of me?" My expression is one of exaggerated hurt. "That wounds me deeply."

Her sharp glare just makes me smile. "Seriously, Westbrook?"

"Aw, but you don't scare me." I slide an arm around her waist, tugging her flush against me. "I like you best when you're feisty," I whisper against her lips, purposely dragging my own against hers but refrain from kissing her. I can practically feel the rigidness of her body ease, and it spurs me on, knowing I'm the reason for it. My lips dust across her jaw. "I also happen to really like being deep inside you, Sunshine."

"Did you just do that little naughty whisper thing?" she whispers softly, and I'm glad to hear the panic has receded slightly in her tone. "Are you *trying* to give me a lady boner while my mother is right down the hall?" she hisses.

Chuckling softly, I press a gentle kiss to her temple. "I sure did. And yes"—I run my teeth lightly over her earlobe, relishing in her sharp intake of breath—"I am."

Backing away and tugging on the last article of clothing— my shirt—I wink before exiting the bedroom, leaving Sarah standing there. Padding down the hallway, I call out to Sarah's mother, "Mr. Sweet Cheeks is fully clothed now, so we can get properly acquainted."

I enter the kitchen to see an older version of Sarah dressed in a long skirt which ends at her ankles, thin, strappy woven sandals on her feet, and a shirt made of thin, flowy material which drapes her petite form.

Her face lights up when she sees me. "You're even better from the front." A wide, exuberant grin accompanies her announcement. "I'll have to commend my daughter on her good choice." Abruptly, her face falls, expression worried. "Are you a vegan?"

"Uh, no, ma'am," I answer slowly because, hell, I'm the farthest thing from a vegan. "I enjoy a good steak as much as the next guy."

"Oh, that's a relief." She lets out a long sigh, reaching over to pat my shoulder. "Oooh!" Her expression perks up. "Nice muscles." She squeezes me and continues talking. "Men who eat red meat normally have healthier levels of testosterone and"—she steps closer to peer down at my crotch—"high libido."

Oh shit.

Thrusting out a hand in hopes to draw her attention away from my dick, I introduce myself. "Jack Westbrook. Nice to meet you, ma'am."

She bats away my outstretched hand and instead closes the distance and tugs me in for a hug with far more strength than I'd imagined a petite fiftyish woman would have. "I'm Lilly." I receive a firm pat on my back and a quick swat on my ass before she releases me to step back.

Her blue eyes sparkle with mischief as she peers up at me. "Had to see what my daughter was working with."

I'm not entirely sure how I feel about Sarah's mother feeling me up...

"Motherrrrrr." Sarah's voice carries, and she slides into view, looking more composed with her hair pulled back in a ponytail and a zip-up hoodie over her clothes. "Explain to me again what you're doing here?"

Lilly pulls her in for a hug, and I can't help but notice she doesn't get the same ass pat I did. When her mother releases Sarah and goes back to shuffling through the pantry with her back to us, I lean in to Sarah's ear to whisper a taunt.

"I got an ass pat, and you didn't."

Sarah's blue eyes narrow on me, but before she can spout off a comeback, Lilly pipes up with, "That's because his ass is nicer than yours."

Sarah merely shakes her head. "What brought you up here from Albany?"

"Oh, you know." More shuffling in the pantry. "I needed your help with something, so I thought I'd stop by and get you. But even better—" Lilly turns from the pantry, expression a mix of hopeful and excitement.

"No, Mother."

"Jack can come with us!"

My eyes dart back and forth between the two women, wondering what in the hell I'm missing. Lilly's expression is one of pure delight while Sarah's eyes are wide with alarm. "No. Say no, Jack."

Lilly waves it off. "Nonsense. He'll enjoy himself."

Sarah's only response is a strangled sound.

Curiosity gets the best of me in this case, so my only response is, "Count me in."

～

Holy. Fucking. Shit. What in the hell did I get myself into?

"I tried to tell you," Sarah hisses at me, shaking her head with a sigh.

She's completely right, too. She tried. I thought maybe her mother needed her help with paint colors or choosing a new couch. I thought her mother would take us into town to help her choose a new refrigerator or washer and dryer. I certainly never thought I'd find myself tagging along to help a woman I'd just met choose something more personal.

And by personal, I mean a *sex toy*.

"So, Jack..." Lilly links her arm through mine as we stroll the adult toy warehouse. "Tell me what you'd prefer the woman in your life to purchase for you."

My head snaps to Sarah, and I know my expression is one that screams, *Please save me!*

She merely grins, and mouths the words I uttered so carelessly early. "*Count me in.*"

"What about anal beads?" Lilly asks.

"Yeah, *Jack*," Sarah pipes up helpfully. "What about anal beads?"

Pinning Sarah with a look, I retort, "I've never used anal beads, *Sunshine*." Lowering my voice in challenge, I add, "Yet I haven't had any complaints."

"Well, then what would you recommend?" Lilly ambles

away about twenty feet to inspect a display of butt plugs beside a variety of silicone vaginas.

Sarah tugs at my wrists, softly tapping her forehead against my chest. "Why me?" she mutters softly. "Why. Me?"

My chest rumbles with a laugh before I dip my head to whisper in her ear. "We're stuck in this together. Might as well make the most of it, Sunshine." Then I raise my voice to call out to Lilly.

"I think the butt plugs might be a fun start, Lilly."

And Sarah and I can't help but dissolve into quiet laughter at our current situation.

CHAPTER THIRTY-TWO

SARAH

"Thanks for the interesting little excursion, Mom." What else can I say, really? *Thanks, Mom, for taking me and Jack along to choose a personal sex aid for you and your new man to try out?* I'd rather not take a stroll down that memory lane, thank you very much.

She enfolds me in her arms, and for a moment, I'm sent back to when I was a young girl. Back to before Dad left. Before she started to reinvent herself each time she found a new boyfriend. Before she decided the original version of herself was lacking.

Before she made me realize what I didn't want to become —what I never wanted to have happen to me.

With a little laugh, she smiles. "It was my pleasure, honey." There's a pause before she whispers in my ear, so as to not let Jack overhear her. He's already bid her goodbye and is sitting on my couch, the sound of the television playing softly in the background. "You should keep Sweet Cheeks around. He's a good one."

Backing away, I flash her a look of warning because she should know me by now. "Don't start." My tone is subdued and weary since we've been over this a million times. "Please."

She cups my cheeks in her hands. Eyes the same shade of blue as my own stare back at me as she expels, "Oh, Sarah," on a sigh.

My lips quirk. "Oh, Mom," I toss back.

Her gaze flickers, and I swear I catch sight of a slight tinge of sadness in the depths. She drops a quick kiss on my cheek and turns to open the door.

She tosses out a, "Take care of our girl, Sweet Cheeks," before stepping over the threshold and into the hallway.

"Will do, Lilly," Jack instantly responds. Neither of them thinks I noticed the whole "our girl" comment, but I did. I simply choose not to acknowledge it.

"Bye, Mom."

"Bye, sweetie." My mom takes two steps down the hallway toward the elevator and then stops, appearing to hesitate. Then she spins back around to face me. "Maybe we can get together for dinner one night soon? Just the two of us?"

It's on the tip of my tongue to ask why. To ask if she'll have the same hair color the next time I see her or if she'll pretend to be on a red meat kick. But I don't because I want our night to end on a good note.

I muster up a smile. "Sure. Sounds good to me."

She gives a little wave and blows me a kiss before making her way over to the elevator. Once the doors open and she steps inside, I close and lock the door to my apartment and lean back against the hard surface. Blowing out a long breath, I mutter to myself, "I really need a drink."

"Want me to pour you a glass of wine?"

I jerk with a start, so caught up in my own thoughts that I'd forgotten Jack was still here. Heading down the hallway to where he's lounging on my couch, I notice his one arm casually stretched across the back of it while the other rests on the arm.

He looks like he belongs here.

The thought is so foreign, so startling that I'm certain my breathing literally stopped for a split second.

"Actually," I start with a sigh, "after everything today, I'd honestly prefer to just veg out."

His eyes hold mine for a beat before his lips curve upward slightly. Reaching over for one of the soft throw pillows on my couch, he places it on his lap before patting it twice. "Then get over here and veg out with me, Sunshine."

I don't acknowledge my lack of hesitation in joining him on the couch. Nor the feeling of contentment that runs through me when he covers me with the throw blanket normally draped over the back of the couch. Nor the soothing way his fingers gently comb through my hair, lulling my eyes closed in blissful relaxation.

Much later, I'm vaguely aware of him slipping me into my bed after I've fallen asleep on his lap. He pulls the covers over me before pressing a featherlight kiss to my lips. But I don't acknowledge it.

Yet a deep, dark corner of my heart does.

CHAPTER THIRTY-THREE

SARAH

"Today is the day. My best friend's getting married to the guy of her dreams who once claimed to be gay so he could rent her available room and figure out a way to woo her."

"Wow," Maggie deadpans. "That was a charming recap."

"Hey." I shrug with a smile. "I'm trying to keep myself from getting weepy."

And it's tough, believe me. Maggie looks breathtaking in her dress. Just as I'm placing her delicate veil in place, there's a knock on the door.

"No, Ry!" I automatically holler.

Ry's made numerous attempts to see Maggie already, claiming he needed to give her a kiss and then a note. I had to put the kibosh on it all.

"It's only me, sweetie," Mrs. James, Ry's mother, calls out before the handle of the door turns, and she quickly steps into the room, closing the door behind her. She stops short at the sight of Maggie, her hand flying to cover her mouth.

"Oh my word," she breathes. "You are breathtaking."

"Isn't she?" I smile over at Maggie, noticing her eyes are glistening slightly, and I know what she's thinking. Her parents passed away a while ago, and I know she'd give anything to have them here today.

Sliding my hand in hers, I give it a squeeze. "You know they'll be watching with the best seats in the house."

Nodding, she presses her lips together firmly before suddenly reaching out to me, and I embrace her as carefully as I can without disturbing her dress and veil. "Love you," she mumbles softly.

"Love you back," I manage to say over the lump in my throat, widening my eyes to keep the tears from spilling over. Finally, Maggie and I part, and I concentrate on righting her veil, smoothing it.

"Ry wanted me to give you this, sweetie." Mrs. James holds out a small square napkin that's folded in half. That's Maggie and Ry's thing; sweet little notes they write when they're out somewhere.

Maggie accepts the napkin, and when she reads it, the smile that spreads across her face is one that affirms everything. Because the smile derived from this small note from her husband-to-be immediately eradicates all traces of sadness, leaving in its place happiness. Knowing Maggie has found a love like this with Ry is everything to me, especially since she didn't always have an easy go of things.

Maggie's eyes flicker up to me and over to Ry's mother before returning to the napkin and reading the message aloud.

I'll be the guy who has the goofiest and happiest smile on his face waiting as his bride walks down the aisle toward him.
I'm ready to marry the love of my life.
I'm ready for Maggie James.

Mrs. James dabs the corner of her eye with a tissue while I

continue to fiddle with Maggie's veil, doing my best to ensure it is perfect. Then I meet my best friend's eyes.

"I believe it's time to go see your groom."

~

There's just something about weddings. It's like you're suddenly encapsulated within some sort of spell or mood which makes you swoony and sappy. Even me, a person who's normally not the least bit swoony.

But, man, this wedding was beautiful, and I guess it was inevitable that the air would be filled to the brim with love and sentiment when it comes to Maggie and Ry.

I watch the couple as they linger at the bar. Ry plucks a small bar napkin from the stack nearby and pulls a pen from the inside pocket of his tux. Maggie smiles up at him as he writes something on the square of paper before sliding it over to her. And, like earlier, the moment she reads whatever it says, the look in her eyes, her entire expression is one of absolute—

"Love."

I jerk in surprise at the sound of Jack's voice in my ear, yet maintain my gaze on my best friend and her new husband.

"Any second now, those two lovebirds will have cartoon hearts shooting out of their eyes at one another."

I'm unable to resist a snicker at Jack's remark because that's exactly what I was thinking.

"Any chance you'll save a dance for me?" he whispers huskily.

Spinning around to face him, I decide to mess with him. Planting a hand on one hip, I gesture flippantly with the other. "Look, just because you're far too handsome for your own good in that tux and have a disarming grin doesn't mean that—"

Oh shit! Abort! Abort! This is how my attempt at harassing him goes? Really, Sarah? By spewing compliments?

"You think I look handsome?" His eyebrows rise in exaggerated surprise. "And what's this about a disarming grin?" Turning his head slightly, he flashes me a wide smile. "Is this the disarming grin?" This smile is more of a smolder—not that I'm going to admit that to him—and he reaches a hand back behind his head to pose dramatically. "Or this? Is this the one? This is the one, isn't it?" He has the audacity to wink at me.

Rolling my eyes at his antics, I redirect my attention to the crowded dance floor without responding.

"Come on, now. Admit it. You thought that was funny." What is the deal with his husky voice? I swear it's giving off subliminal messages. And those messages are something like *Get up on that bar and spread your legs for me.*

Damn vagina. She's such a traitor when it comes to Jack.

He steps closer, his chest against my back, and I swear, I can feel the heat radiating from him. Suddenly, his arm shoots around me, and his fingers hold something small in front of my face.

A foil-wrapped chocolate; the kind I always carry with me. Except today, since amidst the wedding festivities and being Maggie's maid of honor, I had no way of stashing any.

Well, not without putting them somewhere they'd end up melting, that is.

Fighting a smile, I grab it, but he hangs on. I give it a tug, and he leans in to whisper, "Promise me a dance, and you can have it."

"Fine." Another tug but still no dice.

"*Promise,* Sunshine," he says, amusement coloring his tone.

"I promise," I grit out, giving another tug on the chocolate and internally rejoicing when he lets go. Unwrapping it, I read the message inside before popping the small chocolate into my mouth in its entirety.

Something decadent is going to happen.

With a smirk, I fold the wrapper just as Jack's voice rumbles in my ear. "I'd say that's true since you and I"—he startles me by grasping my wrist, spinning me around, and walks backward as he leads me onto the dance floor—"are about to show these people how slow dancing is really done."

My eyebrows rise with skepticism. "To Dave Matthews?"

"Satellite" is playing, and while I love this song, I'm not entirely certain how swaying back and forth will show anyone "how slow dancing is really done."

He picks up on my disbelief and eyes me with a smirk. "Just close your eyes and go on a journey with me."

"Jack." I can't help but roll my eyes.

With a pseudo attempt at a stern expression, he tosses back, "Sunshine," before pulling me closer. In these heels, the top of my head is eye level with him. My eyes fall closed at the feel of his jaw against my cheek, and I find myself concentrating on the masculine, woodsy scent that's one hundred percent Jack—and unbelievably potent.

"Are you concentrating on the song? On his voice?"

My eyes remain closed as I murmur, "Yes."

"Okay." There's a brief pause. "Now tell me you don't think there's a chance that Dave Matthews and Shakira could be the same person."

Wait, *what?*

My head rears back to stare at him incredulously. "Are you kidding me right now?"

"Humor me, Sunshine." I honestly can't tell if he's serious or not. "Listen to his voice and then think of every Shakira song you've ever heard—"

"Which would be a total of two."

"And note the similarities." He raises an eyebrow as if he's made his point. "This song isn't as good of an example as some of his others. Like 'Ants Marching,' for one. That song"—he nods in affirmation—"would totally convince you."

Laughter bubbles up, and I can't help but shake my head. "You're crazy; you know that?"

He makes a noncommittal sound before abruptly swinging me out, then spinning me back into his arms, and dipping me dramatically. Straightening us and continuing to sway to the song, he reaches out one of his hands to brush a few stray strands of hair back from my face. Dipping his head, he presses a kiss to my hairline before resting his lips against my forehead.

"As far as something decadent happening, Sunshine," he murmurs in a low, silky tone, "I'd have to say that having you in my arms like this is it for me."

CHAPTER THIRTY-FOUR

JACK

I'm pretty sure I just grew a fucking ovary.

That's the only reason I can come up with for me getting emotional at Maggie and Ry's wedding—or, more importantly, when I give the toast.

"Ry and I have been through a lot together. We met in college and basically never looked back." With a smirk, I press my hand to my heart and add whimsically, "It was us against the world. Jack and Ry."

There are some snickers and chuckles, but I press on, turning serious as I look over at my best friend and his new wife. "He saved me in a lot of ways, took me under his wing, and became the kind of friend I'd never known I'd been missing. The kind of friend I never knew I'd needed.

"He helped me get through a rough time when my father passed away unexpectedly. I realized then that it didn't have to be Jack Westbrook against the world, trying to pave the way all by himself." I shake my head with a small smile. "I had someone else by my side, a best friend who 'got' me; a best friend who didn't judge too much"—I break off in a laugh—"when he broke the news to me that a pocket protector would, in fact, *not* get us any hot sorority girls."

More people laugh at this, and my expression sobers as I avert my gaze to the linen covered table to maintain my composure. Finally, I allow my eyes to scan the room before coming to rest briefly on the newlyweds and then continue.

"When Ry and Maggie first became friends, it was like it had been meant to be. One minute, they were strangers and the next, best friends. And I had the pleasure of watching that friendship grow into something more. Into a love that's so imperfect to those looking in from the outside, yet such utter perfection for the two of them. I couldn't be happier that my friend has found his other half, and that they both have found their forever love."

My throat grows thick with emotion, and I fiddle with the microphone before turning my attention to Ry whose eyes appear to have a slight sheen to them. "I'm thrilled that you found one another and am incredibly honored to gain a sister in this deal."

Swallowing hard, I force a brave smile, trying to keep my tone light as I address the guests. "I once heard a quote that said, 'You know you're in love when you don't want to fall asleep because reality is better than your dreams.'" Raising my champagne flute, I smile down at Maggie and Ry. "Here's to Maggie and Ry. May your reality always surpass your dreams."

As soon as I'm finished with the toast and the DJ has restarted the music to draw people out onto the dance floor, Ry stands. Making his way over to me, he embraces me in a tight hug, muttering in my ear, "Thanks, man. Love you."

Leaning away, I give him a light pat on the cheek. "Love you, too, cupcake."

He rolls his eyes at the old nickname. Before he can respond further, two additional arms slide around us.

"I want to be a part of this hug." Maggie smiles up at me. "Thank you, Jack. For everything."

Sliding my arm around her, I give her a quick peck on the

cheek before turning my expression quizzical. "This means I get to be a godparent, though, right?"

The couple groans simultaneously. Before I can say more, I catch sight of Ry's father leading Sarah to the dance floor.

"Is your dad about to dance with Sarah?" I pose the question to Ry, knowing his father is usually straight-laced and serious. Not one for doing anything even remotely fun like dancing with the maid of honor or even cracking jokes.

"Uh," Ry falters, appearing at a loss. "Yep. That's him."

Leaning in, my shoulder to his, I hiss playfully, "Is your dad making a play for my—" I freeze, stopping abruptly.

"Go on." Humor fills Ry's voice. "Your…?" he prompts.

Shit. I'd been about to say "my woman." Except she's not. Hell, I don't even know what we are, if anything.

I feel a little nudge at my side. Looking down, I see Maggie peering up at me. "You should go rescue your woman after this song's over."

As I make my way toward the dance floor to Sarah, it doesn't escape me that Maggie referred to her as my woman. I choose to ignore it for now because I know it'll take a whole hell of a lot of work to convince Sarah to be mine.

Note to self: *Start buying those little chocolates she likes.*
In bulk.

CHAPTER THIRTY-FIVE

SARAH

I t's been a few days since Maggie and Ry's wedding, and I've been working like crazy. Am I jealous of my two friends who are lounging in the tropics right now, sipping a fruity drink between their bouts of crazy newlywed sex?

Pffft. Does a square have four ninety-degree angles?

Wow. I really do need sleep if I'm spouting off math facts. That made me throw up a little in my mouth.

I'm also pretty disappointed that I didn't get my hands on Jack after the wedding, but honestly, after a day chock-full of maid of honor duties, I was suffering from bone-deep exhaustion. By the end of the night, the only thing I was fantasizing about was *sleep*.

Today, Clint and I wanted to take advantage of the nice weather and being off work at the same time, so we decided to grab lunch.

After we finish, we stroll along the sidewalk in downtown Saratoga, and Clint spots something in the window of a nearby boutique. "This practically screams my name." He points at a studded belt which has gold and silver designs.

"It will certainly draw some attention to your waist area," I remark dryly.

Clint makes a pistol with his fingers and aims it at me. "Exactly. And there's no such thing as bad attention in that area, honey." Studying the belt on the other side of the window, he lets out a long sigh. "But I promised myself I wouldn't spend frivolously." Tapping his fingers on the window, he mourns, "Bye, little belt. Maybe one day we'll meet again."

I shake my head and laugh. "You're a weirdo." Slipping his arm through mine, he continues leading me down the busy sidewalk. "You planning to head home now?"

He barely stifles a yawn. "Yep. I hear a nap calling my name." Suddenly, he perks up, his face a mask of innocence. "Wait a minute. Isn't Jack's place only two blocks away?"

I'd wondered why we'd continued down to the far end of South Broadway, away from the shops Clint normally prefers. I toss him a look, my face a mask of cynicism. "That was the furthest thing from nonchalant."

He grins happily and shrugs. "It's all good." Stopping at the crosswalk, we wait for the signal and then walk across the street. "I'm going to deposit you on his front step, stork-style, and then he'll—" He stops abruptly, eyes widening on me.

"He'll what?" I ask cautiously, eyeing him.

"Maybe he'll decide he's been lusting over me instead!" he announces gleefully. Untangling his arm from mine, he bounces happily like a Chihuahua before darting down the street to Jack's place.

Tipping my head up, eyes to the blue sky, I groan, "Why me?" before jogging to catch up with him.

Except I'm not quick enough to intercept him before he rings the bell for Jack's apartment.

"Hello?"

Clint leans against the building and smiles coyly into the speaker as if Jack can actually see him. "Jacky, it's me, Clint. I happen to be standing here with a gorgeous blonde who happens to be a complete horndog and secretly writes poems about her love for you. Oh! And sculpting. Can't forget about those clay replicas she makes of your massive pe—"

I lunge in a move that would make Neo of *The Matrix* movies envious, my palm covering Clint's mouth to muffle the rest of his words.

Except it's far too late.

"I'll be right down. Can't wait to hear all about these poems and sculptures."

At the sound of the intercom disconnecting, Clint reaches to open the door and tugs my arm, shoving me inside the lobby. "Go get 'em, tiger."

"But—"

Then he shoves the door closed and runs off. Leaving me standing here dumbfounded in the lobby of Jack's apartment building.

Jack, who'll be down here any minute now.

Shit, shit, shit. What is it about this guy that throws me so off kilter?

Taking a few deep, calming breaths, I spin around toward the elevator. And stop short.

"Hey, Sunshine." Jack stands before me, looking far too delicious in low-slung shorts and a plain white T-shirt.

"Oh hell." Can I, please, get a free pass for once and hurl myself at him? The way they always do in the movies before they kiss each other's faces off passionately?

One eyebrow rises. "That's not quite the reaction I was expecting." He glances past me. "I thought Clint was here?"

"He *was*." I wave a hand toward the outside. "He did a weird, alternative version of ding dong ditch, I guess."

We stand here, a few feet separating us, and I feel awkward as hell. Shuffling my feet, I slide my hands into the pocket of my lightweight hoodie. "Well, um, I should—"

"Come up." He gives a little tip of his head toward the

elevators. "Hang out for a bit."

It's at this moment I realize I've never come over to Jack's place with the intent of just…casually hanging out.

It feels weird.

Okay, so I realize how bad that sounds, but it honestly feels odd. In my defense, the whole "curse" did begin here.

"Try to contain your excitement," he responds dryly when I don't immediately answer. I realize I've been biting the edge of my bottom lip, and my face is probably scrunched up from my contemplation.

"Sure," I offer far too brightly. "I'd love to hang out."

"Stairs or elevator?"

"Stairs," I say quickly. "I had a big lunch."

Finally, I get a tiny smile from him. "Stairs it is." He walks over to the door leading to the stairwell and pulls it open. "After you."

We climb the stairs in silence, arriving at the fourth—and top—floor of the building, and he leads me down the hall to his door. Stepping inside his place, I attempt to shake off the feeling of déjà vu.

"Can I get you anything to drink?" he offers, reaching into his refrigerator and grabbing a bottle of water. "I was about to relax and watch a movie. This week's been hell."

"No, thanks." With a weary sigh, I lean against the kitchen counter and add, "I second that on the week from hell."

Turning, he leans against the closed refrigerator and uncaps his water. My eyes are transfixed on the sight of his forearms, of the play of muscles and veins as he twists off that cap. "Rough time of it, too?" He raises the bottle to his lips, and those biceps stretch the sleeves of his white undershirt.

Oh, sweet Mary Magdalene and Jesus.

Confession time: I have a thing for forearms and biceps, with more emphasis on the forearms. Give this man a fork, a knife, and some food to cut, and I could sit all day long, watching his forearms hard at work. All those flickers of muscle movements and veins on display for my viewing pleasure. Yummmmmm.

And in case you're wondering (let's be honest—you are), yes, I've always been this weird.

"Can I just say that I'm officially in lust with your forearms?" I blurt out.

Jack chokes in surprise while he's drinking and attempts to cover his mouth but not in time to catch some of the water that drips down on his shirt. And I'm not sure what I did this week to deserve this, but it must have been *really* good because Jack's white shirt gets a big wet spot down the front. The cold water instantly makes his nipples hard, and I'm. In. *Heaven*.

Clearing his throat, he sets his bottle of water on the counter. "Jesus, Sunshine." He laughs, and it's almost like he's embarrassed. But it gets worse. Or better. Because in the next moment, he does something divine.

He removes his now wet shirt.

That's right. His fingers grasp the back of the shirt's neck, and he tugs it over his head. In reality, this moment lasts maybe five seconds at most. For *me*, though, it lasts for a half a minute because my mind slows it down.

You know those movies where the sexy, curvy woman is jogging down a beach wearing a skimpy swimsuit, boobs bouncing like crazy, and it's in slow motion? Well, that's what's happening right here, right now. My mind is planning to savor this moment at a later date and is slowing things down as he raises that shirt over his firm abs and pecs. It's like my very own little striptease.

I snap out of it once I realize I'm left standing alone in his kitchen while he heads to get a replacement shirt.

"Don't put on a new shirt on my account," I mumble more to myself than anything.

"What's that?" he calls from his bedroom.

"I asked what movie you planned to watch," I lie.

"I was thinking of *17 Again*."

Walking over to the living room, I peer out the large windows overlooking the busy street and nearby shops.

"Sound good to you?" he asks. I hear his footsteps approach and catch the sound of him inserting the movie into the Blu-ray player.

When I turn around, however, I feel like Jack's trying to pull out all the stops with me today.

"Whoa, whoa, whoa, now. Hold on a second." I toss my hands up. "You never once told me about these"—I circle an index finger in the direction of his face where he's now wearing black framed glasses—"delightfully sexy spectacles of yours."

He runs a hand over his jaw, the sound of his scruff rasping softly against his palm. With a small laugh, as if slightly embarrassed, he shrugs. "I only use them to give my eyes a rest from my contacts."

"Also"—I step closer to him, waving toward his now-covered abs—"I have to tell you, I'm pretty sure you're single-handedly responsible for causing global warming with those abs."

Jack makes a dismissive sound, and I realize that, deep down, he must still see himself as the nerd he was back in the day. I know Maggie has mentioned something about Ry's stories of first meeting Jack during his freshman year in college and how clueless he was. Not to mention, Jack also mentioned something in his toast at their wedding.

For whatever reason, I feel a fierce need to try to get him to realize—to understand—that he's not the geeky, easily overlooked guy anymore.

Placing a palm against the firm wall of his chest, I tip my head to the side contemplatively. "I must say, I really like this more relaxed version of Jack Westbrook." I wiggle my eyebrows. "A lot." Tapping a finger to my lips, I exaggerate a thoughtful expression. "Maybe we could play incredibly sexy nerd entrepreneur who catches his secretary late at night while she's bent over the filing cabinet."

Something flickers across his face, and he looks at me oddly. "You like the whole nerdy thing?"

It's not so much his words as it is the *way* he asks that gives me pause. It's clear there's something more—there's weight behind the question itself.

"I might," I answer slowly. Trailing my index finger down the center of his shirt, I peer up at him. "So, you were a hot nerd back in the day, huh?"

Something sounds off with his laugh, and he avoids my gaze. "I don't know about the hot part of it, but I was definitely a nerd."

"Well, maybe you just hadn't hit your prime." One of my palms slides over his firm pectorals before smoothing down over his abs, the muscles contracting beneath my touch. "I'm sure I still would've been all over you back then."

His eyes crinkle slightly at the corners. "Think so?"

I nod, my voice soft. "Definitely."

"Well, it just so happens I received an invitation to revisit my days of full-on nerdiness." There's a hint of derisiveness in his voice.

Peering up at him curiously, I draw my words out. "An invitation?"

His lips twist. "My ten-year class reunion."

"Ah." I wrinkle my nose. "I don't envy you. High school was painful enough the first time."

"Exactly. But," he hesitates, averting his gaze, "a small part of me wants to go and show all those snotty, rich kids I'm not the same scrawny, nerd who had no sense of style."

The way his blue eyes cloud with what appears to be unhappy memories makes my heart ache. "When is it?"

He snaps his eyes to me. "Two weeks from today."

Mentally running through my work schedule, I pat his chest. "You'd better R.S.V.P. right now."

A crease pops up between his eyebrows. "What are you talking about?"

"We're going to that reunion, Jack. And we're going to rock their worlds." I nod as if to punctuate the sentiment.

He lets out a long, resigned sigh. "Sarah. You don't have to go with me. I didn't bring it up to con you into going."

I don't know what it is, but I find myself disliking any time he uses my name instead of the usual "Sunshine."

Rising on my tiptoes, I press my lips to his in a gentle kiss before moving to settle on the couch. "It's a done deal. Do it now and then put on the movie."

Shaking his head with a chuckle, he heads over to where his laptop is sitting on the dining room table, likely pulling up his email and sending off his quick R.S.V.P. Turning and walking over to me, he centers his warm gaze on me, and I'm relieved to see the shadows are gone.

"All set, Sunshine. Now"—he settles onto the couch, slinging an arm around me—"it's movie time." He picks up the remote, and I snuggle into his embrace as he starts the movie.

And I'm not sure I've ever had a better time simply spending time with a guy.

CHAPTER THIRTY-SIX

JACK

This reunion is a train wreck. A colossal train wreck of epic proportions. I knew it would be, but I think even I underestimated how narrow-minded and caught up in the past people can actually be.

The one major plus is that I have Sarah by my side. She looks so fucking gorgeous that when she opened her apartment door, I nearly swallowed my tongue. Sure, she'd told me earlier that she was pulling out all the stops, but *hell*. She's wearing this long-sleeve burgundy dress with a hem that ends just above her knee. The top part is nude, and consists of a deep V-neckline which has a lace overlay.

"You're the most beautiful woman here, Sunshine," I murmur against her temple before pressing a soft kiss to it.

Her lips twitch with a sexy smirk. "It can't be because I'm the only one without oversized breasts," she whispers back.

Tipping my head back, I can't hold in my laugh at the truth in her observation. It's as though the bulk of my female classmates had taken advantage of a two-for-one breast implant offer and had gone the "make them as large as possible" route. Many of the women appeared far too top-heavy and unnatural.

Sarah's lips part in response, but she's interrupted by a blonde I still recognize even after ten years have passed; Naomi, who pronounces her name "Nay-oh-mee," Salinas.

Naomi and her high school boyfriend, Timmy Collier, enjoyed making fun of me and the fact that my father—a single dad, struggling to make ends meet—drove a beat-up Honda Civic and normally chauffeured me to and from school each day.

In Saratoga Springs, where it seems everyone has money coming out their ears, my accountant father tried his best to give me what I needed. However, he could never afford the latest fashions, let alone afford to buy me my own car.

I was the stereotypical nerd who had big, thick glasses, wore pants that were always a little too short, and was never great at socializing. I had a paper route for extra money to help at home and often watched our high school's football games on the local TV station at home on Friday nights. Make no mistake; I was an outcast to the nth degree. The guy who didn't come from a wealthy family, the guy whose family didn't own a large business or profitable restaurant in the area. The guy who couldn't get a girl to look twice at him.

Luckily, that all changed when Ry took me under his wing in college.

Naomi, in a black miniskirt paired with a ridiculously low-cut pink shirt, swoops in and snags me and Sarah approximately thirty seconds after we enter the banquet room where the reunion is being held. This time, however, instead of staring at me with utter disdain, Naomi's eyeing me like a starving dog eyes a thick, juicy steak.

The moment she catches sight of my name tag is the best, though.

"Hello there, you two. Be sure to sign the—" She abruptly stops once my name registers. Her eyes flicker from the tag to my face, back to the tag, then up to my face as if trying to determine whether it's a joke.

"Jack Westbrook? Is that really you?"

I muster up a polite smile. "The one and only."

"Wow," Naomi remarks slowly. Then she turns to call out to a balding man standing a few feet away. "Honey, get over here and say hi to Jack!" There's no mistaking the false cheerfulness in her tone.

The guy strolls over with one hand in the pocket of his ill-fitting pants, name tag declaring him "Timmy." Huh. Why am I not entirely surprised?

His eyes pass over me, landing on Sarah, and I watch with growing irritation as his gaze travels to her chest, pausing for far longer than acceptable before dropping down the rest of her body. When his eyes drift back up her legs, eyes widening in obvious appreciation, and he licks his lips and grins lasciviously, I feel my entire body grow taut. The fierce possessiveness that washes over me is potent.

The fingers of the hand I have at Sarah's waist flex, and she puts her hand over the top of mine immediately in response.

I reach out my other hand to Timmy, fake smile in place. "Hey, man. Good to see you."

The man shakes my hand, and I catch sight of the wince, barely able to hide my satisfied smile at the result of my punishing handshake.

"Wait a minute." It seems Timmy has finally made the connection. Good to see he's still as sharp as he was in high school. "You're Jack Westbrook? The one we—"

"Made fun of every chance you got back in high school? Yep." I release Timmy's hand.

"Wow." The other man gapes. "You look different."

"Doesn't he, though?" Naomi chimes in. "Who knew you were hiding this handsome guy beneath that horribly dressed nerd?"

I feel Sarah stiffen beside me as I answer in monotone. "Yeah, it's crazy."

"Hey, remember that time I stuffed you into a locker freshman year?" Timmy laughs boisterously. "God, that was hilarious."

Great. Exactly what I wanted to do; take a stroll down memory lane with this asshole.

My voice is flat. "Hilarious." Shifting my attention—and hopefully the conversation, as well—to Sarah, I introduce her. "This is Sarah Matthews."

If I'm not mistaken, there's a glint in her eyes, which means I'm almost certain she's out for blood.

Time to sit back and watch my woman do her thing.

CHAPTER THIRTY-SEVEN

SARAH

I threw up in my mouth. And not a little, but *a lot*.

These two are one episode away from a *Jerry Springer* special. Luckily, I'm trained to deal with people who are hot messes in general, who are a few sandwiches short of a picnic, or those of the mean variety. Working with the public and in a hospital setting has helped me perfect those skills.

There's a small difference here, though, because once they started in on Jack, they changed the tide. My claws have officially come out. No one messes with my Jack.

Wait, what? I mean, *er*…no one messes with Jack. I don't know where that whole possessiveness thing came from.

"So great to meet you both." With an overly bright smile, I reach out a hand to shake Naomi's. "Naomi." I purposely mispronounce the other woman's name as "Ny-oh-mee," re-enacting my own version of the scene from the movie, *17 Again*.

Her expression turns steely. "It's Nay-oh-mee," she corrects.

Never allowing my saccharine sweet smile to slip, I mutter beneath my breath, "Don't care."

"Timmy." I reach out my hand to her husband.

He tugs my hand, causing me to stumble toward him. "I prefer hugs," he says as he pulls me closer. This is when I "accidentally" drive the sharp, pointed heel of my shoe into his foot.

"Ouch!" He instantly releases me, stepping away with an accusing look. Like he wasn't the person attempting to be inappropriate, and like I hadn't caught his eyes lingering on my chest. Gross doesn't begin to cover that. It's even worse since homeboy, here, is married to Naomi, and he's clearly a dirtbag.

"So, Jack..." Naomi practically purrs, eyeing Jack. "When did this transformation happen?"

Can I punch her in the throat? Pretty please?

I fix my attention on Naomi before directing an adoring look at Jack. "You dying to take a bite out of him and these amazing pecs, right?" I run a hand over his chest.

Covering one side of my mouth as though I'm telling her a secret, I lean in and add, "And let me tell you how grateful I am you didn't discover back in the day what he's packing below the belt. Know what I'm sayin'?" I flash her a dramatic wink.

Then I let out a whimsical sigh. "It's like, sometimes, he's just too big, you know? Like he hits all the right places and makes me orgasm"—I pause to add further emphasis to my next words—"*over* and *over* again." Another long, dramatic sigh. "It's *so* exhausting."

Naomi sputters, and Jack interrupts me before I can elaborate. "I think I see someone we should say hello to, Sunshine."

I pout at Naomi. "Awwww, sad!" Jack snags my wrist and begins to pull me away. "Come find me later," I call out to her as I'm being led away. "We can talk more then, Ny-oh-mee."

As soon as I turn my head in the direction Jack's leading me in, I hear the woman call out, "It's Nay-oh-mee."

And in perfect unison, Jack and I both mutter, "Don't care."

~

"Where are you leading me?" I ask as Jack guides us out of the banquet room and down the large hallway of the resort.

"Away from this place."

I stop in my tracks, tugging on our joined hands. "Hold up."

Spinning to face me, Jack's expression is somber. "Sunshine, I'm sorry, but I really don't want to spend the night with those assholes."

Stepping up to him, I slide my hand up to the side of his face and gaze into the depths of his dark blue eyes. "I know that, but," I say softly, "you're forgetting where we are." Confusion etches his features, so I elaborate. "We're at the resort." When it appears that my words are still not getting through, I add, "There are multiple banquet rooms for events like reunions." I pause to flash him a meaningful look. "And weddings."

Dawning interest lights his eyes. "What are you suggesting?"

"I saw that table back there." I wave in the direction near one particular banquet room entrance we just passed. "There are quite a few name tags laying out."

He leans in, and his eyes sparkle with mischief. "Are you suggesting we impersonate guests and crash a wedding?"

"I am." I grin up at him, challengingly. "Are you in?"

"Maybe."

Stepping back over to the table where I spied the adhesive name tags with a silver embossed outer edge and the table number designation listed in small print at the very bottom. I scan the names before plucking two and hold one up for Jack.

"How about it, Michael Wilis?" I raise my eyebrows in question.

Crossing over to me, his eyes flicker to the name tags. "Let's do it."

Peeling the backing from Jack's new name tag, I affix it to the top right area of his button-down shirt. Smoothing it firmly, I recall what I have in my purse. "Ooh! Wait a minute."

Digging into my rectangular clutch, I tug out what I keep handy.

"You keep monogrammed cards in your purse?" Jack asks slowly.

I quickly write a congratulatory message to "Jen and Donny" before withdrawing my checkbook.

"Sunshine." My eyes dart up to find Jack watching me with amusement. "Why do I get the feeling you've done this before?" I finish writing the check out for enough to cover our catered meals and open bar before slipping it inside the card, placing it in the envelope, and sealing it.

Closing my purse, I peer up at him with a smug smile and tap the envelope against his chest. "Ready to make our way to table forty-seven, Mr. Wilis?"

～

"I think it's safe to say that we chose wisely with this wedding," Jack murmurs to me before taking another bite of his seared sea scallops.

"Dang straight." I cut into my stuffed chicken breast. "But," I lean in to whisper discreetly, "I'm not sure which wins out, the company or the food."

As he chews, the edges of his lips tip up at my remark. Before I can elaborate, it's as though the universe wants to reinforce my observation because the best man gets up to make what appears to be an impromptu toast, judging by the surprised expressions of the rest of the wedding party.

The best man is tall and gangly looking, his hair slightly mussed. "For those of you who may not know me"—he gestures with his champagne glass—"I'm Ron, best man, and I've known Donny since we were seven years old." He stares down into his glass before returning his attention to the rest of the guests. "To be honest, I wasn't even sure if I'd be able to make it here because I was in my tenth stint in rehab for my Manga porn addiction."

"Manga porn addiction? Comic book porn?" Jack hisses in my ear, but I wave him off.

No chance in *hell* I'm going to miss this speech.

Ron goes on. "He helped me pack each time I went to rehab." The man appears to get choked up on the memories. "He even got tough with me when he caught me trying to smuggle some Manga in my suitcase." He swipes at a tear before continuing. "I'm so grateful for him, though. Because he got me through, and I feel better." Ron affirms this with a nod before turning to address the groom. "I know that you and Jen will have a happy life together, man." Then he leans toward the groom, obviously forgetting he still has a microphone in his other hand. "That Asian you banged last night has nothing on Jen. She's way hotter."

Ron turns to the front again, raising his unsteady glass to toast. "To Jen and Donny!"

"Ho-ly shit," I breathe, watching as the bride loses it. She flies out of her chair and begins to interrogate Donny while the majority of us sit, stunned.

"This is why I flew in from Florida. Knew it would be worth witnessing in some way." This comes from the woman seated to my right who goes by the name of Randi.

I should also mention that Randi is the self-proclaimed outcast of the family who, at one time, used to be Randall. She grew up outside Saratoga Springs, but after finally declaring to her family that she felt more comfortable as a woman than a man, she relocated to Panama City Beach, Florida, where she currently lives.

Also, I'm certain we're officially BFFs now. She's got a keen eye for fashion, not to mention she clinked her glass against mine after whispering a "Way to go on snagging Hottie McHottieson."

"Oh, and the bride and her crew up there," Randi leans in, lowering her voice as she fills us in on more family gossip, "used to get off on making fun of me when I first started painting my nails and experimented with makeup." She takes a sip of water before continuing. "They were a whole different brand of cruelty."

I lay a hand on her arm. "I'm sorry, Randi."

She shrugs. "It's in the past now. But this"—she waves with her fork toward the scene at the front of the banquet room—"this makes it worth the three hundred bucks I spent for a flight up here." Another shrug. "Those two are meant to be together, though. I have no doubt they'll be fine. But make no mistake"—Randi levels a look on Jack and me—"that was only the tip of the drama iceberg tonight. There's more to come for these families."

And hell if she wasn't completely right.

CHAPTER THIRTY-EIGHT

SARAH

"Well, that was certainly an interesting evening," Jack says with a sigh as we sit in the back of the Uber car on our way back from the wedding reception.

Snickering at the memory, I shake my head. "I'm not sure what the craziest part was."

"The Manga rehab? Or maybe the 'banging of the Asian' the night before?" he suggests helpfully.

"Or"—I draw out the word—"it could be when the groom's father stood to say that it hadn't been Donny, but *him* with the Asian woman."

"Ah, that's right." The corners of his eyes crinkle. "Don't know how I could forget that confession."

"That back there"—I toss a thumb in the general direction of where the reception took place—"was better than binge watching all the housewives of whichever city on Bravo any day of the week. Phew."

Leaning my head back, I let my eyes fall closed. I still feel exhaustion lingering from my shifts at work, and my tone is weary. "Even though Jen and Donny seemed to mend their differences quickly, moments like that reaffirm why I'm opposed to marriage."

There's silence throughout the vehicle, aside from the faint sound of the music playing in the front nearby the driver. Jack's quiet for so long I'm startled when he finally speaks.

"You don't want to ever get married?"

It's not so much his question as it is the way he asks it that makes me open my eyes, fixing my gaze on him. His tone is gentle yet inquisitive with a touch of something else I can't decipher.

With a humorless smile, I blow out a short breath. "My father left long ago. He and my mom would have arguments, and then, one day, he just disappeared. He didn't even stick around to try to fight for her—for their marriage. And well"—I lift a shoulder in a half shrug—"you've met my mother." Turning my eyes down to where my fingers fiddle with the clasp on my purse, I add, "It's as if she's continuously trying to find herself and turn into someone else to please each guy she's with."

"But Maggie and Ry…"

"Maggie and Ry are clearly an exception." My tone comes out sharper than I intend. Attempting to soften it, I offer a tight smile. "They're obviously perfect for one another; like two peas in a pod."

Jack's eyes study me in the darkened interior of the vehicle. "Maybe you just haven't met your other half yet."

Before I can respond, the driver pulls up to the curb in front of my apartment. Jack gets out, coming around to open my door, and helps me out. Sticking his head back inside to murmur something to the driver, he turns and walks me up to the entrance of my building.

Stepping closer, he brings his hands up to gently cradle my face. The look in his blue eyes mesmerizes me as his head descends, kissing me with such a sweet reverence it makes my chest tighten. Once his lips part from mine, his thumbs dust softly along my cheekbones.

"Good night, Sunshine." He releases me and walks back over to the vehicle.

"But wait," I sputter, watching him in confusion. He turns with one hand braced on top of the open door. "You're not… coming inside?"

The smile he gives is one that doesn't quite reach his eyes. "Not tonight." He winks. "Rest up, Sunshine." And he quickly slips inside, closing the door behind him, the tinted rear windows preventing me from seeing him.

Spinning around, I punch in the code for my door, and once it unlocks, I slip inside. I hear the telltale sound of the Uber driver pulling away from the curb once I'm safely inside my building. For whatever reason, I don't turn back but head toward the elevator to take me to my floor.

As I ride up to the third floor to my apartment, an unsettled feeling in the pit of my stomach still lingers.

CHAPTER THIRTY-NINE

JACK

"She blatantly said she's not interested in marriage." I hit the ball with far more force than necessary, volleying it back to Ry.

He returns it flawlessly. "Well, what are you going to do about it?"

"What do you mean? Are you not listening to me? She's anti-marriage." My jaw clenches in frustration as my racquet connects with the ball.

"I heard you loud and clear. But," he says with far more patience, "where's the Jack I had when I thought about giving up when things went to shit with Maggie?"

"Not the same."

"Isn't it?" He raises his eyebrows at me, continuing to return my angry, forceful serves and returns with ease.

"What the hell? You come back from your honeymoon with some super-human strength or something?"

He merely grins, his white teeth contrasting more deeply against his lingering tan. "It's what good love from a good woman will do."

"Yeah, yeah, yeah," I mutter.

As we finish our game, he collects the ball, bouncing it

and catching it. "Look, you wouldn't have let me give up on Maggie, would you?"

"Not a chance." My response is immediate because anyone with half a brain and eyes could see the two of them were perfect for one another. "But this is different."

"How so?"

Tapping my racquet against my palm in thought, I roll my lips inward as I try to explain. "Sarah's not on the same page—"

"So bring her up to speed."

"And she's anti-marriage."

"You can change her mind on that."

"And she doesn't…" I can't even bring myself to say it aloud. Even to my best friend.

"Hey." My eyes lift to Ry's as we both head toward the locker room. "Do you honestly believe she doesn't have feelings for you?"

Shoving open the door, I wind around the corner to our lockers. As grateful as I am that we're the only two guys in this row, I still lower my voice. My words come out sounding terse. "Does she have feelings for me? Sure. She especially likes my dick." I dial the combination on the lock before tugging the bottom and opening the locker. "And my mouth. End of story." I kick off my shoes and socks and stuff them into my locker, my shirt following suit.

"That wasn't what I meant, and you know it."

After extracting my body wash and flip-flops, I shove my locker closed with more force than necessary. "Look, I get what you're trying to do, but you and I both know that sometimes the guy doesn't get the girl in the end." I head toward the showers.

"But the guy doesn't usually throw in the towel before giving it his all either," Ry calls out after me.

Spinning around, I pin him with a stare. "You're saying I

should go all in and just"—I wave a hand—"see what happens?"

"That's exactly what I'm saying."

"And if she doesn't?"

"Then she'll be missing out on the best damn thing to happen to her," Ry finishes.

We stand silent, facing one another for a beat before the corners of my lips tip up slightly.

"Ah, pumpkin pie. You're still sweet on me, aren't you?" I can't help it. I have to bust his balls because I can't take this dreary mood hanging over us.

He whips out his towel, snapping it against my ass. "Damn straight, hot stuff."

"Oh, uh, I'll wait to shower after you guys are done." Ry and I both turn to see a slightly shorter blond-haired man turn and dart down the nearest row of lockers.

Ry shakes his head with a chuckle. "Not everyone can understand our love, Jack."

Shoving him in the shoulder, I head to the shower. "Ain't that the truth, cupcake."

$\sim$

Sarah and I decided to meet for a drink midweek after work. When they didn't have any available tables at Max Londons, and the wait time was atrocious, we settled for two seats near the corner of the bar.

Taking a sip of wine, she swallows and her expression lights up. "Hey, do you want to go apple picking and to a corn maze with me on Sunday? I'm off work."

"Are we going to drink fresh apple cider and eat home-made apple cider donuts?"

"Of course."

"Count me in. Also, I have to say that I find it ironic we're going to go to a corn maze and the fact that"—I lean toward her for added emphasis—"corn actually *is* maize."

"My mind is blown," she deadpans.

Nudging her shoulder with mine, I give her a playful wink. "I'm going to wear you down, Sunshine, and get you to fall for me. You'll see."

"That so?" Her eyes are alit with amusement because she obviously thinks I'm joking.

Grinning, I continue. "Oh, I plan to wear you down until you fall in love with me. I'll keep chipping away at those protective walls around your heart, true erosion hard at work, until you give in and realize you love me back."

Raising my glass of beer, I tip it slightly in her direction for a toast. "To erosion," I say.

When she gently taps her wine glass against it, she has an amused smirk. "To erosion." She laughs.

She has no idea how serious—how determined—I am to wear her down. Because even after all our shenanigans and sexual mishaps, one thing is blatantly—albeit fucking screwy —apparent.

If I have to suffer blue balls for the rest of my life, there's no other woman I want by my side.

CHAPTER FORTY

SARAH

"I always wanted to have the whole 'Have you seen the way he looks at her?' kind of love. And I feel like I have that with Ry." Maggie's face has that concentrated look with the tiny crease between her brows. "And I will do everything it takes to make that continue." Her entire face brightens, and a dreamy, contented smile spreads across her face. Her skin still has a nice tanned glow from her honeymoon with Ry.

Since I didn't have to work this weekend, we'd planned some girl time to catch up on episodes of *Kimmy Schmidt*. But I couldn't get through more than five minutes before my words burst free. Everything bubbled over, and I've just finished telling her about Jack's joking the other night about the whole "erosion" topic.

"The thing is..." She pulls up one leg, placing her foot flat on the couch cushion and wraps her arms around it. Propping her chin on her upright knee, Maggie regards me carefully. "Jack's a good guy—we all know that. But I think you might have thrown him off by coming out and announcing you're not into marriage."

"But—"

She holds up a hand to stop me. "According to Ry, Jack's never been like this—the way he is with you—with any other woman. Which means he has pretty serious feelings for you." Her eyes widen dramatically before she announces in a loud whisper, "Like maybe he really likes you and wants to go steady." Maggie claps a hand over her mouth on a loud, exaggerated gasp, promptly getting one of the throw pillows hurled at her.

"Stop it." I roll my eyes in dismissal.

Replacing the throw pillow on the couch, Maggie tips her head to the side thoughtfully. "But, Sarah, what if he's serious about this whole erosion talk?"

Abruptly sliding off the couch, I begin to pace. "I just…no. Jack can't possibly have serious feelings for me. I mean, come on." Throwing up my hands in exasperation, I add, "It's not like we've even had a full sexual experience together, for God's sake!"

"You and I both know that's not everything," Maggie states calmly.

"He's never said the L-word, at least not in a serious way, either. I mean, no…" Is it just me or is my voice sounding high pitched and slightly panicked?

"Yet."

"Maggie!" I throw up my arms. "You are supposed to be calming me down. Instead, you're inciting more panic." I press two fingers to the side of my throat. "My pulse is crazy right now." Narrowing my eyes, I add, "Because of you and your talk of madness."

She rolls her eyes at me. Because, yeah. What a gem of a best friend. She's *so* supportive.

"Sarah, your pulse is racing because I'm being honest with you. You have feelings for him, and he has feelings for you." Exhaling a long breath, she adds with a wave of her hand, "Then you discover you love one another and live happily ever after." She springs up from the couch and tosses her hands in the air. "Confetti everywhere! The entire city of Saratoga Springs will rejoice!"

Do you hear that sound? That's the sound of my best friend getting kicked to the curb.

"And then"—yes, Maggie continues—"they'll have parades and, ooh!" Her eyes light up excitedly, and quite honestly, she's getting a little too carried away here. "There might even be Clydesdales. And they'll ride right down South Broadway, and everyone will celebrate…" Maggie tips her head to the side, face scrunching in thought. "Wait. What are we celebrating again?"

I can't. I. Just. Can't.

"Happily ever after for me and Jack," I supply in absolute monotone. Doesn't faze my friend, though. Not one iota.

"Right!" Her face brightens as she continues with her little imaginary parade details. I merely sit back on the couch with a long sigh and prop my chin in my hand. She'll eventually tire of these plans.

I hope.

～

"Tell me again how we transitioned from a parade through downtown Saratoga Springs to you and me getting crazy on a girls' night out?" I flash Maggie an amused look as we wait for our drinks at the bar.

She waited for Ry to get home, and he, being the great guy he is, agreed that Maggie and I should head out on the town. Ry said he'd gladly be our chauffeur for the night if we needed him. Knowing Maggie and myself and the fact we're both mega lightweights when it comes to holding our liquor, this night could only go two ways. It could end with us having two drinks tops and then people watching until the terribly late (notice the sarcasm there) hour of nine o'clock at night.

Two wild and crazy girls, that's us.

Or the other possibility—which has probably less than a two percent chance of happening—is that Maggie and I will get crazy and take downtown Saratoga Springs by storm. That's not especially likely considering the fact Maggie and I are the equivalent of two young grandmothers who fantasize about getting into their PJs and lounging around the house with a glass of wine and a snack by seven o'clock in the evening.

But wonders never cease because here we are, in the middle of one of the more popular downtown bars, all dolled up, makeup near perfect, and wearing our favorite jeans that make us feel skinny, paired with tiny tops.

You know what I mean. Women all have that one pair of jeans, that one top, and that one pair of shoes that magically transform how you feel, transform your attitude. That's what we're working with tonight, and I can't lie; it feels good. Just me and my best friend.

Oh, and about a hundred of our "closest friends."

"Oooh!" Maggie squeals, tossing back shot who-knows-what-number, and drags me to the center of the dance floor for a Miley Cyrus song.

Go ahead. Do it. You know you want to break out the judgy eyes on us, but you can't tell me that you can hear Miley's "We Can't Stop" or "Party in the USA" and resist tapping your toe, at the very least. If you try to claim a firm "no," I will promptly call BS on that noise.

Dancing horribly—which is the only way Maggie and I dance, by the way—and singing at the top of our lungs, we are having the time of our lives, and not once does it cross our mind that we're going to be total hot messes by the end of the night. Because, let's be honest. When you and your best friend continue yelling over the loud volume of the dance club, "Best night EV-ER!" to one another, there's absolutely no room for regrets.

Somehow, as the night carries on, so do the drinks. Which can mean only one possibility when it comes to us.

Shenanigans galore.

CHAPTER FORTY-ONE

SARAH

"I've got a secret," Maggie says, leaning toward me clumsily.

We're currently lounging on one of the plush loveseats placed on the outskirt of the large dance floor, far enough away from the speakers so we can manage to hear one another speak without having to shout.

In a dramatic declaration, she leans her forehead on my shoulder. "I'm wrecked." She lets out a long-drawn-out sigh. "So, *so* wrecked."

"Is the room slightly spinny?" I murmur, more to myself than to Maggie.

"I sent Ry a sext." Maggie's face transforms into a wide smile. "I said, 'Pick me up from the bar and take me home or lose me forever.'"

"Nice *Top Gun* reference there." I nudge her shoulder with mine.

"What'd you send Jack?" She eyes me expectantly.

Narrowing my gaze, I frown. "Why do you think I'd send him a text?"

Of course, she just gives me one of those looks. Because, yeah. Best friends. There's no bullshitting them.

So, of course, I fold like a deck of cards. But in my defense, I'd like to blame it on the alcohol.

Tugging my cell phone from my small purse, I pull up the text I'd sent Jack. Or more specifically, the GIF I'd sent him.

Maggie bursts out laughing, her eyes flicking to mine before returning to the screen of my phone. "That's classic. Nicely done. Oh!" She quickly hands my phone back. "You just got a response."

I'd sent Jack a GIF of Long Duk Dong, the foreign exchange student from the movie *Sixteen Candles* where he's hanging upside down, saying, "What's happenin' hot stuff?"

Because, yeah. I communicate best via GIFs. They bring me great joy even if they might not necessarily be the most mature method in the world.

The good news? Jack responded.

Jack: You've been drinking, haven't you? And this GIF is the equivalent of a booty call?

Me: Maaaayyyyybeeee.

In case you're wondering, yes. Drawing out the letters is seductive text-speak.

Says the woman who's been messing around with a guy, suffering one blue balls episode after the next.

Jack: Ry and I are headed your way soon. Stay safe, Sunshine.

"Awwwww!" Maggie swoons dramatically, nearly losing her balance on the small loveseat. "I love his little nickname for you!" And then, of course, she starts singing the song to go along with my nickname: "You Are My Sunshine."

I place my hand on her arm to stop her. "As much as I appreciate you making the connection between Jack's nickname for me to the song 'You Are My Sunshine,' I'm not sure it goes along with the latest Nicki Minaj song they're playing."

My friend merely waves me off, completely unconcerned.

After she's finished serenading me, I let out a long sigh.

"I'm getting too old for this. Maybe we can..." For whatever reason, my shoes grab my attention. "Why am I wearing your shoes?"

"We switched earlier, remember? You made me pinky promise we'd always share fuck-me shoes and the hot fuck-me stories that go along with them."

Huh. For whatever reason, I don't recall that conversation.

I cast an adoring look down at them—*my* heels, the ones Jack bought for me—the ones Maggie's currently wearing and can't help but lean down and stroke the side of the beautiful shoe. Of course, since I've had more than my fair share of alcohol, I take advantage of Maggie's jeans-clad thigh to rest my head.

"Are you really stroking your own shoes?" Maggie giggles. "While they're on my feet?"

"I have no shame. These are beautiful shoes that an equally beautiful man bought for me."

Oh crap. See what happens when I drink? I start spouting off all sorts of sweetness. I mean, really. What's next? Reciting sonnets?

Like the weirdo I am, I leave my head on Maggie's lap and pet my heels. The lighting in this place makes them even more sparkly and beautiful.

Also, I'd like to note that Maggie's lap is super comfy.

"Hey." My head snaps up only to find an intimidating bouncer wearing a black polo shirt with the name *Reggie* embroidered on it staring down at us. "You need to sit up or leave. We can't have people passed out in our place."

I straighten, eyes wide with innocence. "I was only admiring these shoes." I gesture down at them. "Aren't they gorgeous? Especially the way the light hits them just so and makes them sparkle even more?" With a slight pause, I press on. "Plus, this material is not only surprisingly soft but also stain resistant."

Apparently, I'm also trying my hand at being a shoe salesperson tonight. But I don't care because I think I've hooked Reggie's attention.

Gesturing to Maggie's foot, I offer, "Go on. Seriously. You have to feel it for yourself."

Reggie looks torn but finally, his eyes shift to Maggie's as if to ask for permission.

"Go ahead."

He bends down and reaches for the heel. As soon as his fingers make contact, his eyes widen with surprise. "Wow."

"Right?" Maggie says with a wide smile. "Crazy soft. So you see why she was stroking them." She punctuates this with a nod, and even in my drunkenness, I can't help but laugh at her. Luckily, the bouncer is still entranced and inspecting the shoes.

"I've got to tell my boyfriend about these," Reggie remarks. "He has a thing for anything sparkly."

My eyes dart to Maggie's, and we exchange the whole *Did he slip past your gaydar, too?* look. Because this guy's shoulders are massive—like Atlas holding the world kind of massive. I'd guestimate he's pushing two hundred-ish pounds and assume he's BFFs with the weights at the gym.

Then again, as I peer closer at his perfectly coiffed hair, I guess it's probable the overabundance of alcohol in our systems threw us off.

"It's crazy that they're actually that soft and"—Reggie lifts his eyes to Maggie's, still squatting at our feet—"stain resistant."

"This was a total win in my book, especially after I had a terrible experience long ago with a rockin' pair of suede Jimmy Choos. These make it all better." I smile down at him.

"Oh, I completely understand." His face transforms into a smile, and holy shit, he's just too adorable for words. "I had a pair of suede shoes that were ruined by someone spilling their drink on—"

"Are you hitting on my girl?"

All three of us whip our heads in the direction of the male voice, and I can't restrain the smile that spreads across my face.

"Clint!" I shoot off the loveseat in his direction, hurling myself into his arms. "I missed you!"

Patting me on the back, he holds me out at arm's length and peers down at me with amusement sparkling in his dark brown eyes. "Getting a little wild and crazy tonight, huh?" Positioning me by his side, he slings an arm around my shoulders and greets Maggie before turning his attention to Reggie.

"I see you've met my favorite girl."

Reggie crosses his arms, muscles bulging, veins prominently on display. How does he not blow out his shirts around the bicep area? That fabric looks like it's protesting the stretching motion, crying out, *Stahp it. Just stahp ittttt.* "Really, now?"

Clint reaches out to shove Reggie in the chest playfully, and I wonder how he doesn't come away with a broken hand. "Hush. You know I adore you."

I'm having one of those moments where my mind is lagging, frantically trying to catch up. "Wait. You mean that Reggie is your..." I tip my head to the side in question.

Clint grins. "My new boyfriend? Yep." He flashes a sly wink at Reggie.

Shooting an accusing glare at Clint, I shove at his chest. "You didn't tell me this."

"You've been preoccupied lately with"—his eyebrows rise suggestively before he sing-songs—"Mr. Blue Balls."

Maggie's dissolved into giggles, Reggie appears intrigued, and Clint looks pleased with himself, whereas I'm standing here staring pointedly at him.

"I need food." Maggie announces this suddenly. "Preferably greasy food."

"Good thing we're here, then."

Spinning around in surprise, I find Jack and Ry standing there, both men looking far too handsome and garnering appreciative glances from other women nearby.

And what is my initial response to those women and their eyes casting lusty glances at Jack? I totally did one of those feral cat hisses before laying the smackdown on them.

In my mind, that is. Because let's be real here. I'm a big talker in my head. In real life? Not so much. But in my head? Oh, it went *down*. Especially with that one blonde sitting a few feet away who's practically raping Jack with her eyes. First, I'd slap her dramatically, she'd gasp in outrage, and then I'd take her down to Chinatown. Without breaking a sweat or one strand of hair shifting out of place.

Whew. That was intense. I almost feel out of breath just imagining it.

"I know what you're thinking," Jack taunts in my ear.

"That I'm starving and ready to go to Comptons?" I reply sweetly. Comptons is the only restaurant—a diner really—which stays open until the wee hours of the morning, mainly catering to college kids or shift workers.

"This was supposed to be a guy-free night." I pout playfully.

Oh my God. I'm *pouting* now? I've definitely had too much to drink. Time to call it a night, for sure, before I start twirling my hair around my finger and chomp on a wad of bubble gum, too.

"Sorry, Sunshine." Yeah, except Jack doesn't sound the least bit sorry.

"But wait!" Maggie protests as Ry pulls her up from the loveseat. "We never got to try that purple haze shot."

Ry looks like he's trying hard not to laugh. "Mags, we can try that another night."

"Promise?"

"Promise."

I turn to my coworker. "Clint? You want to come along?"

"Nah, I'm just waiting for this guy's shift to end." Clint tugs me in for a brief hug before whispering in my ear. "Have fun with Mr. B.B."

"Have fun with Reggie. Remind him to tell you about the stain resistant fabric."

He wrinkles his nose, and I have to laugh before shoving him playfully. "Not for anything sexual, you dork." Pressing a quick kiss to his cheek, I say goodbye before turning to leave. Just as I turn, Clint takes it upon himself to slap me on the ass with enough force to cause me to stumble slightly.

Jack's hand reaches out to steady me, and I don't miss the sharp look he flashes Clint before carefully leading me toward the exit.

"Sure he's just a friend of yours?" Jack asks as we step out onto the sidewalk.

I laugh. "Of course." A shiver runs through me from the chill of the night air. Maggie and I had gone without jackets because we didn't want to keep up with them and knew we'd be warm enough indoors. Now, however, is a totally different story.

When he removes his light jacket and drapes it over me, I can't help but stop and stare up at him, causing other pedestrians and partygoers to spill around us.

Jack eyes me cautiously. "Why are you looking at me like that?"

"You gave me your jacket."

Wow. *Thank you, Captain Obvious.* I sound like an idiot.

He gives me an odd look. "You were shivering." He says this like it's nothing. Like any guy would give a shivering woman his jacket.

But he's wrong, especially in this day and age.

"Hey! Is everything—" I vaguely hear Ry call out to us a few yards behind with Maggie. I don't respond. Instead, I press my palms flat against Jack's chest and walk him backward until his back is against the brick exterior of the nearest storefront.

His eyes peer down at me, slight shadows playing across his features from the nearby streetlights contrasting with the darkness of the evening.

"Sunshine?" His tone is questioning.

The added height of my heels allows me to easily drag my lips across the dark scruff of his jawline, and I bask in his sharp intake of breath. Bringing my lips to his ear, I whisper, "I want you to take me home."

"That's what the plan was." His voice is gravelly, with a slight tinge of humor in it. "After we get you ladies fed."

My teeth nip at his earlobe. "I want you to feed me." I back away slightly and give him a wicked grin. "I want you to feed me that monster co—"

"Sarah! Are you coming or what?" Maggie interrupts. "I need food. Baaaad."

Turning, I see my friend and Ry catching up to us. "Sorry. No can do. I'm going to take this man home, and we're going to get it on like Donkey Kong."

Vaguely, I hear Jack mutter something that sounds like, "Oh Jesus."

CHAPTER FORTY-TWO

JACK

I f it were anyone else, I'd be immediately shoving food down their throat and seeing them home safely. But something about Sarah makes me lose sight of everything—of logic and, honestly, maybe even some of my morals. Because when she started talking about us getting it on, my dick perked up instantly.

Obviously, there's no way in hell I'll see it through while she's still like this. But, damn it, I fucking want to sink so deep inside her. I want to taste her everywhere. I want to look into her eyes when I make lo—

"Holy fuck."

I don't realize I've spoken aloud until Sarah's voice jars me, teasing, "That's the idea, Westbrook."

Forcing a smile, I try to shake things off. "Let me see about grabbing a cab at the corner." I lift my chin in the direction ahead of us.

"Sweetness!" Sarah pumps her fist, doing some sort of little celebratory dance before tossing her hands in the air above her head. "Hands in the air if you're gonna get lucky tonight!" she calls out, instantly receiving some hoots and hollers from a group of young, college-aged guys nearby. "Whoop, whoop!"

"Simmer down there, horndog." I take her hand, steadying her when she stumbles in her heels. The same heels that nearly stopped me in my tracks when I saw them. Hell, when I spotted her standing in the club wearing those jeans that hug her in all the right places and that black shirt that consists of a full front but only two wide crisscross straps in the back, I nearly swallowed my tongue.

Throwing my jacket over Sarah was not entirely selfless. It was also because her nipples had perked up, and there is no way in hell I want anyone else to get a glimpse of them. They are mine.

Mine. Fuck. Ry was right earlier. I'm so screwed. Worse, I don't know what my deal is in thinking I could deny anything—to myself or to my best friend.

I'm so far gone over this woman. A woman who doesn't do relationships. A woman who's nowhere close to feeling the same way about me as I do her. But facts are facts. She's my sunshine, and I don't want to consider being without her.

Because I know without a shadow of a doubt that my life would be far too dark and lifeless without her in it.

~

"Jack," Sarah calls, drawing out my name languidly. "I cannot wait to get out of these clothes." She's kicking off her heels, removing my jacket, and tossing it onto the nearby chair. Her purse is dropped to the floor without a thought as soon as I lock my door behind us. Toeing off my own shoes, I quickly cinch my fingers around her slim upper arm when she sways to one side.

"Oooh." She wiggles her eyebrows at me. "You saved me again." Then she spins around, out of my grasp, and disappears around the corner toward the hallway leading to my bedroom.

"I hope you are"—she pauses to sing-song the rest of her words—"read-y to roooolllllll." There's a brief pause again. "And I sometimes like to sing-talk. Hopethat'sokay." Her words run together, voice trailing off as she likely enters my bedroom.

Scrubbing a rough hand over my face, a small laugh escapes me. Because this is quite the treat to get to see Sarah like this with those walls not so strongly enforced. She continues softly singing, "No! Sleep! Till Brooklyn!" Not a chance she'll be giving the Beastie Boys a run for their money, that much is certain.

Following the path she's taken, I stop short at the sight of the clothing trail along the hallway, the floor littered with a pair of jeans, her shirt and bra, along with what looks to be the skimpiest black thong.

Shaking my head, I close my eyes and pray for strength. Strength to get through this night in the company of a woman who's got me so strung out over her; who's so fucking gorgeous and doesn't even realize she has me wrapped around her damn finger.

"Jack." Her husky voice carries out from the bedroom. I step past the doorway to find her sprawled out on my bed. In the middle of it, she has her arms thrown out as if she's about to make snow angels. Her nipples puckered and practically begging for my mouth, and her long, slim legs entice me to slide between them.

"Are you gonna snuggle with me?" She remains there, unperturbed by the fact that she's gloriously naked atop the covers. "Naked?"

With a laugh, I shake my head. "No, Sunshine. No naked snuggling tonight."

Her lips form a moue. "Why not?"

I step closer to the bed, tugging my polo shirt over my

head, and letting it drop to the floor. "Because I don't want to take advantage of you." My jeans follow suit, and I remove my socks. Clad in only my boxers, I tug the covers back. She slides and repositions herself beneath them before I slip in beside her.

"Maybe I want to take advantage of you." One palm glides over my chest and slides lower before I catch it, my eyes darting over to her. "We can blame it on abs." Sarah leans over, her lips pressing a kiss to my left pectoral. "Abs made me do it. Abs made me take advantage of you." Her palm grazes over my firm abdominals, and the muscles contract beneath her touch.

Jesus. My dick is at nearly full-salute status right now. Placing my palm over hers, I stop her movement. "Sarah." My tone is pleading. "We can't." *Fuck.* I hear the wavering in my own voice.

Her eyes brighten, visible in the room with the bright moonlight peeking through the slats of the blinds. "What if we play 'just the tip'?"

"Sarah."

She frowns. "I don't like it when you call me that."

"It's your name." My response is slow, drawn out in my confusion.

She gives me a look like *duh.* "I know that. But when you call me Sarah instead of Sunshine, it's like something's missing all of a sudden. And I don't get that warm feeling inside."

If I were a chick, I'd have a fucking field day trying to decipher whether she's just admitted to having feelings for me—stronger feelings, that is—or if it's merely the alcohol talking. As it is, she's already got me tied up in knots.

"Can I have a bedtime kiss? Please?"

I have the most pathetic excuse for resolve around her. "Just a small—"

Instantly, her mouth is on mine, cutting off my words, and

she slides her naked body over mine to straddle me. Inwardly hissing at the contact of her heated flesh, I automatically move my hands to trace over the curve of her ass. The minute she arches and presses her breasts into me, her hard nipples poking me, I feel my resolve begin to crumble.

Just one kiss, I remind myself.

My fingers dive into her hair, tangling in the long strands and tugging her head to the side to deepen the kiss. When my tongue slips inside and greets hers, a shiver runs through me at the mere taste of her. Rocking her hips over me gently, I groan into her mouth as another surge of arousal flows through me, and my cock hardens painfully.

One of my hands unclenches its hold from her hair, fingers trailing softly down over the graceful column of her neck, collarbone, and the swell of her left breast. The pad of my thumb brushes against her nipple, and she breaks our kiss, rising to sit, and gently rocks her hips over me.

Taking my wrists, she moves my palms to her breasts, and I cup their weight. She's so goddamn sexy, and I know this is wrong, but I can't deny her what she clearly wants. If she wants to use me to get off tonight, then I'm all hers.

I'm all hers. Those words linger in the back of my mind, the truth of them reverberating deep within me.

As she rocks herself over me, her eyes flutter closed, and she's got to be the most beautiful sight I've seen. Caressing her breasts, I arch my hips, pressing into her right where she wants it—where she needs it—most.

We continue our own rhythm—arching bodies, rocking hips—until one of my hands slips down to her clit. My boxer briefs are getting more damp from her arousal, and I continue to tweak her clit gently before lightly pressing my thumb to it and rubbing in circles. And then it happens.

Sarah falls apart before my own eyes.

Lips painted a soft pink part on a gasp, her eyes close, and her nipples harden into a lush, rosy shade as she rides out her orgasm. But that's not the most beautiful part of this. It's what slips from her lips. The way it comes out as a little wisp, so airy and dreamy.

"Jack."

CHAPTER FORTY-THREE

SARAH

Why does my mouth feel like a litterbox?

Not that I know what a litterbox actually feels like because I'm allergic to cats, but still. Bleh.

And my eyes are stuck together. That's what I get for taking Maggie's advice and wearing more than one coat of mascara. I have to practically use both hands to gently pull the skin in opposite directions to pry my eyelids open. Talk about gross.

Want to know what's not gross? *Oh-ho*, the sight I'm greeted with, that's what.

Two words: Hello, morning wood.

Okay, that was actually three words. Damn it. I'm still hungover, and my brain is struggling here.

Jack's morning wood is practically pulling an Adele and screaming, "Hello from the other siiiiiiiide!" The other side of those boxer briefs, that is.

The saddest part about a sexy as sin guy you've been naked with a bunch of times but never able to follow through with both of you getting the big "O"—in the same instance—is you always wonder...*you know*. Things like, *I wonder how he tastes when he comes, I wonder what his "O" face looks like, or I wonder what it would be like to wake up to this every mor—*

Whoa, whoa, *whoa.* Hold up. I must have really drunk a lot last night because my mind is veering off into areas I don't dare tiptoe into. That's just not me.

With a sigh, I shift as quietly as I can so as not to disturb Jack, only to realize I have no clothes on, nor any nearby. Approaching his dresser, I figure I can find an undershirt or something to slip on so I'm not prancing around his place with everything hanging out on a Sunday morning.

Just as my fingers touch the handle of the top drawer, my eyes catch sight of a tiny framed photo sitting off to the far corner of the mahogany. Intrigued, I reach for the photo and bring it closer for inspection because the little boy in it is so incredibly awkward looking. Jack really hadn't been kidding when he'd mentioned being a total pocket protector wearing nerd back in the da—

"That was me and my dad a year after my mom passed away." His voice is so unexpected that I jerk, nearly dropping the photo. My eyes fly over to see him watching me with an odd, guarded expression. "He had a heart attack about four years ago."

"I'm sorry," I say gently. I've always hated that response; it feels vapid and useless when it's given to people who have lost loved ones, but it's so difficult to come up with anything else that's appropriate.

He lifts one shoulder slightly, gaze averting to the blinds covering the bedroom windows. "He buried himself in his work, and it was stressful trying to raise a kid on his own. Especially in this area…"

I roll my lips inward, unsure of what to say.

"Second drawer." Again, he startles me, my eyes darting to find him watching me. "You should find your pick of T-shirts there."

Turning back, I hear him release a small groan. "Jesus,

Sunshine. You and that ass…"

Removing a gray cotton undershirt from the drawer he specified, I tug it on, smoothing it down as it reaches my mid-thigh, I turn back to face him.

"My ass what?" My expression is one of exaggerated innocence.

He scrubs a hand over his face, wincing on a tight laugh. "I might not be able to leave this bed for a while."

"What if I, maybe, did something like this…" My eyes widen dramatically as I bend slightly, the shirt riding up my legs, the hem brushing the bottom of my ass. "Would that be terrible?"

"Sunshine," he says in a mixture of a warning growl and a groan.

"Ha-ha," I call out as I jauntily walk toward the bathroom. "Just kidding. My mouth is disgusting, and there's no way you want near it without a hazmat suit."

As I cross over into his en suite, I swear I hear him mutter something that sounds like, "I want more than just your mouth, Sunshine."

But I'm probably mistaken.

～

People totally underrate apple cider and apple cider donuts. Seriously, though. I'm pretty sure I orgasmed when I took my first bite of the freshly made donut at the family-owned apple orchard we're at.

Not only is the apple picking on hold until after I get my fill of this goodness but so is the corn maze. No way do I want to test my maze skills on an empty stomach.

Also, I'd like to go on record and say I have *never* eaten this many donuts in one sitting before. But right now, I have little to no shame. Hangovers will do that to a person.

"Should I have gotten a dozen instead of only a half dozen?" Jack's eyes are sparkling with humor.

"Hmmph," is all I can manage with a mouthful of donut. My eyes are nearly rolling back in my head.

After Jack had carted me back to my place this morning, he'd waited patiently for me to cleanse last night from my body. I put on more appropriate clothing, and he'd driven us up here to the apple orchards.

Currently, we're sitting across from one another at one of the many picnic tables scattered beneath a large white tent while I gorge myself on donuts.

When I feel the granulated sugar from the donut clinging to my lips, I dart out the tip of my tongue because if I don't at least attempt to savor it, that would be wasteful.

The donut gods frown upon such things, I'm certain.

As I concentrate on trying to nab some sugar on the upper left part of my lip, Jack slaps his palms against the wood and pushes himself up to stand. My eyes widen in alarm at the fierceness in his expression.

Warily eyeing him as he comes over to my side of the table, he slides one leg over the bench seat to straddle it, facing me. One hand reaches out, and his fingers thread in my hair, tugging me to him. His lips softly nip at mine, and his tongue discreetly darts out to taste the sugar clinging to my lips. My breath catches in my throat at the feel of the tip of his tongue on my skin, and my nipples instantly harden at the tantalizing thought of his tongue lapping at them in the same manner.

"Jack," I breathe.

"Yeah?"

"This is a family place. A PG-rated thing."

His lips curve against mine. "Oh, Sunshine. You have no idea how hard it is to keep things PG-rated around you."

I lift my eyebrows suggestively. "I'm pretty sure I know how hard it is."

The laugh he gives sends warmth running through me, and the corners of his eyes crinkle as he smiles. Dusting a soft kiss on my forehead, he whispers, "It's harder than you can imagine."

CHAPTER FORTY-FOUR

SARAH

"So did we...you know?" I ask nonchalantly, plucking another apple from the tree and placing it in our basket.

We've already finished the corn maze, and I promised Jack I'd bake an apple pie for us after we get back from the orchard.

Braving a glance over at him, I tack on, "Last night?" The sharp look he gives me stops me in mid reach of another apple. "What? It's an honest question."

He stalks toward me, and I instinctively take a step backward only to find the firm trunk of the apple tree at my back with Jack's tall form leaning over me.

"Do you really think I'd take advantage of you?" he demands almost angrily.

"N-no," I stammer. "I would never think that."

Something shifts between us as we stand along one of the more secluded back rows of apple trees, nearly alone while most of the other apple pickers chose the trees closer to the main entrance.

His eyes darken as he leans in, bracing a hand on a thick

branch above my head. "You don't remember climbing on top of me, Sunshine?"

Oh shit.

My throat is now bone dry, and I work hard to swallow before answering him. "No."

"That's a shame." His lips graze my jawline. "It was hot as hell." Another grazing touch of his lips sends jolts through my system. "Do you know what happened after that?"

Please don't tell me I had hot sex and don't remember it, I chant silently.

Jack goes on without waiting for me to answer. "You fell fast asleep."

I jerk back so fast I knock my head into the tree trunk. But it doesn't register past the look in Jack's eyes.

"You ass!" I shove at him, but it doesn't make him budge an inch. He merely grins down at me. "I was extremely intoxicated."

"And extremely horny."

I work hard at maintaining my stern expression, but it's tough.

"How does it feel to take advantage of such a sweet, inno-cent man such as myself?" He poses the question with such exaggerated seriousness that I can't resist a laugh.

And an eye roll.

"Seriously, though." Jack's expression sobers, backing away from me before his features appear troubled. "I feel so used. Tossed aside like yesterday's newspaper." He places a hand over his heart as if he's experiencing pain. "Oh, Sunshine." With a mournful expression, he shakes his head. "When will you learn to stop riding men's penises with wild abandon?"

I lob an apple at his grinning face only to have him catch it midair and take a big bite out of it. He winks at me, chewing and swallowing before drawing closer.

Dipping his head closer to mine, he cages me in against

the tree. One hand raises to cup the side of my face, and his thumb softly grazes my cheekbone as his eyes lock with mine.

Something is unique about the way he's gazing down at me. Something that feels intense and…intimate.

"Sunshine." His voice is gravelly and low, his full lips drawing my attention as he speaks, and his head dips closer. "Do you have any idea"—he pauses, his gaze searching, and I can't help but feel torn between his entrancing words and the sudden commotion of voices which have grown louder behind him—"that I'm fal—"

"Oh dear." It's something in that unfamiliar voice, in those words that make me tear my attention away from Jack.

"You've got to be kidding me." My tone is part stunned, part exasperation because I'm staring at what appears to be a Catholic church outing, priests dressed casually but with their white collars prominently displayed and a few of the older nuns—including the one I keep running into—with their traditional headpiece.

I sidle closer to Jack, using his broad form to disguise myself from the particular nun who's made it clear I'm on the fast track to hell.

"I swear," I whisper-hiss to him, "it's a conspiracy or something." My eyes rise to meet his laughing ones. Raising a hand and gesturing to the sky above us, I know my voice has a tinge of distress. "I mean, out of all the people in this area, he's assigned her to monitor *me*?"

"You'd best stop riding penises and FaceTiming with your vagina then," he says with a soft chuckle. Then he loops his arm around my shoulders and peers down into the basket of apples that I hold. "That should be plenty for a pie."

Walking in the direction of the entrance to pay for our pickings, we pass right by the group of priests and nuns. Jack's expression grows serious, his eyes flicking over them, and then back at me. This is when he does the unthinkable.

"Would you stop touching me there? No means no! As a female, you should know this!" he exclaims loudly.

Snatching the basket of apples from me, he promptly stalks off. And I could totally stand here and face the judgment but, really, I have no choice.

I turn and run after him like the fires of hell are nipping at my feet.

~

"That was not funny."

"It really was. You should have seen your face." Jack's mouth stretches wide, flashing a smile. He's standing beside me in my small kitchen as he helps me peel the apples for the pie we're going to make.

"Yeah, because it wasn't enough that I'm obviously on God's radar with my sinful behavior."

He cuts the final apple into small pieces and adds it to the pie pan. "I think it's hilarious that you ran into the same nun."

"Just hilarious," I mutter as I pour the batter and spread it over the apple slices in the pan.

We're making Swedish apple pie that requires no crust because I'm no Martha Stewart, slaving in the kitchen and attempting to perfect a pie crust or make soufflés. Nope. Not me.

But I sure do make a mean Swedish apple pie.

Slipping the pie into the oven, I set the timer on the stove, spinning around to grab the bowl and utensils to wash them. Except Jack's already beat me to it.

"You don't have to wash them," I protest as he sets everything in the sink and gets soap on the sponge.

"I don't mind. Then we can sit and check out a movie while we wait for the pie."

I regard him thoughtfully while his attention is trained on

the dishes he's washing. "You're planning on hanging around just until the pie's ready for eating? Then heading home?"

I don't want to admit how much I want him to stick around. Today's been more fun than I expected. Then again, that usually goes hand in hand with Jack.

The side of his lips quirks upward. "Trying to get rid of me, Sunshine?"

"No, I just..." I don't ever ask guys to stick around, so this is incredibly awkward for me.

He finishes and wipes his hands on the dish towel before turning around, his blue eyes locking with mine.

"You want me to stay?" He poses the question softly, but there's a hint of something else in his tone, of something more, but I can't put my finger on it.

Suddenly, my bravery is nowhere to be found, and I merely nod.

"*The Princess Bride*? Or *17 Again*?" he asks, naming our two favorite movies.

"Farmboy," I call out, playfully tossing my own version of a famous interaction between the main characters in *The Princess Bride*. "Fetch us each a glass of apple cider while we wait."

He winks before turning to my cabinet which holds the glasses. "As you wish."

This time, it's not only the wink, but also the secret smile playing on his lips that makes my stomach flip.

CHAPTER FORTY-FIVE

JACK

"That must be the best apple pie I've had in years." I pat my stomach, placing my empty plate on the coffee table. "Maybe the best ever."

Sarah's eyes brighten with pride as she forks the last bit of her piece of pie into her mouth, lips wrapping around the fork in a way that shouldn't be seductive in the least. However, when it comes to her, I think just about everything she does is sexy.

I spot a small crumb clinging to the corner of her lips. Leaning closer to where she sits beside me on her couch, I reach out a hand to cup her chin. Her eyes widen, caught off guard.

"You've got a little crumb"—I lean in closer, holding her gaze—"right here." I dart the tip of my tongue out to nab it, and the way her breath hitches slightly sends gratification rushing through me. My mouth moves across her bottom lip, pressing tiny kisses, and when her grasp on her plate wobbles, I take it from her and place it none too gently on the coffee table to join my own.

The moment her hands are free, she catches me off guard. Sliding her hands into my hair, she fuses her mouth to mine in a frantic, devouring kiss. Rising to her knees, she pushes me back against the couch, straddling me, as our tongues tangle and our breathing becomes ragged.

My hands glide down over her soft curves until I grip her firm ass in my palms, pulling her closer. She tears her lips from mine, mouth swollen from our kiss, and her heavy-lidded gaze meets mine.

"I don't want a repeat of last night."

My brow furrows in confusion. "What do you mean?"

Dusting soft kisses along my jawline, she whispers, "I don't want it to be one-sided again."

Fuck if that doesn't send a surge of blood rushing to my cock as her lips latch onto my earlobe, sucking before she gently grazes it with her teeth. Her hands start untucking my shirt from my jeans, pulling it up and helping me tug it over my head.

"Ah." She sighs, eyes taking in the sight of my bared upper body. "Your body should come with its own disclaimer."

A surprised laugh escapes me. "Like what?"

Her light blue eyes are dancing mischievously. "Like 'Must gird ovaries if in close proximity to this one.'"

My chuckle is cut short when she removes her shirt, leaving her in a simple beige bra. With her eyes locked on mine, she reaches back to unclasp it before slipping it down over her shoulders and tossing it aside.

My hands immediately move to cup her bare breasts with nipples already hardening, and when she arches into my touch, it urges me on. Dipping my head, I latch my lips over one rosy peak, sucking it into my mouth before flicking it with the tip of my tongue.

Moving to the other, her fingers tighten their grasp on my hair, pressing herself closer as if she can't get enough of my touch. Her responsiveness drives me on, my cock painfully hard, and it's as though she recognizes this. One of her hands moves to dip beneath the front waistband of my jeans, and her fingertips graze the head, causing me to jerk at her touch.

Suddenly, I'm desperate for more. Shifting our positions and placing her back on the couch, my fingers are frantic in their movements, working to unfasten and remove her jeans. Sliding them down her slim legs, my eyes feast on the sight of her body clad in only panties and socks. When my hands shift to remove her panties, she stops me.

"You're wearing too many clothes." Her gaze is full of heat as she watches me comply and stand. Removing my jeans and socks, I hitch my thumbs in the waistband of my boxer briefs.

"What do you think? Can you handle all of me? Naked? Or do you need to gird your ovaries?" I tease.

With a pointed look, she lifts one leg, removing a sock then repeating the action with the other before sliding her panties down her legs and kicking them off. With a sly smile, she nods toward my underwear. "I can handle it."

Shoving the briefs down, I kick them to the side before joining Sarah, a hiss escaping our lips at the touch of our naked flesh. My cock nestles between her thighs, pressing against her core. With my forearms braced on either side of her head, I rest my weight on them, hands framing her face, thumbs lightly brushing against the softness of her cheeks. "You're beautiful," I say softly, my gaze direct.

You're beautiful, and I'm falling in love with you.

Something shifts in those light blue eyes as if my declaration has made her uncomfortable. Before she can get herself worked up in a panic, my mouth crashes down on hers, and I find myself kissing her with a unique desperation. Because I'm trying to communicate my feelings to a woman who wants nothing to do with feelings, emotional entanglements, or anything remotely connected to a romantic relationship.

I'm trying to get her to see past her misgivings, to see

what I bring to the table, to see *us*. I want—need—for her to see how well we work.

She returns the kiss with a passion rivaling my own, her palms gliding down my back until she gets to my ass and pulls me toward her roughly, bringing my tip to prod at her entrance.

Breaking the kiss, my voice is hoarse with arousal. "Condom," I manage to get out, shifting to reach for one in my pants pocket, but she stops me.

"I'm on the pill, and I always get tested."

My head turns slowly, my eyes searching her expression before I speak. "I'm clean and haven't been with anyone sin—"

Sarah doesn't let me finish; instead, her palms tug me roughly toward her, and my cock easily slips inside her. Fuck, the feel of her wet warmth surrounding me is almost too much; not to mention, I've never had unprotected sex before. A part of me is dying to know if this means she's on the same page with me, if she's opening up to the possibility of us being...an *us*.

The moment she wraps her legs around my waist, causing me to shift even deeper, my thoughts disappear, my intent only to show the woman beneath me just how good we can be together. To show her I love everything about her.

It's up to me to break down those walls around her heart so my love can finally surge through, filling all those tiny fissures until my name is etched on her heart.

The way she's etched hers on mine.

CHAPTER FORTY-SIX

SARAH

I can't get enough of this, of Jack's frenzied thrusts. His touch is addictive, and the look in his eyes makes me feel like I'm teetering between bursting into flames because of my fast-approaching orgasm or falling victim to a panic attack because... Hell, those eyes, darkened with an unfamiliar intensity, are too much. And I know I can't handle it.

I move to shift our bodies, trying to get him beneath me, thinking that might help. But when I do so, something happens, and I cause Jack to lose his balance, slipping off me and hitting the edge of my glass coffee table.

With his *head*.

"Holy shit!"

I rush to the kitchen to get a clean towel and race back to where he's sitting on the floor with his hand pressed against the gash on his forehead. I quickly assess it with dismay before taking his hand to place it firmly against the cloth in an attempt to help staunch the bleeding.

"I'll be right back. In the meantime, get dressed because you're going to need stitches." I'm pulling on my clothes as I rush to my bathroom for supplies.

"You've got to be shitting me." I hear a rustling and turn to help him tug on his shirt and jeans while he attempts to hold the towel against his forehead.

Minutes later, I manage to clean up his wound a bit and apply some Steri-Strips to the laceration, which will make do until I get him to the ER.

With a wry laugh, I grab my purse and keys and usher Jack out the door. Rushing down the steps to the nearby street parking assigned to residents, we get inside my car, and I drive us to the hospital.

I quickly dial Clint's number using the car's Bluetooth. Surprisingly, he picks up right away, and I'm hoping it's a sign that things have been slow at the hospital.

"Hey, sweets. My break is about to end, but I have to ask: Did you get lucky with Mr. T.D.H. last night? Or should I continue to call him Mr. B.B.?"

I feel Jack's attention on me, but I ignore it...as well as Clint's question. "I'm driving Mr. Tall, Dark, and Handsome to the ER for stitches, as we speak."

There's a brief pause. "I *cannot* wait to hear the story behind this injury."

Frowning as I navigate, and luckily only two blocks from the hospital now, I say, "We're two blocks away. See you in a few."

"Am I on speaker?"

I hesitate. "Yes."

"Hey, handsome." Clint's voice takes on a flirtatious tone.

Jack tosses out, "Hey, man."

"Talking back to our girl is dangerous, huh?"

Jack chuckles. "She's dangerous, all right."

"We'll get you fixed up in no time. See you in a few." The call disconnects, and I turn the corner to pull into the drive leading up to the ER drop-off.

"I'm going to drop you off and park really quick."

"I can walk," Jack protests.

Pulling up and stopping by the doors, I turn to him. "It'll only take me a minute." Frowning with concern, I nod to his head. "I'm worried about that gash, so let's play it safe. See you inside in a moment."

With a nod, he exits the car, and just as he's about to close the door, he stops, eyes meeting mine. "Hey, Sunshine?"

"Jack?"

His features soften, eyes crinkling at the corners slightly. "I had the best day with you. Even this can't put a damper on it." With that said, he closes the door and turns to walk through the automatic doors.

~

"So let me get this straight. You fell into the edge of the glass coffee table when you were shifting positions on the couch?" Clint asks, his features screwed up in an overly serious expression.

"I just told you what happened," I say through gritted teeth. "Three times."

Clint grins. "Oh, but I enjoyed hearing it." His smile widens. "Yet again." Turning to Jack, he asks, "So you're saying you were on top and then Miss Bossypants here had to change it up?"

My eyes fly to Dr. Mills, who's concentrating on the last few stitches in Jack's forehead, before narrowing back on Clint. "Would you please stop?" I hiss.

"Nothing to worry about, Miss Matthews." Dr. Mills finishes up the final stitch before placing a bandage on it. "You know I've heard and seen a lot worse."

"And it's better when it's one of our own," Clint insists, smugly. To me, he prods, "So blue balls strikes again, huh?"

"Clint," I snarl.

He pats Jack's knee consolingly. "You guys are just two Calamity Janes trying to navigate your way to the elusive

Orgasm Island." He pauses. "Or two Magoos, blindly fumbling your way to Bang-Bang-ville. Or—"

"We get it," Jack and I chant in unison.

"All set, Mr. Westbrook." Dr. Mills hands Jack his paperwork. "Schedule an appointment with your family doctor to have the stitches removed in seven to ten days or"—he pauses to glance over at me—"if you feel brave enough, you can have Miss Matthews do it for you."

"And maybe she'll give you a little extra TLC wh—"

"Thank you," Jack interrupts Clint, shaking the doctor's hand.

"—ile finally providing relief!" Clint finishes with a flourish.

"*Clint*," Dr. Mills, Jack, and I all scold in unison.

With a dramatic eye roll, he tosses his hands in the air. "I can't possibly be the only one who finds this so fascinating! I mean, really," he scoffs, "two people who seem like the universe is taking major offense to the prospect of them getting it on that something's always cropping up."

Shaking his head, he lifts his chin toward Jack. "Take care of yourself, B.B." To me, he leans in and winks. "You, missy, had better not shove any other men into coffee tables while Mr. Winky's still inside your hot box."

I'm still sputtering after he's left the room with the doctor in tow, leaving only Jack and me in the quiet room.

Heaving out a long sigh, I glance over at Jack. "Ready to head home?"

He flashes me a weak smile. "Ready to go, Bruiser."

Except this time, his teasing doesn't quite hit its mark. Instead, I'm still wondering about Clint's remarks about the universe.

Wondering if there's any validity to it whatsoever.

CHAPTER FORTY-SEVEN

JACK

Sarah's quiet on the ride back to my place. Far too quiet, actually, and I can't help but wonder as we ride along the streets of downtown Saratoga Springs if she's pondering Clint's unsettling remark.

As if the universe has anything against us getting it on, I scoff internally. Glancing over at her profile as she maneuvers the car through heavier than usual traffic for a Sunday evening, I notice the slight furrow in her brow. The sight of her troubled expression sends a dense rush of foreboding rolling through me.

When she pulls into the numbered guest parking spot assigned to me, the pressure in my chest lessens slightly because I assume she's coming in with me. The tension is still present on the elevator ride up to my floor.

"Thanks for tonight."

Her eyebrows shoot up, lips twisting in a humorless quirk. "You're thanking me for causing you to slam your head into my glass table?"

I eye her carefully. "You know what I mean." The elevator chimes before the doors slide open, and she steps out before I follow suit. "Thanks for sticking around."

Stopping at my door, I reach for my keys in my pocket, sliding the key into the lock before turning back to her. Sarah's leaning against the wall, eyes guarded. Stepping closer, I rest my palms flat against the wall on either side of her and cage her in.

"Sunshine, you have no idea how long it's been since someone's hung around and taken care of me. So thank you." My voice is low, gravelly with emotion, because even within my dim memories of my mother, I recall her being the last woman to take it upon herself to go above and beyond to care for me.

Her features appear to soften, the tenseness on her face easing. "You're welcome," she replies softly.

Opening my door, we enter and remove our shoes. "You should try to get some rest, but..." She trails off, looking uncomfortable, and I know in my gut what she's about to say next.

The knowing doesn't make it sting any less, however.

"What Clint said earlier got me thinking." The crease between her eyebrows pops up, begging me to smooth it out. Reaching into her small purse, the strap across her chest, she pulls out one of those chocolates she keeps on hand. She averts her gaze, focusing on her fingers unwrapping the foil, plucking the chocolate out, and reading the message on the inside wrapper. Taking a tiny bite, she chews and swallows before pressing on.

"Think about it, Jack. We've been through this how many times, right? And every time, something happens. An interruption or something bad happens to throw things off. That's not normal." Shaking her head, she puts the remainder of the chocolate back into the wrapper. "I think we should take it as a sign that it's not meant to b—"

My hand reaches out to grasp her wrist with the chocolate. Stepping closer to her, I watch as her eyes widen. I can see the uncertainty in her expression, wondering what I'm doing.

Bringing her hand to my mouth, I wrap my lips around the remainder of chocolate, licking her fingers clean, and I give her my response.

"No."

Shock is visible on her face. "No?" she repeats in disbelief. "What do you me—"

"I mean..." I swallow, allowing the bulk of the melted chocolate to coat my tongue, then dip my head closer to her so my breath washes against her lips. "No, I'm not letting you take it as a sign."

"But—"

I cut off her response, my mouth crashing down on hers in a deep, chocolatey kiss, pressing my body against hers and trapping her between me and the wall. Our kiss is desperate, needy, passionate, and devouring—all these emotions are running through me at this exact moment.

Nudging her thighs further apart, I press closer, letting her feel my arousal. My hands slide up her sides, dragging the hem of her shirt with them until my thumbs rest beneath her breasts. Her chest is rising and falling with labored breathing, and I wonder if she even realizes she's arching into my touch as if desperately trying to urge me on. Cupping her bra-clad breasts, I brush the pads of my thumbs over her nipples, and at that moment, a moan escapes her.

Practically tearing off her shirt, I make quick work of her bra, and soon, her torso is bared to me. Without allowing her any time for more doubts to cloud her mind, I drag my lips down the column of her neck, placing wet kisses along her collarbone before latching onto one of her nipples while my finger and thumb toy with the other. Loving it with my lips and tongue, I revel in her harsh breathing, the tiny gasps that my actions elicit before moving my mouth to the other hardened peak.

"Jack," she breathes. "Jack, we need to—"

I choose that moment to suck hard before letting her

nipple free with an audible pop as my eyes lock onto hers. "I think you should let me figure out what we need, Sunshine."

Hastily unbuttoning her jeans, I tug them down and off with her underwear and socks following. Without any pause, I slide one finger to her entrance to test her wetness and find her absolutely fucking drenched.

Fuck control. I'm laying it all on the line. She needs to see that nothing—no hokey shit about the universe—will keep us from making love.

Thrusting another finger deep inside her, I swallow her moans with my mouth on hers. My other hand delves into her hair and fists the soft strands. Working her with my fingers, I feel her arousal coating them, and her hips begin to rock, urging me on.

Dropping to my knees, I press her thighs further apart; my mouth goes directly for her clit, lips wrapping around it, and applying a gentle suction. Her hands fly to my hair as my name falls from her lips in a whispered moan. My two fingers continue moving in and out of her in rapid thrusts, and she tightens her grasp of my hair.

"Jack," she whispers my name, again, but this time I can hear it in her voice; I can hear that she's on the precipice.

Fastening my lips firmly to her clit, I use the tip of my tongue to toy with it while my fingers continue sliding in and out of her wetness. As soon as I feel her inner muscles tighten, I speed up my motions, and it catapults her over the edge. Her hips work as she rides out her orgasm, pressing against my tongue shamelessly.

Once her tremors subside, I raise my eyes to meet her languid gaze, holding it as I slide up her body and lift her by the waist. Instinctively, she wraps her legs around my hips and her arms around my neck, and I carry her to my bedroom. As I head down the hallway, she dusts a trail of delicate kisses from my temple downward—opposite of the side where I'm sporting a new set of stitches—and nibbles at my earlobe.

Lowering her to the bed while leaving her legs dangling over the edge, I take a moment to take in the sight of her lying back against the dark gray bed sheets.

Carefully, I remove my shirt without brushing against my bandage before shucking my jeans, boxer briefs, and socks. The way her eyes drift down my body sends a surge of arousal rushing through me, and my cock jerks slightly. Gripping the base, I slowly stroke the length, watching her eyes track my movements and her lips part in anticipation.

I step between her legs, my hands going to her hips. Her eyes widen in surprise when I tug her closer to me, moving her ass to the edge of the bed and placing her feet flat on the mattress. My gaze locked with hers, I guide my cock to her, tracing the tip over her entrance.

"Nothing's stopping this from happening, Sunshine," I murmur, pressing inside her barely a centimeter, my voice hoarse from restraining myself. The heat radiating from her, the scent of her arousal, is nearly more than I can withstand.

"Don't go slow," she protests breathlessly, gently rocking her hips, urging me on.

I have to grit my teeth; the urge to thrust wildly into her fully is so tempting. But I can't do that—won't do it. I need to show her I have finesse. That I will—

"Make me come all over your cock."

Fuck. My groan is loud, and my hands slide over the smoothness of her thighs, gripping them, my eyes still on her. "You don't want finesse?" I inch in further before stopping.

"No." She pants, her fingers clenching in the bedsheets, nipples hard and begging for my mouth. "I need you deep inside me, Jack."

Unable to restrain myself any longer, I drive deep inside her and reach for her breasts. I tug at her nipples, and she throws her head back against the covers, coating my cock with more wetness.

Shifting my hands to her legs, I lift them, draping her knees over my arms to allow me to slide impossibly deeper inside her.

"Look at me," I command. "Let me see those beautiful eyes." I need her to see—to realize that this is happening. That nothing can get in the way of us.

I need her to see that my body's joining hers and that I'm giving her a part of me.

My heart.

My soul.

My everything.

CHAPTER FORTY-EIGHT

SARAH

His dark blue eyes feel like they're peering deep inside me while he works me with his cock, our bodies joined in the most intimate way possible.

He's angled my body so he'll hit the perfect spot, and even though I just came mere minutes earlier, I can already feel the telltale tightening of my muscles and the increasing wetness.

My eyes drift lower to where our bodies join and the sight of Jack, so impossibly hard and thick, pressing deep, then my eyes lift, taking in the sight of his firm abdominals and those slight V-lines framing them. His pectorals are smooth, and when I set my eyes on the slight beading of perspiration in the center of his chest, it sets me off.

My palms press against his chest, drawing him to an instant halt, and his eyes fill with concern.

"I need to be on top." At the sight of his lips parting to protest, I stop him. "Please. Let me. Especially"—my lips curve up slightly—"after I caused your stitches."

There's the briefest pause then his eyes crinkle slightly. "As you wish."

I roll over to make room, allowing him to lie back on the bed before I slide over, my legs straddling him. Grasping his hardness in my hand, my gaze locks with his as I guide myself down over him. Taking him inside me—without any protection—feels like the most decadent thing in the world.

And scary as shit, hisses an inner voice.

Lowering myself in one smooth movement, I feel Jack's hands grip my hips, fingers flexing, as his eyes flit along the curves of my body. "You have no idea how breathtaking you are." The warmth in his eyes is almost my undoing as the quiet, raspy quality of his voice displays his arousal.

Bracing my palms against the hard wall of his chest, I begin to move. His eyes fall closed, and a part of me is relieved I won't have to witness everything within the depths of those dark blue orbs, yet I also feel a slight loss.

Jack's lips part as his breathing mimics my own, coming out hot and fast. Sliding my palms up and over to rest on the mattress on either side of him, I latch my mouth onto him, and I'm caught off guard by his response. It's as though he's been anticipating my move. He slips one hand to the back of my head, and his fingers thread through my hair, tugging me even closer. Our kiss deepens, becoming an intoxicating combination of feverish, desperate, and devouring lust.

My motions speed up, and he works his hips, thrusting upward to match my pace, which is becoming more frantic as I edge closer to release. I ride him with a near desperation until he finally tears his mouth from mine.

"Ride me and touch yourself, Sunshine," he whispers his words hoarsely, heavy with lust, and I find myself obeying his request.

Spurred on by the intensity of his gaze, I rise off his chest, and we both inhale sharply at the change in angle and how good it feels. Pressing a finger to my clit, I begin to rub in slow circles, my gaze locked with his own heavy-lidded one. Jack continues rocking his hips, working me over his cock.

As my movements quicken, on the brink of reaching climax, he murmurs huskily, "Beautiful."

It's the reverence in his tone that pushes me over the edge, my orgasm crashing over me in fierce waves. I vaguely register the sound of his accompanied groan, his fingers clenching my hips as he rides out his own release.

Collapsing onto his chest, our combined ragged breathing the only sound in the room, I feel one of his hands gliding over my back in a light, soothing caress.

"Universe be damned," Jack's low murmur settles over me before he presses a soft kiss to the top of my head.

~

"You're the first guy who's let me eat my chocolate in bed."

I meant for that to be flippant, teasing, but after I say it, I instantly wish I could take it back because it makes me sound like one of *those* women. The type who gets into hardcore commitment mode and shares morning coffee in bed with her boyfriend.

Does it count that I'm sitting here, in bed, propped against what have to be the softest, fluffiest pillows known to mankind beside the man who rocked my world mere minutes ago? Jack poured us some wine, and we're curled up on his bed, watching *17 Again* on his small flat screen mounted on the wall across from us. He surprised me with a small handful of the brand of chocolates I love, apologizing for them being milk chocolate instead of my favored dark chocolate.

"Sorry, Sunshine," he'd said. "I picked the wrong bag and didn't realize it until I opened it just now."

"It's chocolate," I'd stated firmly, picking one from his proffered hand. "One should never scoff at chocolate."

Now, unwrapping the foil wrapper, I scan the inner message written on it before taking a small bite of the chocolate.

Let delicious happen.

Allowing the milk chocolate to melt in my mouth and coat my tongue in its sweetness, I'm startled when Jack turns his face, nuzzling my neck. "I'd like to let some more delicious happen."

"Oh, really?" I toss out playfully. "I'm intrigued, Westbrook. Tell me more." A slow smile curves my lips at his playful grunt before I pop the remainder of the chocolate into my mouth.

"I'd rather show you." He slides over me, my naked breasts pressed against the hard wall of his chest. Taking my mouth in his, his tongue dips inside, tasting me, and eliciting a groan from us both. The flavor of Jack combined with the chocolate must be one of the best things I've ever tasted.

When he tears his lips from mine, I can't restrain a whimper. My eyes watch as his darken with heated lust, his bottom lip smudged slightly with chocolate. Reaching out, I'm intent on swiping my thumb over his lip, but as soon as the pad of it touches his skin, his lips close over it. And he sucks. Hard.

How is it possible that I feel it—his suction and his tongue—all the way down deep? Arousal pulses throughout my body at his touch, and I'd give anything to feel that tongue, that mouth, on my pussy.

Abruptly, Jack shifts to his knees on either side of my legs, reaching over to the end table and grabbing another foil-wrapped treat. Cupping his hands around it, it takes me a moment to realize what he's doing.

He's heating it up with his hands, using his body heat to make it more malleable. Then he straddles my legs, unwraps the chocolate, tosses the wrapper aside, and runs the tip of it around one of my nipples.

Jack ducks his head, eyes locked with mine, and runs his tongue along the track of chocolate, lapping it up and sucking up every bit. He repeats the motion with my other breast, and this time, when he flicks the tip of his tongue against my nipple, I can't stifle the low hiss that escapes my lips.

"What do you think?" he murmurs against my skin, still holding my gaze. "You ready to let delicious happen?"

"Not sure if I'm entirely interested since you're getting all the chocolate," I retort.

His lips twitch into a smirk that's so incredibly sexy, my breath catches slightly. "Oh, but I plan on you getting it." At my confused expression, he slides down my body until he's cradled between my thighs.

With the remainder of the chocolate between his finger and thumb, he drags it along the crease of my opening and around my clit before he dips it inside briefly. Withdrawing it, he places it in his mouth, eyes falling closed as if to savor the sweetness now mixed with the wetness of my arousal.

When his eyes open, they're burning hot with lust, and his head slowly descends. "Delicious is about to happen," he whispers seconds before his mouth and tongue devour me in the most intimate of kisses. The scent of chocolate fills the air, and Jack alternates between using his tongue to dart inside and taste me deeply, and fastening his lips over my clit and sucking it gently, applying the right amount of pressure.

He senses when I'm fast approaching my release by pressing my thighs wider and seals his mouth over me. His tongue darts wildly, deep inside me, urging me on; the fingers of his hands nearly painful in their grip on my knees spread wide. Shudders of release overtake me as I ride out my orgasm, my hips moving wildly of their own accord. My breaths are coming out in harsh pants as I work myself over his tongue while he ravages me with his mouth.

Once my breathing has evened out, I watch Jack as he rises from between my legs, his chin slightly smeared with melted chocolate and a smugness tugging at the corners of his lips. Sliding up my body, he braces himself above me on his forearms.

"What do you think?" One eyebrow rises expectantly. "Did delicious happen?"

I pretend to ponder this, looking off to the corner of the room. "Hmm, it's a tough call, really."

"Is that so?" he asks, humor lacing his tone.

Meeting his eyes, I lift a shoulder in a slight shrug, trying to maintain nonchalance. "It's hard to judge such a subpar job."

His face stretches into a wide smile, eyes alit with amusement. "Oh, Sunshine." He laughs before pressing a soft kiss to my lips, his expression softening. "Now we can agree that the universe has nothing to do with any of this." He pauses, dusting a trail of tiny kisses along my jawline. "Nothing to do with any of this, let alone love."

My body instantly goes rigid at his words, and it's clear that he picks up on it when he lifts his head to peer down at me with a quizzical expression. "What's wrong?"

"No one said anything about love, Jack." I try to say calmly, but I know there's a tinge of panic there.

He doesn't immediately respond, his eyes studying me carefully. Finally, his gaze softens, and he murmurs the last thing I expect.

"I guess I'm saying it now." Those blue eyes of his appear a darker, deeper shade, his tone tender. "That I fell in lo—"

"No!" I press my fingers to his lips to stop him from spewing anything more. My entire body is in fight or flight mode—the adrenaline pumps through me, and my heart is racing. Shoving him off me, I fight against the tangle of bedsheets, frantic to get free.

Nearly toppling over onto the floor, I right myself in the nick of time. Rushing to the small plush chair beside the bedroom window where Jack was thoughtful enough to place my earlier discarded clothing, my movements are jerky as I tug items on, uncaring whether they're on inside out or backward.

"What are you doing, Sarah?"

The calmness of Jack's tone grates on me. How can he be

so calm right now? After nearly saying outright that he loves me? I feel like someone punched me in the solar plexus. I thought we were on the same page.

"Look, just because we've finally managed to screw to"—I stutter in my haste at finding my words— "completion doesn't mean the universe hasn't been telling—no, *screaming* —that this isn't meant to be. I mean, really." I make a derisive noise. "It shouldn't be this challenging to actually have sex and follow through with things!" My voice edges into hysteria.

"It's not all about sex, Sarah. There's more to us than just that." I don't miss the fact that he's using my name. *Sarah.* Not Sunshine.

"Obviously, you're expecting a lot more out of this."

His expression closes off, features tightening. "Out of what? What am I expecting?"

I circle a finger, gesturing between us. "Out of us. You're expecting a happily ever after like Ry got with Maggie. But you and I both know"—I break off with a brittle sounding laugh—"I'm no Maggie."

His gaze holds mine before speaking slowly. "I know that." There's a brief pause. "I don't want what Ry and Maggie have." When he steps toward me, the fierceness in his eyes makes me subconsciously take a step back. "I want what you and I started to have; I want that to continue." His gaze drops to his feet, both hands running through his hair, disheveling it slightly as if gathering his thoughts before his eyes find mine again. "For us to figure out our own happily ever after."

Shaking my head, I gape. "*What?*"

"What the hell do you think we've been doing, Sarah?" He stares incredulously. "We've spent time together doing just about anything and everything!"

"And getting interrupted at every turn when things turned sexual!" I shoot back. "Come on, Jack." My voice rises as my indignation escalates. "We. Hang. Out." My words are practically bitten out in short staccato bursts. "Don't make more out of this!"

Examining my features, he seems to be desperately trying to detect something. "What was all this, then?" He waves a hand wildly. "All this time we spent together? For shits and giggles?" His expression turns hard. "Because you had to know I wasn't hanging around just to *fuck* you, Sarah."

My entire body jerks at his crass words. I don't think it's possible that his features could become more disgusted.

Huffing out a short breath in frustration, I level my gaze on him. "I never led you to believe I was looking for more. I told you about my parents. About my mother. I refuse to ever be like her. I mean"—I wave a hand wildly—"just look at her. She's a fifty-something hippie bouncing from one boyfriend to the next, still searching for affirmation after my dad left. I've seen how that works." Gaining more steam, I surge forward. "I can't do forever, Jack. That was never my deal."

He stares at me without saying a word. The silence seems to drag on forever even though I know, in reality, it only lasts a few seconds.

"What if that was mine?" He delivers his question softly, and the way he utters it slips deep inside, sending shards of panic running through me.

His jaw works, eyes narrowing on me. "Tell me this," he demands, stepping closer. "What other guy knows about your 'menstrual snacks'? How you like to have a stash of those special chocolates with the messages written on the inside of the wrapper? Or how your breath hitches when he places a kiss at that certain spot on your neck, just below your ear?" He pauses for a beat. "What other guy have you gone to —what other guy has held you in his arms—after you've lost a patient?"

He drags in a harsh breath. "You need to let me in, Sarah. Yes, you let me see past some of your everyday façade, but you won't let me in." Shaking his head slowly, the hurt is etched upon his handsome features. "Not entirely."

The room is closing in on me while, simultaneously, the air is being sucked out of it. My chest feels like an elephant is sitting on it, and the tightness is excruciating. Gasping for air, I push past him, desperate to make my escape.

"I need to go." Rushing out of the bedroom and down the hallway, I grab my purse and slip on my shoes, practically sprinting toward the door.

"If you leave, that's it." The finality in his voice carries down the hallway, giving me pause when my fingers touch the door handle. "I won't force something you don't want."

It takes great effort to get the words out. "I know." Pulling open the door, I ignore the faint inner voice whispering that I'm making a mistake.

"Goodbye, Sarah."

As I tug the door closed behind me with a soft click, I whisper, "Goodbye, Jack."

CHAPTER FORTY-NINE

SARAH

"**L**ovely to see you again, Miss Moodypants."

I don't bother turning to Clint as I finish inputting notes on a patient's chart. My only acknowledgment is when I raise my left hand to discreetly scratch at my hairline.

With my middle finger.

Clint laughs and slides in closer, lowering his voice. "Did I mention I checked in on a certain handsome man we both know and removed his stitches? Which means"— he nudges me slyly—"that I had to get all up in his business—"

My head whips around; my eyes narrowed in irritation. "We both know his stitches were on his forehead, so there's no need for you to get up in any type of his business."

His lips curve upward, and he shrugs. "Maybe all that time spent pretending to be his friend's gay lover a while back changed the game for him. *Maybe*"—his eyes light up, widening dramatically—"he realized he wasn't in love with you all this time but, in fact, *me*." Clint places his palms on his chest with a whimsical sigh. "How sweet would that be?"

I glare at him, and my words are nearly a low snarl. "So sweet."

"You know what's wrong with you?"

"No, but I'm sure you're about to tell me."

He doesn't bother to acknowledge my sarcastic response. "You need an inspirational story to help you get your head on straight."

"Really?"

He nods. "Yep. And I'm gonna need you to listen carefully for a moment." He pauses for a beat. "There was a young woman from a steel town who had a dream. That dream was to dance. But the odds were against her."

My face scrunches in disbelief. He cannot be referring to what I think…

"That young woman had to believe in herself, give herself over to the risks, and give it her all. And finally, when she did, when she got the chance, do you know what happened?"

"She became a maniac?" I deadpan because this sounds an awful lot like the premise of the movie *Flashdance*. "On the floor?"

"Well, yes. But more than that." He leans in close, lowering his voice. "She found love."

Our gazes lock and hold until, finally, we both burst out laughing. "*Flashdance* references, Clint? Really?"

He merely shrugs. "It was the best I could come up with on the spot." He holds up a finger. "And I think it's quite applicable."

Studying him, I ask. "What exactly are you saying I should do?"

"Besides getting a unitard, some leg warmers, and dancing your ass off before dousing yourself with water?" he immediately responds.

I blink. "Besides that."

"Give it your all. Put yourself out there. Because"—he lifts a shoulder slightly—"I think he has potential." His lips curve into a shit-eating grin. "To be more than Mr. Blue Balls."

Before I can form a response, we're interrupted, and Clint makes his way down the hallway to check on a patient. And I'm left with two things lingering in my mind.

One, the idea of putting myself out there and giving things with Jack a chance.

And two, that damn *Flashdance* song whose chorus includes something like "She's a maniac on the floor" is on replay in my mind.

~

"Let me get this straight. You turned down a super sexy, sweet guy because he wanted to love you and have a relationship?" Maggie asks nonchalantly. Chopsticks in hand, she waves them at me. "Are you just semi-nuts or one hundred percent?"

"Hey! What's this about him being sexy?" Ry mutters, shooting his wife a hurt look before devouring another piece of sushi.

My friends decided we needed a sushi dinner night out. I know what it really is, though.

An Intervention.

Except I'm not an addict; I'm just a hot mess of emotions. Who knew I'd miss Jack so much? That I'd miss his text messages or his seemingly endless supply of chocolates? His humor? His smile? His kisses? The way his lips were so incredibly soft and tender when he—

Whoa. What the hell? My mind is betraying me. Clearly.

Maggie rolls her eyes, not even sparing a glance at Ry because she knows he's messing with her. "Sarah, have you thought about this? Like *really* thought about it?" Concern is etched across her features.

Suddenly losing my appetite, I toss down my chopsticks. "Of course," I answer in heated exasperation. "I thought about it every single time my mother went above and beyond, trying to cater to a new man in hopes he'd stick around. I still think about it while she continues to do the same thing."

Maggie levels a look at me. "Do you care for Jack?"

I eye her warily. "Of course, I care for him. I care for you and Ry and—"

"Do you care for him as more than a friend?"

My lips press thin, entire body tensing. "As someone I was intimate with, sure."

Maggie's eyes narrow. "Not what I'm asking, and you know that."

Ry lets out a loud, exasperated breath, slapping down his chopsticks, and locks his eyes on me. "Do you get excited when he's around? When you talk to him?" Leaning his forearms on the table where he sits across from me, he continues. "Do you get that little flutter of excitement when he smiles at you? Are you generally happier with him around?"

I don't answer immediately, mulling over his questions. "Flutter of excitement? Did you read that in one of Maggie's magazines?"

My flippant question meant to derail the line of uncomfortable questioning does nothing. Ry and Maggie stare back at me, stonewalling me.

Covering my face with my hands, I let out a tiny groan. "Everyone's against me, I swear."

"We're not against you, Sarah." Maggie's response is immediate and gentle. "We care about you. That's all it is."

"And Jack, too. We care about him," adds Ry. "I mean, he *was* my fake boyfriend for about a year, so I kinda have—"

"We care about both of you," Maggie interrupts. "And we want you to be happy."

My hands slip from my face to shoot back in irritation, "But I am—"

"No, you're not," Maggie and Ry say in unison.

My lips part to argue, but they both hold up a hand to stop me. My sigh borders on petulant, but I don't care. I don't appreciate them ganging up on me. First Clint, and now these two.

Maggie's tone gentles. "You're not happy, sweetie. We can all see that, and I know deep down that you realize it, too."

"I've met your mother, Sarah," Ry offers, his expression sobering, "and while I adore her, you're nothing like her." He tips his head to the side, thoughtfully. "You're ambitious, kind, fun, incredibly smart, and have a huge heart. A woman with all that going for her isn't meant to be alone, drifting through life without attachments. A woman like you is meant to—"

"Love and be loved," Maggie chimes in as she and Ry finish together. Turning to one another in surprise, they laugh before their attention returns to me.

Toying with my wooden chopsticks on the table, I murmur, "But what if Jack and I aren't meant to be together? I mean"—my voice grows softer, more faint—"he did what my father did. He didn't stick around. And he...let me leave."

I focus my gaze on the table, continuing to mess with my chopsticks when a large hand moves to cover mine. Raising my eyes to meet Ry's somber gaze, I feel the warmth of his hand seep into my suddenly cold, clammy one.

"You hurt one another. It takes time to get your mind right and get your feelings sorted. The question is, are you going to let him slip away? Would you be able to face him at some point when we all get together and meet his fiancée? His wife? To see him with his wife and kids?"

My stomach clenches painfully at the thought of Jack marrying someone else. Of him having a life, having kids...without me.

"The look on your face tells me all I need to know." Ry's

hand squeezes mine before releasing his hold and drawing back. "Now what are you going to do about it?"

Well, hell. That really is the million-dollar question. What am I going to do about it?

I have no freaking clue.

CHAPTER FIFTY

JACK

"New suit?"

My head snaps up to find Ry standing in the doorway of my office. "Hey." I glance at my watch, noting it's before five, which is much earlier than he usually cuts out of work. "You're out early today."

He shrugs, closing the door before walking over to take a seat in one of the chairs in front of my desk. Crossing a leg over the other, he leans back casually.

Too casually. Which can only mean one thing.

"You look handsome." He grins at me, increasing my suspicions.

"Stop hitting on me, cupcake. You're married," I scoff jokingly.

My best friend releases a dramatic sigh. "I'll always have a soft spot in my heart for you."

Shaking my head derisively, I click the mouse to save my latest notes on the computer. "What can I do for you?"

"I was trying to figure something out." Again, Ry's somber expression sends up red flags. "Would you be cool with going to dinner with us some night next week?"

My brow furrows in confusion. "Why wouldn't I be okay

with having dinner with you and Maggie? We've done dinner a million times."

"I didn't say only me and Maggie."

Ah. He wants to know if Sarah and I can be civil around one another…

"I meant me and Maggie along with Sarah and her date."

Everything stills, my breath hitches, and I have to work hard to swallow past the sudden lump in my throat. My voice comes out sounding hoarse, my response far from the nonchalance I'm trying for. "Date?"

Ry stretches his arms up and laces his fingers behind his head. "Yeah. She's seeing this new guy…"

I spring out of my desk chair, rushing over to the large windows overlooking the busy street below. Spinning around, I stare at my friend. "We just... It's only been..." I sputter in disbelief. "She's seeing someone?"

He simply stares back at me, not answering.

My vision blurs as I turn to face the windows, and a dozen different memories flit through my mind. Sarah's spunkiness, her smile, her laugh. Holding her when she needed me. Her kiss. Her touch.

"Fuck," I mutter quietly, bracing both palms flat against the cool, flat surface of the window.

"Hey."

"Yeah?" I don't bother turning because if I thought it was fucking painful to watch Sarah leave me over a week ago, the idea of her dating twists my stomach up in tenuous knots.

"I was just testing the waters."

It takes a moment for Ry's words to sink in. My head whips around, and I stare at my best friend.

The best friend I might end up punching in the throat.

"You *what*?"

His lips curve up at the corners. "Just testing the waters to see if you're as torn up about things as she is."

"You're an assh— *Wait*." My head tips to the side. "She's torn up?"

Rising from his seat, Ry rakes a hand through his hair. "You two just had to be hardheaded, didn't you?"

My eyes narrow. "Funny, but I seem to recall you wallowing on my couch at one stage," I point out.

He heaves out a sigh. "Are you going to get your shit together or what?"

I clench and unclench my jaw, attempting composure. "She made it clear what she wants and, more importantly, what she doesn't want."

"And you're going to let it go at that?" Ry's features take on a sudden intensity as he steps toward me. "You and I both know you wouldn't have let that fly with me when I had the fallout with Mags."

My eyes lock with his, holding it for a long beat before I avert my gaze. Running a hand through my hair in frustration, I gesture with the other. "What the hell can I do?"

"Do you love her?"

Meeting his gaze, I nod, and he tosses out, "Even if she gives you a near constant case of blue balls?" I nod again. Ry rubs his hands together, his eyes alit with excitement. "Well, then, we've got some brainstorming to do."

An hour later, Ry and I find ourselves sitting at my conference table. Pushing away from my laptop after one final entry, we look at one another.

"Finally," he says.

For the first time since Sarah walked out my door, I feel the start of a smile. "Finally, we have a plan." Tossing my best friend a look, I have to ask, "You think it'll work?"

"Without a doubt," he affirms, nodding with a grin. "Mark my words, Mr. Blue Balls will be getting the girl."

CHAPTER FIFTY-ONE

SARAH

"You look like someone on one of those Skittles commercials. All happy and bright with color."

I pin Clint with a sharp look. "Seriously?" I forgot to do laundry and am wearing a set of the more colorful scrubs I wore while in school, working my rotation in pediatrics.

He rolls his eyes at me. "Well, with that kind of attitude, you'll be like the 'before' part of a Snickers commercial. Sheesh."

"Clint," I say on an exhale, checking the time. "I'm about to end my shift."

"You're implying I should cut you some slack? Be nicer? Maybe give you some chocolate since you ran out unexpectedly?" His eyebrows rise in question.

Releasing a groan, I frown. "I swore I had plenty."

Cocking an eyebrow, he flashes me a secretive smile. "How much would you love me if I told you I had some for you?"

Immediately, I pounce on him, my hands dipping into his back pockets in search of my fix. "I can't believe you're holding out on me," I say accusingly.

Clint grasps my wrists and tugs me away from him, staring at me incredulously. "Jesus, Matthews. You're like a junkie." Steering me a step away from him, he holds up his hands and eyes me. "Stay there."

He reaches into his front pocket, and I'd like to say I wouldn't have gone there, but I've not experienced a desperation for my chocolate fix quite like this.

And if I'm being completely honest, I have to admit I think of Jack every time I eat one of them.

When Clint withdraws two foil-wrapped treats from his pocket, I snatch them from him like a junkie about to get their fix. My fingers begin to peel the foil back when his voice stops me.

"What? No thank you?"

My eyes rise to his, and I give him a grateful smile. "Thank you, Clint."

Removing the chocolate from the foil, I bring it to my lips just as I look at the message on the inside of the wrapper. My hand freezes an inch away from my mouth as I stare down at the wrapper in confusion.

Give yourself up to love.

Huh. This one is unlike their usual messages, but maybe they're adding variety. Mentally shrugging, I take a bite, only to have it fill my mouth with its sweet goodness and remind me of him.

Damn it.

Finally, I register that Clint's still standing there, watching me with an odd expression. "What?" I ask cautiously.

"Any fun message on the inside?" His eyes flick down to the foil wrapper in my hand before they return to mine.

Suspicion rolls through me because Clint never asks about the messages. Wordlessly, I hand over the small square foil and try to gauge his reaction as he reads it.

His gaze meets mine, and the corners of his lips curve upward. "You should follow through on this one."

"Right," I scoff. "Because I normally take advice from chocolate wrappers." Turning, I head to the hall leading to the room housing our lockers. His hand on my arm stops me, his brown eyes thoughtful.

"Don't forget to check the other wrapper, too."

I nod, eyeing him oddly...because I always read them. And he knows that. "Catch you later."

It's not until much later that evening that it registers how odd it was that Clint doesn't prefer those particular chocolates, yet he had two on him.

For me.

~

Love might not come easy, but it's always worth it.

"Home sweet home," I mutter to myself, unlocking my apartment door. The message on the second wrapper kept me distracted on the entire ride home.

It's eerily quiet as I close the door and lean back against it with a weary sigh. Maybe I should get a pet. Something that doesn't require much attention due to my long shifts. Then it wouldn't be so god-awful lonely to come home to an empty apartment.

And no, it doesn't escape me that it's never bothered me before. I never really cared about coming home to a quiet, empty home before …

"Jack," I breathe out on a wisp. Simply saying his name aloud causes the pinching in my chest to increase painfully.

I still haven't found the nerve to talk to him. Because, *really*. How does one even go about saying, *"Hey, um, remember when you basically professed your love for me, and I practically left skid marks on the floor trying to get away from you? Well, I've changed my mind. I really do love you."*

Trying to shake off my funky mood, I kick off my shoes

and walk into the apartment, ready to set my bag on the kitchen chair.

Except I don't make it that far.

My keys and bag drop to the floor with a loud thud. Transfixed, I stare at the sight around me.

Vases cover every possible flat surface of my kitchen and living room. And I'd recognize the flowers that fill them anywhere.

Blue balls.

Arrangements of the pitifully plain blue flowers decorate my kitchen counters, kitchen table, end tables beside my couch, and the coffee table. Blue balls are everywhere, on every available surface.

It's a massive allergy attack waiting to happen...and the sweetest thing I've ever come home to in my entire life.

I notice the largest arrangement on my coffee table has a small florist's envelope clipped to it, drawing my attention to it. Dozens upon dozens of foil-wrapped chocolates are scattered on my coffee table, but three in particular are propped up against the vase.

Stepping closer, I carefully tug the envelope free and pull out the small card.

Please read the messages of these three chocolates first, Sunshine.

With trembling fingers, my heart feeling as though it's about to burst from my chest, I set the card down and pick up one chocolate, unwrapping it and setting the chocolate on the surface of the table.

If I could, I'd go back and fight for you.

My breathing stutters, and I immediately reach for the next chocolate, unwrapping it hurriedly.

I never got to tell you how much I love you. I hope I get a chance.

Moving to the third chocolate, I don't realize I have tears streaming down my face until one drops onto the foil.

You are my Sunshine. Still. Always. Forever.

The vibrating sound coming from my bag alerts me that my phone is ringing. With my heart in my throat, still grasping the foil wrapper, I dig through my purse for my phone. The screen is alit with the person's name I've ached to see over the past two weeks.

Swiping my thumb across the screen to accept the call, I place it at my ear. "Jack." My voice comes out sounding breathless.

"Sunshine." That one word, that deep, husky voice filled with such emotion washes over me, warming me through and through.

"You did this for me?" I ask in disbelief. Wiping at another tear trickling down my cheek, I fix my eyes on the sight of all those chocolates wrapped in what must be custom-made wrappers.

"I'd do anything for you," he answers immediately. "But I do have to warn you..." I swear I can hear the smile in his voice. "After a while, my creativity waned."

Now curious, I walk over and pick another chocolate from the random pile, unwrapping it quickly in anticipation of reading the message.

I'd give anything to get FaceTimed by your vagina again.

Laughter bubbles up, bursting free. "You want to Face-Time my vagina again, huh?"

"If you had to come up with dozens of messages, you'd get pretty desperate, too." I detect the sheepishness in his voice.

Unwrapping another, I smile down at the wrapper in my hands.

I'd suffer blue balls my entire life if it means I get to spend each of those days with you.

"Jack." I sigh into the phone. I wish he were here right now so I could thank him and tell him... "Where are you?"

"Open your door, Sunshine."

I still before turning slowly, eyeing my door. The hand holding the phone drops to my side. My feet carry me to the door, and when I open it, I'm greeted with a sight I've ached for.

"Jack Westbrook," I murmur, drinking in the sight of him in soft, worn denim and a long-sleeved gray Henley. "How did you manage all this?"

Closing the distance, he steps inside and shuts the door behind him. Resting one hand on my hip, he dips his head, and eyes bright with emotion, he presses a kiss to my forehead.

"I had the wrappers specially made and used my time before and after work for two days unwrapping those damn chocolates and rewrapping them with my wrappers."

"You had Clint and Maggie in on this," I murmur, realizing he must have given the chocolates to Clint and had him nab my usual stash. Then he'd used the key I'd left with Maggie in the case of an emergency.

"I had to enlist their help with something this important." His eyes search mine. "I should've fought harder, Sarah. I'm sorry."

I press a finger against his lips and speak softly. "No. I was wrong...and scared. You were right."

His brow furrows, a crease popping up between his eyebrows, and he tips his head to the side. "I'm sorry. I didn't quite catch that last part. Can you repeat it?"

As my lips part to do so, I catch sight of that telltale sparkle in his eyes. Shoving against him playfully, I scoff. "Nice tr—"

His lips swallow my words, and I kiss him back with everything I have, going to my tiptoes, and wrapping my arms around his neck. Jack's fingers thread through my hair, tilting my head to deepen the kiss.

And that's when I realize what I've been missing.

Jack doesn't taste sweet and indulgent like my chocolates. He tastes like something far more decadent, far more delicious, and far more addicting.

Jack tastes like love.

CHAPTER FIFTY-TWO

JACK

One Year Later

"Just give me a little peek."

I grin at the screen, watching her try to scowl at me and fail. The corners of her lips are twitching, and her blue eyes sparkle with amusement.

"I am not going to point the phone down there, Jack."

I give her a pointed look. "You never had an issue with FaceTiming me with your vagina before."

Sarah releases an exasperated sigh. "That happened once. And we both know it was an accident."

"Best accident ever." I flash her a smug smile.

"I need to go, or I'll be late."

I can hear Maggie and Clint's voices in the background complaining about bad luck and letting me see Sarah's face. Luckily, neither of us cares about any of that.

Her expression softens into one of those tender smiles I've come to know. I classify those smiles as *mine*.

"I love you, Jack," she murmurs. "I'll see you soon."

I wink. "I'll be the handsome guy with a blue balls boutonniere waiting for you."

She raises her bouquet, filling the screen of my phone with the same blue flowers and baby's breath before lowering it. "I'll be the woman heading your way with these in tow."

"Love you, Sunshine."

After she murmurs her goodbye and we disconnect our FaceTime, I turn to Ry, my best man. "All set?"

He slaps a hand to my back. "All set."

As we head toward the front of the large ballroom of Saratoga Springs's historical Hall of Springs, I take in the sight of the large pillars at the front and the tall, ornate ceilings. No doubt about it; this place is beautiful in its own right.

However, the one sight which literally robs me of breath—because of the indescribable beauty—is the moment I watch Sarah approach, walking down the white linen runner leading to me. It's not because of her dress—which is gorgeous. It's not because of her makeup or the fancy, elegant way she's styled her hair.

It's because she's walking toward me with the intent of becoming my wife.

The moment she draws near, smiling up at me after handing her bouquet to Maggie, I take her hands in mine.

"Hey, Sunshine," I whisper, waiting for her to realize I'm pressing something into her palm. Luckily, I've already told the minister to wait for my cue. I wait as Sarah curiously looks at what I've given her.

Her eyes lift to mine, rich with curiosity before she carefully unwraps the single, foil-wrapped chocolate. I wait for her to read the words I know are on the inside.

Suddenly, Sarah throws her head back on a laugh, her eyes sparkling as they lock onto mine.

"Ready to do this?"

Nodding, she rewraps the chocolate, hands it back to me, and I quickly pocket it. "I'm ready, Jack."

On that cue, I nod at the minister, and he begins the ceremony. And throughout the I dos and afterward at our reception, I recall the message in that foil-wrapped chocolate I'd given Sarah earlier. Hell if that message isn't God's honest truth.

Can you believe blue balls ended in our incredible happily ever after?

EPILOGUE

SARAH

Four Years Later

"Mommy! Look what I have for you!" The blond-haired, blue-eyed toddler runs up to me.

Flashing a knowing smile at Jack as he and Ry return from getting coffees around the corner, I bend down to greet my daughter and accept the flowers. "Did you bring me flowers, Ella?"

"Daddy said they're special ones." She nods as if to affirm this fact, her adorable face solemn. "He got them from Ms. Paisley's shop."

Reaching to smooth back the young girl's hair, I press a kiss to her forehead. "They are special. When you get older, I'll tell you the story behind these flowers."

"When I'm older next year?"

Laughing softly, I smile down at my daughter. "Maybe a few more birthdays."

"Can Mauve and I have a chocolate?" With eyes a dark shade of blue like her father's, she peers up at me.

"As long as you're careful not to make a mess."

"Promise, Mommy."

Reaching into my purse, I withdraw two foil-wrapped chocolates and press them into Ella's palm.

"Thank you!" Ella darts off to Mauve who's on one of the swings at the playground, her little legs pumping as she goes to and fro.

"Nice one, Westbrook." I turn to narrow my eyes on my husband, setting the flowers on my lap. He hands me my coffee before taking a seat beside me on the bench over-looking the playground.

"I can't imagine why you didn't tell your daughter the name of those flowers," Ry comments from where he sits on the other side of Maggie.

"Hey, cupcake," Jack admonishes. "Don't throw shade." Barely concealing his smirk as he raises his coffee to his lips, he adds, "You've got napkin notes, and I've got flowers and chocolates. It's clear who the suave one is here."

"Simmer down, you two." I roll my eyes at their friendly ribbing before Jack rises from the bench to heed Ella's request to push her high on the swing. He takes my hand and presses his lips to the top of it before slipping something into my palm. Ry follows suit and rises from his seat on the bench. Knowing Mauve will want the same, he leaves Maggie and me sitting alone.

We watch in comfortable silence as the two men push our daughters on the swings, smiling at the happy squeals as they go higher.

"Sarah?"

"Yes?" I turn to my best friend, but her eyes are trained on the sight before us.

"Did you ever imagine this?" Her cheeks have that trade-mark rosy glow that only accompanies a woman who's bliss-fully pregnant. One of her hands rests on her large belly.

Shaking my head, I peel back the foil-wrapped chocolate Jack slipped me. "Never in a million, sweetie." My breath catches at what the message on the inside says.

RC BOLDT

With glistening eyes, my throat grows tight with emotion when I meet my husband's eyes from across the playground.

As my best friend and I sit here watching our beautiful families, I allow the chocolate to melt in my mouth, and my hand holds the foil wrapper tight.

I'd love to make another beautiful baby who has your smile, Sunshine. What do you say?

Holding my husband's gaze, I mouth my answer.

"Yes."

DEAR READER,

Thank you so much for taking the time to read this book! I'd love to hear what you thought about Sarah and Jack's story. If you would be so kind as to leave a review on the site where you purchased the book, it would be appreciated beyond words. And if you send me an email at rcboldt-books@gmail.com with the link to your review, I'll send you a personal 'thank you'!

Please know that I truly appreciate you taking time from your busy schedule to read this book! If you'd like to stay up to date on my future releases, you can sign up for my mailing list (I'm the most anti-SPAMMY person ever—promise!) via this link: http://eepurl.com/cgftw5

ALSO BY RC BOLDT

Standalones:

Out of Love

CLAM JAM

Out of the Ashes

The Teach Me Series:

Wildest Dream (Book One)

Hard To Handle (Book Two)

Remember When (Book Three)

Laws of Attraction (Book Four)

STAY CONNECTED TO RC BOLDT:

Facebook: https://goo.gl/iy2YzG
Website: http://www.rcboldtbooks.com
Twitter: https://goo.gl/cOs4hK
Instagram: https://goo.gl/TdDrBb
Facebook Readers Group:
https://www.facebook.com/groups/BBBReaders

INTRIGUED BY MAGGIE AND RY?

Keep reading for a sneak peek of *CLAM JAM.*

CLAM JAM

PROLOGUE

M y name is Maggie Finegan, and I'm the continuous victim of a "clam jam."

To answer your questions:

No, I'm not Irish—I was adopted.

And, yes, clam jamming is a thing.

I'll wait until that one sinks in. *Taps toe of shoe quietly.*

Okay, ready? I'll go on. It's a pretty crazy story. It all started one dark, stormy night—wait, don't roll your eyes at me, people. Fine. So it *might* have been more of a typical Upstate New York overcast kind of day. I had left work early since my boss, whom I fondly referred to as Sybil, left work at lunchtime for a meeting in the city. I took advantage of him skipping out early, knowing that I could hurry home and clean up the apartment I shared with my fiancé, Shane, and set the mood to get lucky. Things had been a little off lately, with both of our work schedules usually residing in the "heinously hectic" realm, and I wanted to remedy this.

Sliding my key in the lock of our apartment door, I stepped one heel over the threshold, and my favorite pair of Jimmy Choos slipped, sending me off balance. I barely caught myself as one hand flew out to brace against the entryway wall to steady myself. Prepared to take offense with whatever object had made me nearly land on my butt, the next moment happened in slow motion.

You know what I'm talking about. Slooooow mooooooooootion. Where a moment in your life is too freaking weird, crazy, or just all-around effed up, and your brain does some weird thing with the synapses, immediately slowing everything down. Like an out-of-body experience. That's what I had going on. Because the offensive object that had me nearly falling on my butt was a pair of woman's panties.

Fact: Those panties weren't mine.

You know. In case you were wondering.

My slow motion continued as I bent down to make sure my eyes weren't playing tricks on me because, yeah, that was my initial thought. They might be my panties. Because no way would my fiancé be getting "jiggy"—thank you, Will Smith, for that term—with someone else, right?

Go ahead. Say it. Say exactly what you're thinking. *Maggie, what the hell is wrong with you? Stop being delusional!*

I kicked those panties to the side, slid my briefcase's straps off my shoulder, and set it in the corner of the entryway. Walking down the hallway, I could hear my heels clicking along the hardwood floors. And do you know what I thought the entire walk to the bedroom—to our bedroom? I thought, *Wow, these floors are gorgeous. And those oversized windows looking out onto downtown Saratoga Springs have a gorgeous view. I'm so glad I chose this apartment.*

Weird, right? I think I had an idea of what I'd find in that bedroom, and my mind had officially gone into full-blown protective mode.

The noises were the worst. Let's be real here. I get that, in the heat of the moment, you're probably going to have harsh breathing and some moans, but what I heard as I approached that bedroom was something you'd likely find on the Discovery Channel. Elephants mating, perhaps? Something large scale. Maybe if wooly mammoths still existed, that would be the closest thing to what I heard coming from that bedroom.

That's right. I know you're cringing right now. It was absolutely *mammaliciously* awful. Yes, I made up that word, but you have to understand that mammals everywhere were shaking their heads in disgust at that moment.

I'm going to fast-forward a bit now because I'm pretty sure you know how what I call "the discovery" went. They both shrieked, he pulled out of her—out of her mouth, by the way—and claimed it wasn't what it looked like.

Because, you know, his penis inside of a woman's mouth was one of those blind taste tests or something. Like back in the day when they were all like, *"This is Coke? Wow! I can't believe it. I've drunk Pepsi my whole life."*

First of all, you should not be that amazed and mystified by a freaking beverage. That's just lame.

Let's move on.

I kicked them both out. Luckily, his name was not on the lease since he'd moved in with me. Not so lucky was the fact that this place was on the pricey side of things, so I'd have to watch my spending on happy hours, takeout, and dinner nights out.

Here's the quick rundown:

1. I left all of Shane's belongings outside the door. ALL of them.

2. Okay, so I *might* have tossed some of his things in the trash. My bad.

3. Luckily, our lead building attendant, Mr. Charlie, has adored me from day one and once I informed him of what went down, he told me not to worry about anyone reporting the overabundance of crap piled up near the trash chute.

4. I Craigslisted the *hell* out of that mattress. Because God only knows what had gone down—pun intended—on that thing when I hadn't been home.

5. I did the whole bawling my eyes out to my best friend, Sarah, between bouts of inherent desire to maim Shane. Because, let's be honest, that's what women do. After too much Pad Thai—wait, I'm kidding; *no one* can have too much Pad Thai—at my pity party, I made some new decisions about my life.

a) I was not going to date for a while. Now, I'm not saying I refused to ever date again because, really. It's not like I have my sights set on being *that* woman with seventy-two cats or anything. Plus, I'm allergic, so that's a no-go.

b) If I were going to be single, footloose, and fancy-free — thank you, Auntie Patsy, for that phrase that I hope never spills from my lips again—I'd need to get a roommate because I'd need the extra money. You see, I'm not a fan of women who expect guys to buy them drinks. We all know those drinks often come with expectations. The single's world is flooded with douche bags, you know. Then again, so is the attached world, as my situation served as a prime example.

c) My roommate could in no way be a straight man. It couldn't be a woman, either, because I've never been able to cohabitate with another female. I know it's weird. But it is what it is.

d) I couldn't exactly put out an ad for a "gay roommate" because, uh, discrimination? Who doesn't want to get slapped with a lawsuit and has two thumbs up? *This* girl.

This is the point where the story really begins. Get comfy. Well, as comfy as you possibly can when preparing to read about a year of my life being clam jammed.

Shall we begin?

CHAPTER ONE

MAGGIE

October, One year ago-ish

Saratoga Springs, New York

Holy shadoobie. This guy is hot.

No, scratch that. He's the kind of hot teenage girls spell out as H-A-W-T. He's *that* kind of hot. And he's applying to be my roommate, which means only one thing.

I have to send him packing.

There's no way in h-e-double hockey sticks I'll be able to maintain any self-control around a guy like this. I mean come on, people. It's like the moment you decide to diet, and you catch a whiff of pizza or walk past a bakery when they're putting new pastries in the display case.

Temtorture at its finest. I know, I know. I made that word up—a mix of the word temptation and torture. It's accurate, though, isn't it? You know you shouldn't have it because it's so bad for you, but you know once it touches your tongue, it will be so *gooooood*.

Wow. That sounded more sexual than I expected. Because I wasn't exactly thinking of having this guy's anything touching my tongue. But now, the seed has been planted, so …

"I appreciate you taking the time to meet with me."

Ryland's voice brings me back from my not-so-G-rated thoughts. I am a terrible, horrible, no-good person, just like that Alexander kid in those children's books they turned into a movie. I nod, trying my best not to let his lips mesmerize me because, whoa, they're so nice and full and soft looking. And his hair makes me want to run my fingers through the short, light brownish-blond strands.

Sigh. Long, long sigh. There I go again.

"I admit"—he leans in, and I find the sparkle in his eyes captivating—"I was grateful you chose to meet in this spot since my company's offices are right above here. I had a few things to take care of this morning. And the fact that your apartment building is within walking distance is another plus."

Flattening my palms against the small table as we sit across from one another in Starbucks, I let out a slow exhale. Because it has to be said.

"I have to be honest with you, Ryland. You have great references." I gesture to his résumé and list of references, both work and personal, he submitted to me when he'd contacted me about the room for rent a few days ago.

After printing off a sheet with some key information about the room for rent as well as photos of the spare bedroom, I'd posted it on the corkboard located in the lobbies of a few of the large, well-known office buildings—both mine and a few others I was familiar with nearby. I had hoped that would decrease my chances of ending up with some college kid who would end up being a slob and skip out on rent. I had a few decent applicants, but Ryland James had stuck out amidst the others.

He's not only educated but also quite successful, as was clear from both his résumé and company's website. He'd explained he had been renting a room, but the guy had recently gotten married, and he didn't want to cramp the newlyweds' style, so he'd been temporarily staying with another friend. Ryland wasn't interested in buying anything —house or condo—at this point as he wasn't entirely sure his job would keep him local and didn't want the hassle of trying to sell a property or rent it out if he relocated.

Everything had checked out with him. Everything. He seemed like he had his act together. And his photo from the Eastern Sports company website didn't disappoint. Which was why I had been planning to nix him altogether. He was exactly what I didn't need right now. So why am I here, meeting with him face to face?

Sarah. She'd coerced me to meet with him. She went over each applicant's information with me, and she kept coming back to Ryland's. She'd hassled me about giving him a shot.

Inhaling deeply, I continue, "But I have to be honest with you. I've recently broken up with my dirtbag fiancé"—I break off with what I hope is a lighthearted laugh, but I swear it comes out sounding strained and a touch maniacal—"and I'm not interested in having a roommate who's a guy and—"

"I'm gay."

I jerk, startled by his interrupting admission. And if I didn't know better, I'd swear I detected a little hint of surprise in his eyes.

My eyebrows arch. "Really?" Shoot. That's rude because even I hear the tinge of disbelieving doubt in my voice.

"Yes." He nods, clasping his hands together and leaning forward to rest his forearms on the table. "Jack and I have been together for years now." One of his hands reaches up to tug on his earlobe. "We still have a bit of an"—he pauses, lips pressing thin as though he's trying to word it correctly —"open relationship, and I feel it's best … to have a separate place and not be continuously underfoot."

Huhhhhh. I'm still processing this information when he continues.

"So"—he flashes a smile that makes my insides all gooey —"you wouldn't have anything to worry about with me."

"Okay," I say slowly, "but what about guests and sleep-overs? Because I'm not a huge fan of having to listen to moaning and—"

"Not a problem." He waves a hand dismissively. "I can totally stay at Jack's place. He doesn't have a roommate. It's no big deal." He flashes me another smile, and I feel my ovaries weep his name.

It's a good thing he's gay. Otherwise, let's be real. I'd likely end up being that roommate who accidentally-on-purpose "sleepwalks" into his bedroom—naked— and has sex with him.

Holy crap. Did I really just think that? Bad, Maggie. *Baaaad,* Maggie.

Glancing over his paperwork, I say, "If you don't mind, I have a few other applicants to interview." Lies. I'm totally stalling. Raising my eyes, I find him watching me expectantly; that gaze centered on me in such a way that I feel like I'm the only person who exists right now. "But, tentatively, I'd like to offer you the room for rent."

If I thought Ryland's smile was ovary-lurch inducing before, this one trumps that. *Big* time. It's blindingly bright and infectious, and I can't help but return it. We sit there for a moment before he clears his throat, and I remember what else I have to tell him.

"So, as I mentioned earlier, the utilities normally run this much per month." I use my capped pen to point at the sheet I had printed, which includes all the pertinent financial infor-mation. "We'll split it fifty-fifty. Rent is due on the first of the month, and a late fee will be imposed if it isn't in by the fifth day." I recap a few other details and ask him if he'd like to look at the room.

He agrees, and when we stand, pushing in our chairs, he helps me slip into my coat once I pluck it from where I'd draped it over the back of my chair.

I repeat: **Ryland took it upon himself to help me put on my coat.**

I know, right? He has to be gay. Because no normal guy would take the initiative to do that for a woman. Especially not in this day and age.

Exiting the busy Starbucks, we fall in step along the crowded sidewalk full of the usual Saturday foot traffic as I lead him to my apartment building. He rushes up to beat me to the large, heavy doors to the building, reaching out to hold it open for me. Flashing him a smile, I thank him.

Such a gentleman, this one. Jack is one hell of a lucky guy.

"Hey, Mr. Charlie!" I smile, greeting our lead building attendant. He's become like an adopted father to both Sarah and me. He's sweet as pie and always watches out for us.

"Have to use your handcuffs on anyone recently, Chad?" I can't resist teasing our security guard since an older woman on the second floor flirts with him *shamelessly*. It wouldn't be as funny if she weren't pushing ninety. I never knew women that age could still be hoochie mamas.

I introduce Ryland to them, and Chad steps around the desk where he was chatting with Mr. Charlie and walks with us to the elevators. I had already asked him if he'd be willing to accompany us up to my apartment in case I chose to show it to Ryland.

Chad waits in the hallway while I show Ryland around. After a quick peek in the spare bathroom, I lead him to the spare bedroom.

"Obviously, I still have a few more things to move out of here since it's been used as storage more than an actual bedroom. But no worries, it'll be cleaned out and ready to roll." I gesture to a few small boxes I've yet to toss out—mainly mementos of my relationship with Shane—one, in particular, is a box of photographs of Shane and me from over the years. I've been putting off getting rid of it, which is dumb because it's over and I know it. But those photos of us —especially the ones from early in our relationship—show us so happy and in love. It's painful to think about throwing those away.

"Looks good." Ryland's deep voice behind me sends shivers down my spine.

"Well"—I turn, facing him—"that's it." I reach out a hand. "It was great meeting you, Ryland. I'll definitely be in touch."

When he slides his hand in mine, grasping it firmly but not too tight, I feel tingles.

"Call me Ry," he offers with a soft smile.

"Ry," I repeat and inwardly wince when it comes out sounding a bit breathless. "It was great to meet you."

"Likewise, Maggie."

He turns to leave, exchanging a quick good-bye with Chad at the door before I quietly lock up behind them. Leaning my back against the door, I let my eyes fall closed.

God just gave me an olive branch of sorts. A way to ease my financial situation a bit and eliminate any possibility of being tempted by a guy—just like I'd planned. No fear of getting involved with my male roommate because he's not into women. I should be relieved.

I am relieved.

Maybe if I keep repeating that, I'll start believing it.

ACKNOWLEDGMENTS

This book was so much fun to write and none of it would have been possible without a team of people helping me each step of the way.

My readers! The fact that I actually have readers is just ... incredible!! Thank you for choosing to read these books. Without your support, your sweet emails and reviews, and you sharing my books with others, none of this would be possible. I am forever grateful.

My husband and my daughter, thanks for being freaking awesome beyond words.

My parents, for their continued support. And for my mother who has no qualms about telling others to read my books—even the ones with "questionable" titles. Also, FOR THE LOVE OF EVERYTHING THAT'S HOLY, just admit that I'm your favorite child, already. Geez.

Sarah, my Australian BFF. There's no way I could have made it this far without you or our WhatsApp texting, voice messages or phone dates. #LYLT

Amber G., I adore you and your gracious generosity! I'm so incredibly grateful for all of your help!!

Boldt's Beach Babes—you guys are the most stellar individuals! I am beyond grateful for your support, excitement, and feedback when I share my ideas with you. I'm clearly biased but I think I have the best readers group!! Love you all!!

All the book bloggers out there who have been so wonderful to me! I could never manage to truly show my gratitude for all of your support. Please know that the time you take to read and review my books and/or do promo posts is appreciated beyond words.

My beta readers who spent their own time to comb through my book and help me refine it! You all are freaking stellar and I'm so grateful for your help!!

Leddy, Steph, Brandi, Jen, and Hazel—You have been such an incredible help and I'm so grateful to you ladies! I freaking love the hell out of you!!!

To wine and coffee (don't judge me, people) for being there when I'm under duress because of deadlines. Without you both, this book wouldn't be possible.

ABOUT THE AUTHOR

RC Boldt is the wife of Mr. Boldt, a retired Navy Chief, mother of Little Miss Boldt, and former teacher of many students. She currently lives on the southeastern coast of North Carolina, enjoys long walks on the beach, running, reading, people watching, and singing karaoke. If you're in the mood for some killer homemade mojitos, can't recall the lyrics to a particular 80's song, or just need to hang around a nonconformist who will do almost anything for a laugh, she's your girl.

RC loves hearing from her readers at rcboldt-books@gmail.com. You can also check out her website at http://www.rcboldtbooks.com or her Facebook page https://www.facebook.com/rcboldtauthor for the latest updates on upcoming book releases.

Made in the USA
Lexington, KY
30 August 2017